THE ARNASAID SERIES

Storm Winds

OVER

TRANNOCH

FIONA H. PRESTON

@iamselfpub
www.iamselfpublishing.com

For my daughter Emma and my Mum

In memory of my beloved Dad
And Calvin
*'Tis better to have loved and lost
than never to have loved at all.'*
Rabbie Burns

People live and die, but the land, the elements and the beauty remain unending as the turn of the tide.

Chapter One

Ailsa Fisher picked up her coat and left the office with a sigh of relief. It wasn't that she didn't enjoy her work, she loved it, but this week had been a particularly difficult one in the recruitment advertising company where she'd worked for the last fifteen years. The contract with one of the UK's biggest energy companies had been a difficult negotiation, and, now that it was finally signed, she felt like celebrating.

Connie and Jan were already in their favourite pub waiting for her, white wines duly bought and on the table as Ailsa swung in, looking great in a bright royal blue dress and black jacket. Her blonde hair was short, expertly cut by her favourite London stylist, and at six o'clock in the evening she looked almost as fresh as she had done at six o'clock in the morning.

'Hi darling, you look fab!' said Connie in appreciation, as their friend joined them. Connie was a short, plump, spikey-red-haired lawyer whose appearance belied the fact that she was a respected professional dealing specifically in employment law. Jan was another blonde, curly and wild, with a hippyish appearance. Jan had her own business in London, a small tea shop tucked away in a cobbled street, where she did her own home baking and had more customers than she could serve in a day. Their differences had drawn them together, and they had been friends for more than twenty years.

'Thanks honey, I feel done-in,' said Ailsa, taking a gulp of her wine and visibly relaxing as she climbed up onto the proffered bar stool. 'Contract is signed, and I'm celebrating!' She lifted her glass, chinking it together with the other two.

'Great news,' answered Jan. 'It's been a long one, but hey, it's Friday, and we are not talking shop!'

'Agreed!' chorused the other two. This was the line spoken by Jan every Friday which drew a line in the sand and moved them neatly from work to leisure. It was a ritual to say the words, and they all laughed, just as they did when it was said each week.

After the fourth glass of wine, they were looking at the menu, although they knew it inside out, deciding what food they would order to soak up the alcohol.

'Anyway, I have some mysterious news!' Ailsa said suddenly, with slightly slurred words. The other two put down their menus and looked at her in appreciation. It was always good to have something out of kilter happening, and this opening was promising.

'Yeah? Well, come on, spill the beans!' Jan said, with enthusiasm.

'Well, I got a strange call yesterday from a James Tarbett, who wants to meet me to talk about a long-lost relation who has been trying to track me down!' she said, and sat back to watch the reaction from her friends.

'What long-lost relation?' Connie asked. 'Wait a minute, you are adopted, so do you mean that this person is talking about your birth family?'

'I'm not sure.' Ailsa had fretted over this very question since the previous day. 'He called me out of the blue. I have checked his credentials online and he is kosher, from a decent law firm. Henley and Swanson?' she questioned Connie, who replied with a nod of approval. 'What did he want?' Connie asked.

'He wants to meet me tomorrow, to talk about this relation. As you know I know nothing about my birth family; my 'parents' were the best I could ever have wished for, and I have never tried to make any enquiries about who might be my birth parents.'

'Yes, but Annie and George have passed away now, darling,' said Jan gently. 'It's really up to you if you want to pursue this.'

'I'll come with you.' Connie was all lawyer now. 'I'll know what to ask, and I'll be able to understand any jargon better than you. You know what these lawyers are like!'

'Oh, thanks Con!' said Ailsa feelingly. 'I was hoping you would say that!'

The next day saw Ailsa and Connie, slightly hungover and giggly at 10 a.m., walking into the coffee shop suggested by James Tarbett as the meeting place, and where a tall, dark-haired man in his late fifties rose to greet them. It transpired that Mr Tarbett was acting on behalf of his client, who wished to meet Ailsa and explain the family connection. Disappointingly, he would not divulge any details, as his client wanted to speak directly to her. The surprising thing was that the meeting needed to take place in Scotland, on the North West coast, where his client lived.

'My client wishes to meet you in his own surroundings, in the North West of Scotland, chiefly because he is in poor health and cannot travel. He is willing to pay for any travel arrangements and would be delighted if you could meet him in the next week or so,' James stated, monotonously, almost as if he were reading from a book.

'Okay, we will agree to travel, but I will go with my friend Ailsa as her representative, and therefore the travel arrangements will extend to me too.' Connie was completely in command now.

'I shouldn't think that would be a problem,' James Tarbett said, with a tight smile.

A week later, Ailsa and Connie were on a flight from Heathrow to Glasgow. They had both taken a weeks' holiday from their respective jobs and were viewing the trip rather more as a holiday than a realistic attempt to connect Ailsa with her past. They were both enjoying the prospect of an unexpected break, and, as neither had been to Scotland before, were looking forward to seeing this particular part of the world and having a relaxing time off work.

When they landed at Glasgow Airport, there was, surprisingly, a car awaiting them. It was quite an old and battered looking Range Rover, and the driver took their cases and loaded them into the boot. 'How far is it?' Ailsa asked, shyly. The man looked a little surly, almost as if he had been interrupted in doing something by the request to pick them up from the airport. 'Aroon fower oors.' It was almost a snap, and the two girls eyed one another sceptically. Ailsa had no idea what he had just said.

'Around four hours,' Connie supplemented, as they climbed into the back seat together.

'Four hours! It was quicker flying from London!' Ailsa had not realised how long the onward journey would last.

'That's why I bought that bottle of red wine duty-free, and two sandwiches on the flight!' Connie touched the side of her nose in a conspiratorial way. 'I've got the plastic glasses from the flight too, so we can have a picnic!'

'You're a star! Should we ask Grumpy if he wants a sandwich?'

'Would you like a sandwich?' Connie asked in a sugary voice. 'We've got chicken salad or egg and . . . '

'Naw, goat crisps an' that,' he answered, and turned his radio up, presumably to drown out their talking.

'Nice!' Ailsa muttered, and bit into her meal with relish.

Four hours later, as Ailsa and Connie lay in the back of the car, covered with a fleece blanket which smelled suspiciously like dog, the driver drew into a long rumbling drive, and pulled up at a dimly-lit front door. It was impossible to see anything of the landscape or surroundings; it was a cloudy night and had rained on and off on the journey northward. The two were roused, with difficulty, and then jumped out of the car. Without a word, the driver picked up their cases and had a quick conversation with someone standing in the lighted doorway of a looming building, looking huge and black under the night sky. The hallway was dark and felt like the inside of a castle, with its numerous passageways and ancestral pictures on the walls. A young woman of around twenty asked them, in a musical accent, if they would like some supper. They both refused, saying they would rather get to their rooms. They were escorted to comfortable bedrooms, where they found their cases, and curled up under their respective duvets, sleeping soundly until the next day.

At seven twenty the next morning, Ailsa was roused by the sensation of a dry throat and reached out to where she usually kept her glass of water on the bedside table. After some fumbling about produced no glass of water, she turned slowly and opened her eyes. The picture which greeted her was not her comfortable bedroom at home, but a vision of an unknown bed, ceiling and wallpaper which was far removed from her own normal existence. It took a few moments before Ailsa remembered that she was in an unknown house in Scotland, and had arrived here, the previous night, after a long, dark and wet drive from the airport. The house itself had been dark and cold and unwelcoming to their tired eyes, and even the bedroom, as she'd rummaged through her case for her jammies, had felt dismal and chilly. She was finally in Scotland, here for the meeting with the prospective relative of whom she knew nothing.

She dragged herself from the bed and over to the French window. The scene which met her was nothing like what she might have imagined. There was a rough hillside, dropping steeply from the house, and the sea beyond was turquoise and frothy and could have been a picture of the sea in the Mediterranean, not the North West of Scotland. Near the shore was a group of rocky islands, tiny places with sandy shores, some no more than twelve or fourteen feet long, big enough to pitch a single tent and no more. It fuelled her imagination, and she thought how she would have loved that as a child, rowing out to one of them, building a fire and perhaps staying there all night listening to the rush of the sea all around her. The water here looked shallow, she imagined you might be able to paddle out to some of the rocks when the tide was out. The sand was white and fine, and glistened in the sun. She shivered in anticipation at the sight, opening the sash windows to breathe in the breeze from the ocean.

Immediately in front of her were lawns, well-kept and surrounded by rocky flower beds, with forests to the west of the house climbing up mountains in the distance. From her viewpoint she could get some scale of the house. It was huge, built of grey stone, and probably several centuries old.

A tap came at the door, and a tall woman, with wiry flint-grey hair combed away from her face, wearing a navy blue high-collared coat dress buttoned up under her jutting chin, stepped into the room when Ailsa called, 'Come in!' The woman stood just inside the door, with her hands clasped formally in front of her, her face frowning wrinkles as she slowly raised one eyebrow and spoke in a low steely voice.

'Good morning, Madam. I am Miss Cochrane, the housekeeper here. I am sorry I missed you last night, but it was late when you arrived, and I trust Eileen saw to it that you had everything you needed?'

Ailsa expected Eileen was the young woman who had met them at the door. She remembered the driveway, the shallow steps of the sweeping staircase and the hurried tumble into bed.

'Yes, thank you,' Ailsa mumbled. The journey was very tiring, and it was good to get here and into such a comfortable bed.'

Miss Cochrane raised her eyebrow again but did not answer this. 'I have arranged for breakfast for you downstairs. Eileen will come up and show you the way in around ten minutes, if that suits? The doctor will arrive at 10 o'clock, and then, if Sir Angus is fit enough, he will be moved to the library for an hour or so, and I will come and fetch you then to speak with him. You understand, though, that he is very ill and weak, and we need to keep an eye on him so that he does not overtire himself.'

Ailsa looked startled. 'Sorry, did you say *Sir* Angus? I'm sorry, but I have been told very little about this situation other than I am here to see a relative of mine and that they are very ill.'

Miss Cochrane looked her up and down, then spoke again. 'I am afraid I am not party to any further information about your own situation,' she said, with derision in her voice. 'We need to monitor Sir Angus' condition on a daily basis, and, if the doctor doesn't think he is fit to get up today, then I'm afraid whatever you are here for will have to wait.'

'Of course,' Ailsa said, with finality. 'We, that is my friend Connie and I, are here for the week anyway, so hopefully we can speak to him at some point.' She hadn't meant to sound flippant, but the look from Miss Cochrane, as she spoke, caused Ailsa to wish she had kept her mouth firmly shut. 'This is going to be a difficult week!' she thought to herself, grimly.

When the housekeeper left, Ailsa slowly turned to look at her room as if seeing it for the first time. It was a large room, with original plastering cornices on the ceiling, heavy brocade wine-coloured curtains, and the same shade of wine-coloured rugs adorned a floor almost black with many years of polish and wax on the floorboards. The bed was tastefully decorated in cream covers, with a wine throw and cushions, and the heavy wooden theme continued in the huge oak wardrobe, dressing table and chest of drawers. A door led to a well-appointed en suite, with warm cream towels and tiled floor, a deep bath and a walk-in shower. It was a pretty room, obviously refurbished in recent years to provide a modern upgrading to the old house.

Ailsa speedily dressed, pulling on grey trousers and a navy jumper, combing through her blonde hair and adding a touch of mascara, and a flash of light pink lip gloss. She opened her door in trepidation and found herself on a corridor with several other doors, leading to a square balcony overlooking an oak staircase which she remembered from last night. It was like stepping back a hundred years, as she took in the heavy-framed portraits hung on the stairwell, the patterned carpet and the highly polished dark oak wood. A chime, from a grandfather clock, startled her as she walked down the stairs, and, at the bottom, met with doors on all sides and passageways leading off in all directions, she was at a loss as to where she should go.

'Are you okay, Madam?' An enthusiastic high voice broke into her thoughts, and she turned to see a young red-headed woman, presumably in her early twenties, her pretty features and high ponytail making her seem younger than her years.

She was wearing a white blouse and black trousers, like a waitress in a hotel. A faint recollection came to Ailsa – this was the 'Eileen' from last night.

'Hi!' Ailsa said, in a friendly way. 'Miss Cochrane said there would be breakfast somewhere down here?' she said, hopefully.

'Oh, deffo!' Eileen said, laughingly. 'The breakfast room is just over here. Your friend is already down.' She opened a door to the left of the stair and showed Ailsa in to another room heavy with oak and old furniture but lightened by a duck egg blue colour scheme, which modernised it considerably.

'Ailsa!' Connie looked up from a table which would have seated at least ten people. She put down the paper she was reading, and her coffee cup back on the saucer. Eileen shut the door behind her and the two women were left alone. Ailsa smiled and took up a place opposite her friend.

'This is scary,' Ailsa said, outright.

'What is?' asked Connie, cautiously.

'All, this!' Ailsa said, waving her arms around her. 'Have you met the formidable housekeeper yet? She came into my bedroom this morning and introduced herself, and I honestly felt that she was the headmistress and I the naughty pupil!'

'I know, she came in here and showed me the sideboard, with all that food, but looked at me like I was some sort of mud under her feet,' Connie said, cheerfully. 'I must admit though, she looks like her bark is worse than her bite. Anyhoo, fill your plate with eggs and bacon and grab a coffee. I want some of that square sausage. Have you ever seen square sausage? Apparently, it is quite a thing here in Scotland! We'll make ourselves comfy and talk.'

With plates laden with food, they sat and discussed the house and its people. Ailsa explained how she wakened to take in the surroundings and been amazed by them, and the house itself. 'It's like another world,' she told Connie. 'I loved the view of the beach and all those little islands, and I had no idea the house was so big. It's enormous, an actual mansion! Have you seen that sea? It's positively turquoise! That was all *your* fault of course, drinking that wine you bought in duty-free.'

Connie laughed. 'Yes, I poured it down your neck,' she said, sarcastically. 'Never mind, it was a good gig, and definitely helped to put in some of the miles – what a journey! I'm looking forward to what your relative has to say –'

'Miss Cochrane, the housekeeper, said that the relative is a 'he' and wait for it – called *Sir* Angus. I'm related to a 'Sir!' she said, with a mixture of amusement and confusion in her voice.

'Really? Wow, how you have moved up the ranks Ailsa!' Connie said, with a grin. And she took a bite of sausage, pointing her fork at Ailsa as she spoke. 'Anyway, we need to wait and see just exactly how related to you he is before we jump to conclusions.'

'Your grammar is pathetic for one so learned,' Ailsa rejoined with a chuckle. 'I mean, why does he suddenly want to see me? Has he done a bit of genealogy and tracked me down or something?' She poured out more coffee, frowning deeply. 'I mean, Con, this could all be some sort of ridiculous set-up, and we could be captured and murdered and there is no blood relation to speak of!'

Her friend laughed as she buttered another piece of toast. 'You know, you should write novels, you have a fantastic imagination.'

'But, you know what I mean?' Ailsa persisted. 'That lawyer guy, he could have looked up that law firm and acted out the part of the bearer of good news when all along he was some sort of criminal acting for whoever this Sir Angus is! Who's to say this whole thing isn't a sham?'

'Some sham!' Connie retorted, 'I mean, who would pay for us – two of us! – to travel from London up here, and put us up in this huge gothic pile just to murder us, or whatever, when we are nothing but London birds, and no use to anything or anyone? Talk sense mate!'

'Well, maybe you are right. But, it's just like some kind of mad dream at the moment. I really hope we can see Sir Angus today.'

Chapter Two

It turned out that Sir Angus was in no fit state to talk to anyone that day, so the two friends resigned themselves to making the best of their little holiday and decided to fully explore their surroundings. They found the path which led to a quiet secluded beach overlooking the crop of islands Ailsa had seen from her window. The late April weather was warm, with a light wind, which suited them as they scrambled over the rocks and found the cliff paths overlooking the rough and colourful landscape of this particular part of the coast.

Miss Cochrane advised that the handyman and jack-of-all-trades, Jim Hutton, would drive them into the nearest village if they so desired. They glanced quickly at each other before Connie enquired falteringly if that was the 'gentleman' who had driven them home from the airport. Miss Cochrane said it wasn't, and that man had done the trip as a favour to Sir Angus, because Jim had been otherwise engaged. With relief, the two answered that they would take him up on the offer, and they visited a local pub and had a lovely lunch whilst overlooking a decidedly calmer bay than the one back at the house. The two were, after all, on holiday and were determined to make the best of it, whatever the outcome of the conversation with Sir Angus may turn out to be.

On the second day, they discovered the wine cellar, and, giggling like two schoolgirls, they picked a few bottles out of the hundreds there and took them down to the rugged beach at the house. Connie had asked Eileen if they could get a packed lunch, as the weather was so fine and sunny that they wanted to go walking. Eileen obliged by bringing them a packed lunch of homemade brown bread sandwiches, filled with locally cured ham and cheese, crisps and bottles of Highland Spring water.

They had a long walk along the coastal path which was rugged and rocky, making it heavy going in some parts. The wind started to get up and tossed the waves onto the rocks, throwing up spray and making them scream in delight. They could walk all the way to Arnasaid, the village they had visited yesterday. The busy bay was full of boats bobbing in the water, their little bells tingling musically. It was a lovely sight.

Later, the two ensconced themselves on a secluded part of the beach and opened the illicit wine to have with their meal. They enjoyed it thoroughly and decided, in the wake of the alcohol, to have a paddle in the sea, which, in early spring was like plunging into the ice of the North Pole. They dried their feet, laughed some more, and finished off the meal and the wine.

On the third day, Miss Cochrane came into the breakfast room while the two friends were making their plans for the day. She clasped her hands in front of her and advised that Sir Angus was a 'bit better' today and would be happy to see them both in the library at 11 a.m. that morning.

Ailsa and Connie looked at each other after she left. 'Now that I need to meet him, I am absolutely terrified,' Ailsa said, her face turning white, and her hands shaking with trepidation.

'Don't be daft, Ailsa.' Connie tried to be all-professional. 'This is what we came here for, if you remember. We've had a few days pottering about, getting tipsy and loving the area, but it is back to business. You need to talk to Sir Angus and try and gauge exactly what it is he wants out of this meeting. He says that you are a relative, but we need to know what the connection is, and why he has suddenly come into your life.'

'I know, sorry, I'm just a bit overwhelmed with this whole experience. I'm just wondering what the conversation with Sir

Angus will involve and how it might change things. I have no idea how I fit into all this, it is so alien to me, and before we came here a few days ago, I had never even been to Scotland. It is all totally new to me.'

At eleven o'clock the two friends went to the library. The room seemed dark inside, despite the brightness of the day, and there was a faint smell which Connie would have described as mustiness, and Ailsa would have described as the natural warm and comforting smell from the second-hand bookshops she frequented. There was a log fire alight in the grate, and three winged-back chairs sat in a circle round the fire. The one on the left was occupied by a hunched figure, in a dressing gown and slippers, with a shawl draped over the shoulders. He had a full head of thick silvery hair, his eyebrows were shaggy and silver also, and he had remarkably bright blue eyes. He moved his head to stare directly at Connie, then his gaze shifted to Ailsa and a flicker of emotion passed over his sagging countenance.

'Come away in and sit,' he said, in a drained voice. It was as though the effort of talking was too much.

They sat, and looked expectantly at their host, and, although he held their gaze, he remained silent for several minutes. When he spoke, they were surprised by what he said.

'Are you enjoying Storm Winds?' he asked, in that rasping forced tone he had used earlier.

Ailsa looked stupefied, then asked, 'Sorry, what is Storm Winds?'

'Storm Winds is this house, of course. It has been in our family for several generations,' and he took a gasping few breaths, as if the sentence had been too long for the air in his lungs.

'Sir Angus,' Connie had cast a glance at Ailsa, and, seeing her floundering with this new information, thought she would intervene. 'I'm sorry, but no one told us that the house was called Storm Winds. Also, you said 'our' family and I think that is why we are here, to establish what relation Ailsa is to you.'

Sir Angus took a long hard look at Connie. His eyes glinted with a spark which told of his spirit, long stifled by ill health. 'Of course,' he said, with gentle authority. 'That is why I instructed my lawyers to find her.' He started to cough, then wheeze, and the attack lasted for around five minutes before he could gather himself together and talk again.

Connie, however, was trying to move the conversation along and said, 'Sir Angus, do you know . . .' but, she got no further as he interrupted in an abrupt manner, which belied the state of his condition.

'Ailsa, I am your Father,' he said, as a large log shifted and crackled in the grate.

Ailsa was rooted to the chair in her astonishment. Connie was taken aback to the point of sheer amazement, which rendered her unusually dumb for several minutes. The old man looked at Ailsa with a softening expression, tears shining in his eyes.

'I met your mother when she was very young, in her early twenties, and she became pregnant two years into our relationship.' He spoke slowly and in a rehearsed manner as if he had practised this speech for half his life. 'Georgina was a beautiful, wild, exciting woman with long blonde hair and a face so similar to yours, Ailsa, it takes my breath away. She was known as 'Hunter', we all called her Hunter as she was the best markswoman anyone around here had ever known, and she hunted grouse and deer like it was second nature.' He paused, wheezing for some time before he could continue.

'So, why did you give Ailsa up for adoption?' Connie said quietly, although she knew the answer before it was spoken.

'I was already married,' Sir Angus said, his face seeming to sag even farther in his obvious distress. 'Elizabeth Douglas and I were married very young. It was an arranged marriage. Yes!' he insisted, as Connie looked thunderstruck at such a suggestion. 'You must understand, I come from a highly respected titled family which has been here in the North West of Scotland for more than three centuries. This house was built in 1794, and generations of Hamilton-Dunbar's have lived here since. Your name Ailsa is Hamilton-Dunbar, not Fisher as you thought.'

The tears streamed quietly down Ailsa's face, as she sat there trying to take in what Sir Angus was saying. Connie gripped her hand and squeezed it sympathetically, her own eyes welling up at the sight of her friend's bare emotion. Ailsa was numb with the shock of what Sir Angus had just said. Out of the corners of her eyes she could see the tall bookcases of the library looming around her, seeming to envelop her in gloom.

'Have a look at that portrait over there,' the old man said, sadly, and still in that rasping voice.

Connie helped Ailsa from the chair as if she was the invalided one, and not Sir Angus, and they walked arm-in-arm to the portrait on the wall behind them. The sun streamed in the long window facing south, bathing the portrait in yellow light. It was a picture of a woman in riding clothes, carrying a shotgun halved over her arm, mountains in the back drop and purple heather bringing colour to the scene. The woman looked to be in her twenties, and Ailsa looked like her. The colouring was the same, the blonde hair and the features which were dark, rather than the pre-supposed light colouring which normally accompanies such fair hair. It immediately made both friends gasp as it was so like Ailsa's colouring. In the bottom of the portrait, there was one simple phrase, 'Hunter, by James Wilson.'

The door opened, and Miss Cochrane entered, followed by the doctor, a specialist from Glasgow. Sir Angus was checked over, and given some medication, while Ailsa and Connie stood gazing at a picture which illustrated, more than any document ever could, the true family line which Ailsa had never known, or indeed, wanted to know. Eileen brought in a tray with tea and cakes and laid it on a small table next to the fire. The doctor tried to persuade Sir Angus to return to his bed, but the old gentleman was resolute. 'I'll stay here until I have divulged it all!' he said, melodramatically, in a wavering voice with a high degree of dramatic doggedness in its tone.

'I was weak,' Sir Angus continued, as he sipped his tea, half of it going over his dressing gown, as his shaking hand brought it to his lips. 'Hunter begged me to leave Elizabeth, and I couldn't bring myself to do it. Elizabeth was the sweetest, gentlest person I have ever known. Hunter was fierce and demanding and challenging and exciting. My father was still alive at the time, and I was a coward and did not want to face him. Hunter threatened me with giving you up for adoption. She was not the maternal type and would probably not have kept you anyway. I know that sounds harsh, but, unfortunately, it is true. She had her way, set the wheels in motion, and I met your adoptive parents and was very impressed with them. Hunter moved to Australia and died ten years later. She was only in her thirties when she died, Ailsa. I put her portrait up here when my own Lizzie died. Everyone thought she was just a friend. No one knew the truth.'

There was silence for almost ten minutes. Tea was sipped, cakes were untouched. The fire grew low and the room dimmed.

Ailsa was at a loss for words. There seemed no words to say. Not in her wildest dreams had she thought that by coming to Scotland she would find her actual birth father. She had thought maybe a distant cousin or great-aunt or uncle. Not her father. Did he seem like her father? No. Not what she had imagined. But what had she imagined? Every time she thought of who her parents might be, where they had come from, what their story was, she had forced the thoughts firmly out of her mind. She had built a wall of protection around herself, keeping the past and the present firmly bordered. She didn't allow herself to think about the past. She had felt it was self-indulgent to do so, so she had thrown herself into her life and work. But secretly, she knew that this was not the way to grow and heal from old wounds, that there would be a time when she would have to face the past, not her past, their past, and try to accept what she had always believed, that her birth parents did not love her enough to keep her.

'So why now?' Ailsa asked quietly, after some time.

'Because, I am dying,' Sir Angus said, plaintively. 'I need someone to take on the ancestral home. Lizzie and I were not blessed with a child.'

Ailsa was startled out of her maudlin mood, shaped by the events of the last hour. 'I'm sorry, but are you trying to tell me that I will actually inherit all this?'

Connie answered for him. 'Of course, that is what he is telling you. You are the only heir to this estate, honey. That is why we are here.'

'Yes, of course you will. I have loved this house all my life, and I hope you will love it too. This is my favourite room, I spend most of my waking hours in here. It is part of me. My books are part of the fabric of this place, some of them extremely old and valuable. My favourite is *Treasure Island*.' The old gentleman seemed to sink into the chair even more after this long speech, and, as if on cue, Miss Cochrane stepped back into the room to see him bed-ward.

Ailsa and Connie walked out onto the headland, the wind in their hair and so much on their minds. They sat on the edge of the rocks, looking across the sea to the island of Eigg. The sun was high in the sky, late spring flowers waved in the breeze, the sea was still choppy, and the waves joined the shore in slapping frothy gulps.

'What's happening to me?' Ailsa asked her friend, in a strained voice, her face streaked with tears and real consternation in her expression.

'Well, you have become an heiress overnight,' Connie said, carefully. 'It's the stuff of dreams for some, but when you are thrust into a situation like this, it is very, very hard to take and accept. We came here thinking we were having a freebie holiday, to learn about someone who was trying to trace their ancestors and put you firmly on their family tree. This is nothing like either of us expected. I don't blame you for being shocked. I am feeling a bit overwhelmed myself.'

'I feel no affinity to him whatsoever.' Ailsa looked at her friend desperately. 'I am to inherit a huge estate in Scotland,

I have been speaking to my birth father, and I felt absolutely no connection to him. I mean, apart from anything else, there is a huge age gap. I am in my thirties and he must be late seventies. If I thought of it at all, and those times were few and far between, I thought that meeting my real parents would give me a wham bam kind of feeling, like a vibe that I was part of them. I got nothing at all.'

'Sorry to say it, sweetie, but that is the stuff of fairytales. It takes a lifetime to build connections and closeness and whatever you want to call it. Sir Angus could have given you the world, all of this, a rich upbringing in a beautiful part of the country where you would want for nothing, but he chose to give you away for his own selfish reasons. I believe this is all about him trying to recompense for the past.'

Ailsa sprang to her feet, suddenly angry. 'That may be, but I couldn't have asked for a better or more loving upbringing than I had with Annie and George. They didn't have huge amounts of money, but they always managed to give me everything I needed, and most especially love. If I had been brought up here, I would have been devoid of love, an unwanted reminder of an affair he never should have had.'

'Of course he shouldn't,' Connie agreed, and she looked at her friend before putting into words what they both already knew. 'And, there is the estate. He said himself, he wanted it to carry on . . .'

Ailsa looked at her friend in shock. 'You don't mean you actually expect me to *live* here do you?'

'Darling, I expect nothing of you,' Connie said gently, 'but, old Pop in there has brought you here to hand over the estate to you, and I guess you have a life-changing decision to make.'

Ailsa, lost for words, turned and walked slowly down the cliff path to the beach.

At dinner that evening, Ailsa and Connie picked at their food. Connie had just plucked the second bottle of red wine from the rack, when Miss Cochrane came in and stood in the usual pose with her hands clasped in front of her. 'Madam, Doctor Stevenson wanted me to inform you that Sir Angus has taken a turn for the worst. He is with him at the moment, doing all he can.'

It was Connie, again, who answered, 'Thank you, Miss Cochrane. Ailsa and I will be in the blue sitting room, if needed,' and she dismissed the housekeeper with a nod.

They took their wine to a small sitting room which faced due west, and where the brilliant red sunset could be seen through the tall sash windows. Eileen had lit the log fire after they had suggested sitting in there for the evening, and it was as comfortable and cheery a room as they could have wished for, under the circumstances.

At around 11.45 p.m. there came a knock at the door, and Miss Cochrane came in followed by the doctor. Sir Angus had slept peacefully away to another world, and Ailsa Fisher was now Lady Ailsa Hamilton-Dunbar, Baroness of Strathkinnieford, and Marchioness of Dunlivietor and Arnasaid.

Chapter Three

Ailsa pattered on bare feet through her London flat side-stepping the boxes, which held all the trappings of her life so far, strewn across the three small rooms. She wanted a coffee, but the percolator was packed, and had a can of diet coke instead. Her mobile chirped companionably, and she picked it up from the empty worktop.

'Hi darling, just me,' Connie said cheerfully. 'How are you getting on?'

'All packed and ready to go,' Ailsa said, with as upbeat a voice as she could muster. In the last three weeks since Sir Angus had died, (she still couldn't bring herself to think of him as her father) she felt as though her whole world had been turned inside out.

When she and Connie had landed back at Heathrow, Storm Winds, and its inhabitants, had all seemed like an impossible dream. The rugged coastline, the windswept grand house and estate, the woods, beach and village, all of which now belonged to her, very quickly seemed like a distant memory. She had gone back to work but couldn't concentrate. She hadn't told her boss about what had happened in Scotland, chiefly because she didn't really get on with him, and by the end of the second day she had handed in her notice. She met with Jan and Connie that Friday, as usual, and she had broken down in floods of tears, her confusion and angst apparent to her friends. They had talked and talked about the options she had: she could sell the place and go travelling; she could stay in London and visit occasionally; she could turn Storm Winds into a hotel. She had the money to do this, as well as leaving her the estate, Sir Angus had left her a villa in Italy and a fortune amounting to around twenty million pounds. With all this wealth, it just didn't seem right to her to keep her job, and she started to think about what she wanted to do with her life, now that money was no object.

'You know I have always wanted to write,' Ailsa had said that evening, to her two best friends in the world.

'I know you have always written,' Jan said, with a grin. 'You just didn't finish anything or keep the momentum going.'

'True, but now that I don't have to work, I could throw myself into it. I have so many stories in my mind, all jumbled up, which I need to sort out and get down on paper, so to speak. And, I have to say, Storm Winds is such an inspiring place. I really think I could do it.'

Her two friends exchanged startled glances. 'You mean you are seriously considering moving to Scotland?' Connie ventured, in complete surprise at this apparent turn around in her friend's thoughts.

'Maybe,' Ailsa smiled, cautiously. 'What have I got to lose? My marriage ended in divorce after three short years, and since then I've not managed to hold together a relationship for more than a few months at a time. I have no job here now, and, although I love the fact we are in the most exciting city in the world, the fast pace of it all is starting to get to me a bit. Not that I noticed it before I went to Scotland, I just feel that I can't go on commuting on the tube, rushing here and there, going to parties and bars and restaurants. All the things I loved up until now seem a bit empty and meaningless. I have both of you, of course, and I love you, and I'll miss you more than I can say, but you can always come up for visits. There are plenty of rooms in the old ancestral pile after all.'

'Sounds like you've made up your mind already,' Connie said, resignedly. 'What about Adrian?'

Ailsa hesitated before she answered. 'Adrian and I are going nowhere. I hardly see him as it is, and, when I do, all we do is argue. The only thing we have in common is that our names both begin with 'A'! His work is his life, takes him all over the world, as you know, but whenever I need him, I turn around and he is gone, off on some journalistic trip somewhere. I need someone who needs me, otherwise I feel useless and un-loved. I called him last night and told him it was over.'

'Wow, this is serious stuff!' Jan said, taking a gulp of her wine.

'I think it's just being able to talk it through that's made me realise that this is actually what I want. I hadn't sorted my thoughts out finally until now, but everything seems to be falling into place. I am going to sell the flat and move to Scotland.'

'I don't think either of us can blame you, Ailsa. I've seen Storm Winds, and I think it is the most romantic place I have ever seen. Arnasaid is a gorgeous little place too, and, you're right, if you're looking for inspiration for your writing, you couldn't really pick a better place. It's just that it's so big! Anyway, you've got the lovely Eileen and the horrible Miss Cochrane and the other staff too, to look after you.'

'Well, contrary to what Connie has just said, I haven't seen Storm Winds, but I think it sounds amazing! I can't wait to come up for a holiday!'

'I can't wait to have you, Jan! Both of you.'

'Well I think this calls for a bottle of champagne!' Connie said, and suiting action to the word, she jumped up and ordered one at the bar.

The flat had been sold within the week, and the boxes packed and ready two days later. Connie and Jan helped with this task, and also with the cleaning which inevitably followed. Three weeks to the day when she and Connie had landed back at Heathrow, Ailsa was back there, waiting for her flight back to her new life in Scotland. The removal van had already dispatched to the North West, with a few of her favourite pieces of furniture which had come from her adoptive parents' house. Connie and Jan had gone to the airport to see her off, with the promise that they would visit soon.

The flight from Heathrow to Glasgow is no more than an hour, although the plane taxiing and waiting to take off takes up time. Ailsa was on the five o'clock flight, which didn't depart until almost six. She made use of the cabin service and ordered white wine and sandwiches, munching her way through them as she read her book. She enjoyed the flight but didn't take in a word of her book. She wondered what her reception would be like, this time, when she got to the house.

Fiona H. Preston

depart until almost six. She made use of the cabin service and ordered white wine and sandwiches, munching her way through them as she read her book. She enjoyed the flight but didn't take in a word of her book. She wondered what her reception would be like, this time, when she got to the house.

Jim Hutton was waiting for her at the airport, and, for this, she was relieved. Glad that it wasn't the surly guy who had transported her and Connie last time. She sat in the front with Jim, although he spoke seldom, and she enjoyed just seeing the little villages lit by street lamps as they passed through. She fell asleep not far south of Fort William and was roused at nearly 11 p.m. by Jim shaking her gently and telling her they had arrived.

She awoke the next morning to a fierce wind and driving rain lashing against her window, and, when she woke fully to see that she was in a bedroom at Storm Winds, she felt a little thrill of excitement. She knew Miss Cochrane and Eileen were still in the household. It had been Sir Angus' expressed wish that if Ailsa decided to keep the house the present staff should all stay on, if they so wished. Ailsa, arriving late the previous night, had not seen anyone but Jim. She cuddled back down into the warm bed. It was late April, but the room was really cold, and the weather was more like a winter's morning than a spring one.

'No wonder the house was named Storm Winds!' she mused, as she watched the rain battering at the house, and the wind howling down the chimney.

A few minutes later, Eileen knocked on her door and brought her a cup of tea. Eileen was smiling broadly as she looked at the new mistress of the house. 'Cup of tea, Madam? I've put breakfast in the breakfast room, as usual. It's good to have you back!'

'Thank you, Eileen,' said Ailsa, 'but I would prefer it if you didn't call me Madam, it makes me feel ancient! Please call me Ailsa, won't you?'

26

'Oh, Miss Cochrane would never allow me to call you by your first name.' Eileen looked shocked at the prospect. 'I could call you Lady Hamilton-Dunbar, if you would prefer?'

'Definitely not!' was the reply. 'Although,' she added, with a mischievous glance at the younger girl, 'you could always call me Lady HD, you know, high definition, like the TVs?' Her humour was lost on Eileen, who looked at her quizzically, but did not respond.

Halfway through Ailsa's breakfast, Miss Cochrane made an appearance. She stood beside the table, hands clasped in front of her, with a grimmer than normal expression on her face. Ailsa put aside her paper and looked at her, long and hard, before she said anything, all the while trying to remind herself that she was in charge now and need not be intimidated by this controlling woman who stood before her. Ailsa amazed herself by falling neatly into the 'Lady of the house' role, as she said, eventually, 'Well Miss Cochrane, here I am! Was there something you needed?'

Miss Cochrane drew a deep breath and said, 'I just wanted to let you know, Madam, that I welcome you back to Storm Winds.'

Ailsa literally gaped. 'Thanks, Miss Cochrane, but could you please call me Ailsa? All this is really new to me, and having a title isn't really my style. I would love it if you could just call me by my first name.' She was quite pleased with her plea, she felt it sounded friendly and comforting.

Miss Cochrane thought differently. 'I am afraid, I am unable to do that, Madam,' she said, with disdain in her voice. 'You see, I have worked here all my life, as housekeeper, for Sir Angus, who always insisted on keeping the distinction of rank. I was happy with knowing my place, and I shall always defer to a title.'

'Well, that is quite a statement, Miss Cochrane,' Ailsa said, in surprise.

'The trouble, Madam,' she continued, 'is that Sir Angus told me about your mother, who she was and why you were not brought up here, and although I realise you are Sir Angus' only living relative, you are . . . you are . . . '

'A bastard?' Ailsa said, calmly. 'Don't you think you are being very old-fashioned? We are in the twenty-first century, for God's sake, no one bothers about that kind of thing now.' Ailsa was more amused than angry.

Miss Cochrane looked at her new employer with distaste. 'I am afraid I cannot stay here,' she said, with finality. 'You say it is old-fashioned, and yet you are willing to accept a title which has gone back generations. This family used to mean something in the area. They were role models for the local community, looking after the land and its tenants, and providing shelter and help for the poor in times of trouble. You seem to take over the estate as if you were taking over a holiday camp, with no responsibility connected to it.'

Ailsa caught her breath before she spoke carefully. 'I don't know how you come to such a conclusion when I have only been back here five minutes. You have no idea what my thoughts or feeling may be, never mind my approach to the responsibility the estate throws up and also the title I hold. Just because I don't want to stand on ceremony with the staff doesn't mean I don't want to take my responsibilities seriously. I think you misjudge me, Miss Cochrane.' As she said the words, Ailsa suddenly woke up to the fact that, in a way, her housekeeper was actually correct. She had not thought about the responsibilities such a role and inheritance would bring, she had selfishly thought only about what it provided her in order to carry out her dream of writing. It suddenly dawned on her that being First Lady of Storm Winds meant that she would need to immerse herself in the community, carry out certain tasks, work hard on the estate, and take care of people almost like a Vicar took care of his flock. She would need to be a pillar of the community. She almost laughed out loud at the thought. Miss Cochrane turned and left the room, and Ailsa pushed aside her plate.

She pulled on sturdy boots and went for a long, wet walk across the cliffs, needing to think. Had she been too hasty, accepting all of this? Was it merely a selfish reason to leave London, just because she suddenly realised that she was almost done with the rat race? She had changed her mind relatively quickly. Had she given herself enough time to decide if the move was right for her? How naïve she had been to think that the Storm Winds community would welcome her with open arms. Her title had been bestowed on her because there was no one else suitable alive who could take it on instead. Sir Angus had had no love for her, there had been no connection, just a cold, calculated decision to hand over the estate into the only hands which were free to take it on. Sir Angus had been besotted by Hunter, that much was apparent, but Ailsa's very presence at the end had reminded him of that love which he had cast aside, of his ineptitude, his weakness and cowardice as he sent her away for adoption to save his own reputation. Was she over-thinking the situation? She had come to Storm Winds looking for a fresh start, a new beginning, but, unfortunately, Storm Winds didn't seem to want that same fresh start.

Eileen made up the fire in the small blue sitting room where Ailsa and Connie had sat that fateful night when Sir Angus passed away. Ailsa had the radio on Classic FM and curled up on the squashy sofa with a glass of red wine. The curtains were still open wide, although at nine thirty in the evening, darkness enclosed her. The wind and rain had died away, and the night sky was clear of clouds and dotted with stars. She thought fleetingly that this was the first time in years she had actually looked at a sky and seen the stars. Such a thing was almost impossible in the centre of London, with the tall built up landscape and the light pollution of the largest city in the UK.

'I don't know what to do,' Ailsa told Connie on the phone that evening, her thoughts in turmoil.

'It sounds like it's a bigger job than you imagined, darling,' Connie said cheerfully. 'Miss Cochrane is a right bitch. She should be helping you, not condemning you because she thinks you were 'born out of wedlock'. Shit, she would fit into Jane Austen's time rather than now.'

'Yes, I know all that, but I think she makes a valid point about the responsibility,' Ailsa said desperately. 'It's more than just enjoying myself up here and taking the time to immerse myself in the scenery and landscape, it's about being someone to people who need a figure to look up to. I don't believe I can do that,' she finished tearfully.

'Course you can, don't be daft. Okay, you were not brought up with a pre-conceived notion of your own self-importance, but what you need to remember is that none of this is your fault. You didn't ask to be born, you didn't ask to be adopted, and you certainly didn't ask to be given a title and a fortune which most people would kill for, but which comes with a responsibility which I know you take seriously. I think you need to try and get under old Cocky's skin. Ask for her help. I know you think she doesn't rate you, but you need to try and make a friend of her, and she may well be the key to helping you to run the estate. Think about it, honey, as a challenge, not a curse.'

Ailsa finished the bottle of red wine. She thought she would like to read in bed, so made her way to the library, switching on the nearest lamp as she entered. It was a lovely room. Tall bookcases framed the walls, with a moving staircase to reach the higher shelves. There was a huge oak table in the centre, and the room was split-levelled. The lower part was like a cosy study, with a fire and the winged-back chairs Ailsa remembered from her meeting with Sir Angus. As was the same in most of the rooms in the house, this one too had an open log fire. She scanned the shelves for something interesting and picked up '*Kidnapped*' from a shelf. On the way out, she suddenly remembered the portrait, and back-tracked into the room to stare at the picture of her mother, 'Hunter'. What a strong figure she portrayed. What steely determination could be read in her face. Had any of that passed on to her? She was the daughter of a remarkable woman, by all accounts. Why couldn't she harness some of that spirit and determination and run Storm Winds the way Hunter might have run it? Ailsa Hamilton-Dunbar decided, at that moment, that she would not be beaten. She had never been tested in this way before. She would try and step into the shoes of her illustrious ancestors. She would be a modern 'Lady', but she would try and espouse the values of that bygone age, and her inherited title. She would do it her way, but with sympathy for the traditions on which this empire of Storm Winds was built, *her* empire. Could she do it? By God, she would certainly try.

The following morning was white with the mist of spring, and the wind was fresh and cold from the north west. Ailsa got up and dressed early, going out for a walk before breakfast. The dew lay thick on the grass, the mist hanging over the cliffs like a muffling blanket. The sun, making a concerted effort to burn the clouds of mist, was not making a very good job of it so far. She walked down the rocky cliff path to the beach, her mind in a tumult with the events of the day before, trying to make sense of all that she and Miss Cochrane had discussed.

After breakfast, she went looking for Miss Cochrane. Alisa found her, putting linen away, in a small room on the first landing. 'Hello!' she said, to the housekeeper's back, which went rigid before Miss Cochrane stiffly turned around. 'I wondered if we could have a chat? I've been thinking about what you said last night, and I really want to talk to you about it. I've asked Eileen to bring some coffee to the library. Would you join me there?'

Miss Cochrane hesitated, for more than half a minute, then, without speaking, she briefly nodded her head, before she turned back to her task. Ailsa thought to herself, 'Is that a yes, Cocky?' and moved away, towards the stairs and the library.

The sun had come out, though there was a decided chill in the air, and Ailsa was glad to see that Eileen had lit the fire. A small table had been drawn up in front of it, with a coffee pot, two mugs and a plate of chocolate biscuits. She decided not to sit until the other woman came in, as tactically, she didn't want to be in a disadvantaged position, especially if Miss Cochrane refused to sit down.

Miss Cochrane came in five minutes later. Ailsa motioned her to a seat, and then proceeded to pour two cups of coffee.

She proffered the plate of biscuits over to the housekeeper, who took one as if in slow motion. The log crackled in the hearth, and Ailsa took in a long silent breath before she spoke.

'After we spoke yesterday, I had a long hard look at what I had taken on. I have been in a bit of a daze since Sir Angus spoke to me, trying to work out what was for the best all round.' Miss Cochrane raised an eyebrow, but said nothing. 'You see,' Ailsa went on, 'I was perfectly happy with my life. I hadn't ever sought out my real birth parents because I could not have asked for a better childhood and upbringing than my adoptive parents gave me. They both worked hard and taught me the same work ethic. They brought me up in the Church, helped me with my homework, and took me on picnics in the summer. They loved me and made me feel special. When I found out that someone was trying to 'find' me, as I was a relation, I thought it was somebody doing it for a hobby and bringing me up to Scotland only added to the mystery and excitement. I did not expect what awaited me. I never imagined I would meet someone who would claim to be my father.'

Miss Cochrane looked at her with a steely expression. Obviously, the niceties of her life and the stability and love she received from her adoptive parents had no effect on her housekeeper's emotions, so Ailsa tried another tack.

'I didn't ask for this, Miss Cochrane. But, you are correct, I did not think about the responsibility of running a great estate. I did not think about the position, and how it might affect people in the community. I did not think about the hard work, the effort or the input that Sir Angus had to this estate and collection of villages. I did not realise that the estate was his life's work and that this had passed to me. I was in shock. I was not thinking clearly, if at all, and I did not consider the huge responsibility connected to Storm Winds. I think that, if I had thought about it, I might have shied away from it. I need your help Miss Cochrane. I need your help to make the right decisions for the good of the estate. Please don't go.'

Chapter Four

Miss Cochrane had decided to stay. Not that she made it easy for Ailsa. She let Ailsa have her say, then gave a derisory sniff and stood, saying she would think about it, but that she was unsure if Sir Angus would have given Ailsa the position and inheritance if there had been anyone else suitable to hand it over to. Ailsa was quite sure that she was right, but certainly didn't tell her so. It was an uneasy beginning, but at least the housekeeper had decided to stay, and, if nothing else, she was the most credible link with the past Ailsa was ever going to meet.

So, what to do now? Ailsa had no idea how to begin to run an estate. For a start, apart from what her titles told her, she had no idea what she actually owned, neither did she know who to ask. In the end she decided to contact Sir Angus' lawyer whom she had met when the affairs and estate were being settled. Then she thought about a routine. A day's work where she could focus on the estate for a certain amount of time and concentrate on her writing too. She had not given up on this idea, she felt she needed this outlet as well as the 'day job' of being in charge of Storm Winds.

'Do we have an estate manager at Storm Winds?' Ailsa ventured to ask Miss Cochrane as she brought in a mid-morning cup of tea.

'We had an interim manager on loan from a neighbouring estate owned by Colonel MacKenzie, whose family has been in this area almost as long as the Hamilton-Dunbars. His house is only about five miles away, and, when Sir Angus became ill, Stephen Millburn stepped in at Colonel MacKenzie's request and worked half his week at Storm Winds.'

'I see,' Ailsa was churning all this information around in her head, 'and do you think we could get him back, even for a short period, until I found my own manager?'

'Probably. Stephen would be able to help you find a suitable person,' Miss Cochrane said, then started, and looked taken aback at her own alacrity. 'Sorry, I mean to say, "Madam",' and Miss Cochrane added, to hide her own confusion, 'Colonel MacKenzie has invited you to dinner on Saturday.'

'Oh really?' Ailsa said. 'Can you tell me anything about the family, Miss Cochrane?'

'Colonel MacKenzie lost his wife around twenty years ago. He is a very prominent figure in the area, like Sir Angus was,' she paused to catch her breath and her emotions. 'He has four sons, all of whom live at home, with their respective families.'

Ailsa pondered on the invitation. It would be good to meet other members of the community, but why had the Colonel invited her? This 'old money' family of Colonel MacKenzie's sounded worlds apart from anything that she had ever known. Would she have to sit through a huntin' and fishin' diatribe, and be quizzed about her good fortune in landing one of the biggest estates in the West of Scotland? She thought she would have to attend the dinner to get any answers to her questions, but, as well as experiencing a thrill over her first dinner invitation, the thought of meeting a large family, who were lifelong neighbours of Sir Angus, made her blood run cold. Four sons, all with their respective families, was a lot of people. She feared she was going to be completely out of her depth, and, worse than that, the centre of attention and the butt of their high-class jokes. But, she had an agenda too. She needed to meet them and to get to know them and even make allies of some of them in order to find her own feet here at Storm Winds. Not least, she needed help with an estate manager. She went online to look for dresses, so that at least she would feel good, although she knew she would fret about the invite from now until Saturday.

'You've got mail!' Eileen said, as she waltzed into the library the next day with three large packets, one on top of the other. She plunked them down on the nearest table and looked at Ailsa expectantly.

'My dresses!' Ailsa said, with a smile. 'I hope at least one of them is okay for Saturday, otherwise I'm stumped!'

'Are you going to try them on?' Eileen urged. She had dropped the 'Madam' when Miss Cochrane was not around; she had not discussed this with Ailsa, and Ailsa, wanting nothing more than to be called by her first name, gleefully and silently accepted it.

'Yes, come on up to my room and tell me what you think,' Ailsa said, with a grin.

The first was an off-the-shoulder deep purple dress, with a bow at the back.

'D'you think it's a bit fussy?' Eileen was perched on the end of the bed, her nose twitching, head to the side, as she pondered the dress. 'I just think it looks a wee bit like a bridesmaid's dress.'

'God, you're nothing if not honest,' Ailsa laughed. 'I thought as much myself, but I don't know what the Colonel's mob are like at all, whether it will be really formal, or quite casual.'

'Try on the next,' Eileen urged.

The next one was a royal blue wrap around dress, very fine silky material, the skirt tied at the left-hand side, with a flattering narrow bow, both plain and sophisticated at the same time.

'That's it, without seeing the third one!' Eileen hugged herself in glee. 'Deffo the right one, not too fussy, but classy, and the colour is exactly right for you.'

'I quite like this one myself,' Ailsa said, as she turned this way and that in front of the full-length mirror.

The third one was bright red, simple and straight and showed off her curves. 'I'll keep this one too, but I think I'll wear the blue one on Saturday,' she said, and Eileen agreed.

Ailsa was determined to establish a routine. She wanted to write, but she also wanted to devote time to the estate; not that she knew what she was doing with either at this particular time. She decided to work in the library. She loved this room. There was a separate study, which Sir Angus had used, but she found it cold and clinical, with no atmosphere, so she decided to use the library. She loved the smell of it. The shelves of books reminded her of Saturday afternoons when she was young, scouring the second-hand bookshops for bargains, and returning with two or three treasures clutched under her arm. Books she had bought with her pocket money. Books she read in the living room of the terraced house where she was brought up. Saturday nights were always special. Her father would sit with the crossword and periodically read out loud the clues for her and her mother to try and solve. Her mother would sit with some knitting and a glass of wine, and the glow of the fire would make the room seem comforting and welcoming and secure. Then her mother, at around 9.30 p.m. would go to the kitchen and make milky coffee and a pile of toast, or toasted teacakes, and they would eat contentedly while they enjoyed their various pursuits. It was Ailsa's favourite memory of home.

She moved a table over to the window, so that the fire was near, and she could work looking out of the window at the back kitchen garden and the mountains beyond. She knew that to write something successful she would need to write every day, so she decided to be quite regimented and work between 10 a.m. and 1 p.m. each day for the immediate future, then spend time in the estate office in the afternoon. She also wanted to incorporate a walk at some point every day, as she needed to explore her estate but also get fresh air and exercise. She shared her plans with Miss Cochrane, who looked at her with a blank expression when she said she would 'write' in the mornings. The housekeeper, however, did not challenge the plan, and saw to it that Ailsa had peace in the library during this time.

'I need to get a dog,' Ailsa thought, as she walked down the windswept path to the beach. Having a dog was one of the things she'd longed for, but the complication was that she was asthmatic, and suffered from allergies. Her doctor in London had told her that small dogs which didn't cast were the best bet, and, although it had not been possible to keep a pet in her confined space in London, she didn't see why she couldn't think about it here. She would need to make enquiries.

Arnasaid was a lovely village, the now familiar harbour bobbing with boats, and a small collection of shops including a store with a post office on its premises, a hotel, a few cafes, and a nice restaurant. There was a village pub, where Ailsa and Connie had enjoyed lunch a few weeks ago, although it now seemed like months to Ailsa. When Ailsa ventured into the village store, following her return to Storm Winds, a few people were entirely different in their approach towards her than they had been previously. Mrs Brown, who was at the checkout of the store when Ailsa went to pay, was like a completely different person.

She became extremely flustered as she put through the items Ailsa had put in her basket.

'Everything okay up at Storm Winds?' Mrs Brown asked, sweat beaded on her brow.

'Everything is fine, thank you,' Ailsa smiled. She wondered what all the drama was about. She hadn't changed, but Mrs Brown seemed to think that she was a different person and treated her as such.

'That'll be £15.29, Lady Hamilton-Dunbar,' she said, in an unnaturally loud voice, with a watchful eye on her customer's face.

'My name is Ailsa, please call me that,' Ailsa said, as cheerfully as she could. She felt that she was being tested.

Mrs Brown's taught features relaxed. 'There's your change, *Ailsa*,' she said, with a tight smile and obvious emphasis.

Ailsa picked up her bag and turned so abruptly that she almost knocked into the man standing directly and silently behind her. He was tall and fair, with blue eyes and a boyish grin. He looked around mid-forties, and he was very good looking. Ailsa, to her annoyance, found herself flushing as she thought that he would easily have heard the exchange between her and Mrs Brown.

'I beg your pardon,' he said, with a grin, his eyes twinkling at her embarrassment. He stepped aside to let her pass, and she did so without a word. She had just got to the door when she heard Mrs Brown's voice lifted in friendliness, 'Well hello, Mr MacKenzie, what can I do for you today?'

'So, that was one of the MacKenzies. One of the sons, as he must at least be in his forties, and Eileen said the Colonel was in his late sixties. But why hadn't he introduced himself when he had obviously overheard the exchange and would know that I've been invited to the MacKenzies' on Saturday? It was almost as if he was mocking me, keeping his identity to himself when he knew who I was,' she thought, 'well, I suppose I'll find out which one on Saturday!'

When she got back from Arnasaid, she decided to have a look at the estate offices situated in a clutch of old stables in a cobbled courtyard which used to house the horses. There were no longer any working animals and the buildings had been made into a suite of rooms where the affairs of Storm Winds were ordered and put to rights. Eileen had told her that there was one member of staff who worked for the estate manager, though at the moment there was no estate manager.

Gennina was a general office worker. She was a peroxide blonde, red-lipped, black mascara-eyed, epitome of a dumb blonde, and, unfortunately, nothing in her manner or dress disproved this particular theory. She was, however, the kindest, most helpful and happy person that Ailsa thought she had ever met. It was like dealing with a happy child who wanted to do everything she could to please her parents.

'Oh, hello Mrs ... er ... Ailsa ... er Lady Dun, sorry, Lady Hamilton . . .' Gennina searched for the title which would please her new boss.

'Gennina, isn't it?' Ailsa held out her hand, which Gennina took and shook vigorously. 'Please call me Ailsa, it's my name, and I would prefer it to the title which I think is really too long winded and a bit of a mouthful for anyone to pronounce!'

Ailsa looked at her with amazement which turned to something short of hero-worship. 'Great! We'll just be Gennina and Ailsa, like two pals,' she said, with a gushy red-lipped smile.

'What are you working on at the moment?' Ailsa said.

'Well, just events really, you know, cos since Sir A left,' she made it sound like he had gone on a trip somewhere, 'there has been a drop in the applications for the shooting parties and balls and stuff.'

Ailsa nodded. 'Okay, so what sort of events do you co-ordinate?'

'Sir A was involved in a lot of charities, so we organise charity balls, concerts and other fund-raising events. We also had grouse shooting and deer stalking as annual events, and lots of other wee things like Christmas parties for the local children and things like that.'

'So, are you carrying on with these events?' Ailsa asked.

'Oh, yes,' Gennina said, with enthusiasm, 'if you want to?'

'Of course, I would like that, and please just let me know what's happening, as I'll be working on the estate from now on,' Ailsa said with a smile. She walked over to what she imagined to be the estate manager's own office and spent the rest of the morning going through the files, trying to get a grasp of all the things going on at Storm Winds, which she very decidedly wanted to continue. There was a lot of good work generated by the household which she wanted to retain and be a part of.

Gennina brought Ailsa a coffee later on, it was almost time for her to leave, she worked from 8 a.m. to 4 p.m., and it was around 3.30 p.m. She had been feeling very enthusiastic since meeting her new boss, as she had thought when Sir Angus passed away she would have been out of a job. Gennina was engaged to a local boy, and they were trying to plan their wedding in the next year. The last thing she needed was to lose her job.

Ailsa walked thoughtfully back to the main house later, well after Gennina had departed for home. The sun had gone down, and it was cold for spring, much colder than it would have been in London. She turned full circle to see the mountains, still heavy with snow, their giant peaks clearly outlined in the unusually blue, clear skies.

She had a solitary dinner that evening. Jean Morton was the part-time cook at Storm Winds, and Ailsa had made it plain that she was quite capable of seeing to her own dinner now and again, although she was aware of the fact that the cook, a bustling, heavy set woman in her sixties, would be out of a job at her discretion. So, she took small opportunities to have her own way, and other times allowed herself to be waited upon in the dining room much as Sir Angus would have done.

Ailsa looked round the huge old-fashioned kitchen. Mrs Morton had gone home for the evening, having left the place looking like it had been scrubbed within an inch of its life. There was a wooden table in the centre, a range, and all manner of antiquated appliances around. She took out a small frying pan, laid out a chopping board, and found some ingredients to make a simple pasta sauce. After cooking a tasty supper, she opened a bottle of red wine and took her meal into the small sitting room, where Eileen had already laid the fire. Ailsa left the curtains open, so that she could watch the last of the light outside, and settled herself down to enjoy.

She felt, later, that she needed a breath of fresh air and walked to the head of the cliff overlooking the coast and the rough sea which she couldn't see in the darkness of the spring night.

She breathed in the freshness, her hair tossed in the wind and her face tingled with the salt spray from the Atlantic Ocean. The turf felt springy beneath her feet, and she walked, hands in pockets, for a short way along the cliff path.

She felt his presence before she saw the dim outline. She took a sharp intake of breath, then steadied herself stammering, 'Hi, sorry, I didn't see you.'

'I'm really sorry, I didn't mean to give you a fright,' the man said, with real concern in his voice.

'No, it's fine,' she said, looking anything but fine, 'I just got a bit of a fright, that's all. I haven't bumped into anyone on these cliffs before.'

'Ah, right to wander,' he said, with a smile. 'Scotland prides itself on its allowing trespass rule. I come to this cliff quite often, I love the views and the path is good.' When he hesitated, a bundle of wet, lolloping energy launched itself at Ailsa, almost knocking her over. She shrieked and almost stumbled, and his arms were around her waist pulling her to her feet before she hit the turf.

'Sheila!' the man shouted urgently, at the brown animal whose tail was wagging ferociously. 'Sheila, sit down! And where is Sandy?' he asked, almost as if the dog understood his question. She looked behind her, just as another bounding wet mass of joy came up to them, and, sensing his master's stern voice meant that she had to sit, they both sat side by side watching with intelligent eyes.

Ailsa laughed. 'What lovely dogs!' she said appreciatively. 'Are they spaniels?'

'Yes,' he grinned. His voice was musical and low. 'I take it you are the Lady of the house?' he added, motioning his glance across to Storm Winds.

'Ailsa,' she said, simply but firmly.

He nodded and held out his hand for a friendly shake. 'I'm Stephen Millburn. I work up at Trannoch, Colonel MacKenzie's estate, and I've worked here, off and on, over the years.'

'Oh yes!' Ailsa was just able to make out the dark hair and strong dark features of his face. Miss Cochrane told me about you. On impulse, she said, 'Look, it's quite cold out here for a 'Softie Southerner' like me, would you like to come in for a coffee?'

He hesitated just long enough for her to feel uncomfortable. 'Well, I've got a long walk back to Trannoch from here, so I'd better get on my way.' He smiled, and with a few more pleasantries, walked away, his two dogs following in his wake.

Ailsa had a disturbed sleep. It was full of dogs of all shape and size, men who swept her off her feet then dumped her, and people who insisted on calling her 'Lady'. She woke up in a cold sweat and found it very difficult to drop back off to sleep.

Chapter Five

Ailsa had spent some time reading up on the area and learned that Fort William is a thriving tourist and shopping centre, and only forty-five minutes from Arnasaid. She decided she needed to get away for the day, so she took the Land Rover and drove down the picturesque A830, with its wild barren landscape, through the beautiful Glenfinnan with its 'Harry Potter' arched bridge, and loch which had provided the escape route of Bonnie Prince Charlie around the time when Storm Winds was built.

After parking the car, Ailsa spent the next few hours buying cushions, books and other meaningless items, which made her feel so much better. She trawled the DIY store and ordered paper and paint to be delivered for her bedroom and her favourite sitting room. She bought a pair of silver high heeled shoes and a clutch bag for her outfit on Saturday and bundled into a coffee shop with her new possessions, picking a small table by the window which overlooked Loch Linnhe.

Ailsa enjoyed the time by herself, away from the confines and complexities of her new life at the house. She passed by a small newsagent, which had a board in the doorway stuffed full of adverts for local services and informal sales and wants. While she took a note of a local painter and decorator advertising on the board, her eye caught sight of a small pink card in the uppermost area of the board which simply said, 'Adorable pedigree Yorkshire Terrier pups for sale, £500 each.' She wrote this number down too. Ailsa wasn't sure about Yorkies, but she knew that they didn't cast.

When she got back to the house, by dint of questioning Eileen about the phone number for the pups, Ailsa discovered it was a local number, a landline, and further enquiries uncovered the fact that the number belonged to a smallholding on the outskirts of the village, and Eileen knew the family in question.

'Could you take me there to have a look?' Ailsa asked.

'No problem, I'll give Sandra a ring and see if we can have a look at the pups,' Eileen promised.

The next day Ailsa drove the Land Rover, with Eileen at her side, a few miles up the coast to the house with the new puppies. Sandra MacDonald was in her early fifties, and an attractive looking woman. She was smallish, with long brown hair piled up on her head, well-cut-features, and dressed in wellies, jeans and a red jumper. She met them coming in the gate and led them to a back room in the house where the pup's mother, and lots of pups, seemed to fill the room.

'The wee black one is spoken for.' Sandra pointed to a frolicking fat little pup with a fiercely wagging tail. 'Other than that, you can take your pick! Take your time and have a look, I'll put on the kettle.'

Ailsa knelt down and immediately three puppies pranced around her legs, one pulling at her sock above the rim of her ankle boot. Another sat by her mother's side, eyes forlorn and expressive, quietly taking in the scene in front of her.

'Oh, they're adorable!' Eileen cuddled them each in turn.

'The little quiet one.' Ailsa pointed to this pup, and Eileen lifted her up. She seemed smaller and more timid than the other pups. 'Perfect!' Ailsa snuggled up to the tiny little bundle, who shivered apprehensively in her arms.

'Yes, she's a wee pet!' Eileen passed her to Ailsa.

The others gradually got bored and moved away, but the one who was playing with her sock persisted in trying to get it out of Ailsa's boot, a determined little rump moving to and fro in the conquest.

'This one too!' Ailsa said, with shining eyes. She will be perfect for my little quiet one, and will look after her.'

'I think that's a brilliant idea!'

So, it was decided that Ailsa should have two little pups, not one. They completed the transaction at the large kitchen table which was strewn with papers, food, the teapot and a selection of the most delicious cakes Ailsa had ever tasted. 'I like to bake,' was Sandra's only explanation for the most generous and delicious fare.

An hour later, Ailsa and Eileen made their way back to Storm Winds with a basket with two puppies in it, in the back of the Land Rover. 'What will you call them?' asked Eileen, as they sped along the road.

'Bluebell is the little quiet one, and Rosie is the adventurous go-getter!' she said, with a huge grin. She was quietly delighted with her new pets.

Miss Cochrane was less amenable to the new pups than her mistress. 'We've only ever had working dogs at Storm Winds, never dogs in the house,' she said, with a look of distaste. 'I think they should stay in one of the outhouses.'

Ailsa eyed her calmly. 'I have wanted a dog for ages, Miss Cochrane, and I am very excited about bringing two new pups to Storm Winds. I have spoken to Jean and she is happy to have them sleep in the kitchen next to the big range.'

'But Molasses lives in the kitchen!' Miss Cochrane said, insipidly. 'How will that work?'

'Apparently, Jean's cat already seems to have taken to the pups. It isn't unusual for cats and dogs to live happily together,' she added, drily. 'I think the big cat will mother the little pups.'

There was nothing more for Miss Cochrane to say, she knew when she was beaten, so she pursed her lips and turned away.

Ailsa was more nervous about the dinner at the MacKenzies' than she cared to mention to anyone, even Eileen. A figurehead Colonel was bad enough, but four sons and their respective families thrown in was enough to intimidate anyone, and Ailsa was no exception. She had no idea what any of them were like, except the one she had met in the village, and he was handsome enough to be disconcerting to her.

She had quizzed Eileen about them. She was not terribly sure of them, individually, but she could tell Ailsa that the Colonel was a legend in his own right, large and blustering and some would say bullying. He ruled the estate and his family with the proverbial iron rod, and a few of Eileen's friends who worked at Trannoch, were happier away from his presence than in it. Eileen had seen or met all of the family during various functions and meetings and was aware that the two estate families had always 'socialised' in the past. Three of the sons were married, with their families living at the Trannoch estate. One was living apart from his wife, and the fourth was the local doctor, and widowed. All the children of these respective sons went off to boarding schools, and the wives were influential members of various committees and groups in the area.

'Apart from that, I don't really know anything!'

'I think you know quite a lot! Thank you for filling me in, I feel more nervous than ever.'

'Well, what I mean is, I don't know any of them personally. I do know that one of the sons has a bit of a reputation with the women but can't remember which one.'

'Okay, that's helpful.' Ailsa threw back her head with a sarcastic laugh.

Colonel Mason Smith MacKenzie had been born with the proverbial silver spoon in his mouth. The MacKenzies, like the Hamilton-Dunbars, had owned vast areas of land in the North West of Scotland, and like most of the landed gentry, had become more powerful in their own particular area than local government. In days gone by, they actually governed the area. The Colonel owned, like Sir Angus, many of the nearby villages, and had private tenants who were beholden to their landlords. They were central to the decision-making councils in the area and were members of highly influential commercial enterprises. All this added to their power, and substantial 'voice' in the area. In addition to this, the Colonel was an astute political leader and figurehead in his own right. He was an outspoken blunderbuss of a man, fiercely Royalist, with a strict right-wing conservative viewpoint which would allow no debate or challenge. He was quite firmly and unashamedly stuck in the past. He had led troops in Afghanistan and the middle east, and his strategic enterprises had spilled over into the way he managed his own 'kingdom' – and his family.

None of this, however, was conveyed to the unsuspecting Ailsa; Eileen did not move in the illustrious circles which would furnish her with the personality traits of their rich and powerful neighbours, so Ailsa was perfectly unsuspecting about her future encounter.

Ailsa had a long hot bath, and Eileen brought her a glass of chilled wine to sip as she got ready for the dinner at Trannoch. All the time she was wondering how on earth she was to keep her nerves at bay when she met the MacKenzies. If the son she had met in the village store was anything to go by, they would be intimidating and probably arrogant. She was beginning to wonder why she had bothered accepting the invitation, but she had felt it was part of the 'duty' which she had undertaken with the inheritance. She knew that Sir Angus and the Colonel had been figureheads, but were they friends? She was beginning to wonder if all wasn't as it first seemed. And now she was a living product of that long line of tradition. She knew she could never be the type of person Sir Angus was, she still couldn't think of him as her father, apart from anything else they had lived in very different generations, but she hoped that she could bring a youthful freshness to the 'role' and her situation in the district.

'You look lovely, Ailsa,' Eileen breathed appreciatively, as Ailsa descended the sweeping oak stairway.

'Thanks, Eileen. I am a bit nervous about meeting them all, I must admit.'

'You'll be fine.' Eileen handed over her coat. 'Jim's got the car out front,' and she gave her employer an encouraging hug.

Ailsa gasped when she first caught sight of Trannoch. Made of the same grey stone as Storm Winds, there the similarities ended. While the latter is a substantial estate mansion Trannoch is at least three times the size and stature, commanding an imposing vista over the most perfectly-cut lawns and weed-free terraces. Sitting around five miles through the rugged hills more inland than Storm Winds, and thus enjoying more shelter from the mountainous backdrop, Trannoch had a much more nurtured feel about it, the flowers and shrubs cultured and well-tended almost like a garden which would be open to the public. The lights from the windows shone invitingly through the dusk from the tall rounded windows, not gothic ones like Storm Winds Ailsa noted. A pillared porch big enough to drive a double-decker bus through was the centre of the building, through which came striding soldierly the figure of a tall older man. Ailsa sprang forward, determined to show that she was not nervous or intimidated by the situation. Before anyone could say a word, she pushed forth her hand to shake, 'Colonel MacKenzie? Hi! I am Ailsa,' she announced in a high voice. There was a startled silence. The tall man, who had his hands behind his back, kept them there, and in what seemed like slow motion, turned slightly, chin jutting upwards, and said, 'Lady Hamilton-Dunbar, I am Denbeath, Colonel MacKenzie's butler. Will you please come this way?'

Ailsa and Jim Hutton exchanged glances, Jim with a half-apologetic smile that could have meant, 'awkward!' hurried back to the car. Ailsa sheepishly followed the other man into the vast hallway of Trannoch.

She thought, 'What a start!'

If Ailsa had been amazed by Storm Winds, it was a miniature version of Trannoch. The hall was literally cathedral-like, with old oak panelling and huge pieces of fine antique furniture, tapestries and a whole arsenal of weapons displayed on one wall. A log fire burned sleepily in the grate, and a woman dressed in black approached to take her coat. Just as Denbeath turned to lead the way, a loud bellowing voice was followed into the hall by a tall, red haired giant of a man, with a chiselled face, jutting chin and an aura of command about him which told unquestioningly that this was indeed the Colonel.

'There you are!' He came forward and pumped her hand in an enthusiastic shake. 'I was beginning to think young Jim Hutton had driven off the road!' and she joined in his loud infectious laughter, especially the description of the ageing handy man.

The Colonel stood grasping her hand and searched her face with fresh interest. 'You look . . . you look so like . . .' he paused and gathered himself together. 'You look very nice,' he finished lamely, and with a characteristic throwing up of his hands added, 'come away in and meet the hooligans! They are all here to meet you!' and he strode purposefully up the hallway and flung open a door to the left. Ailsa almost had to run to keep up with him, trying not to go over on her new silver sandals.

They were standing and sitting in little groups around the ornate high-ceilinged room, commonly known as the 'Great Room,' having pre-dinner drinks. Italian marble furniture adorned the place, which was decorated in a light green paper and had soft green furnishings throughout. A fireplace, the inside of which was big enough to fit a table seating six, was the centrepiece, logs burning assertively in the grate. High, gilded-framed paintings were hung on each wall, and the waiting staff were mingling with silver trays upon which stood champagne flutes. The Colonel lifted one and placed it into Ailsa's hand which she found to be shaking. She did not notice the surroundings, she was at this moment only nervous about and concerned with the people. They had stopped talking as she entered, eyeing her, in the main, with expectation, and in some cases amusement.

'Well, here we are, everyone!' The Colonel commanded silence with his statement. 'Lady Ailsa Hamilton-Dunbar is amongst us, daughter of my very great friend (he hesitated ever so slightly before 'friend') Angus Hamilton-Dunbar.' There was a general murmur of what could be construed as a welcome, then the Colonel proceeded to make the introductions. The four sons were there, all tall like their father, but all different in appearance. Noel was the eldest of the sons, tall, broad and red haired like his father. There was no mention of his wife, who lived apart from the family. Ailsa got the impression he was a bit surly and bad-tempered. Malcolm was the second son, tall and fair, and the best looking of the sons, the one she had bumped into in the village store in Arnasaid. Ailsa felt herself flush when she was introduced to Malcolm.

'Well, hello again!' he said, grasping her hand and coming near enough for her to smell the whisky on his breath. He held her hand just a little longer than was necessary, and Ailsa felt a fluttering feeling in the pit of her stomach which she had not felt for a long time. He introduced a mousey looking woman with lank bobbed dark hair and a perpetually tragic look on her face, as his wife, Belinda. The black dress did nothing to enhance her appearance. She said hello in a small voice, which was almost a whisper, before the Colonel, with some impatience, propelled Ailsa over to the next group consisting of Maxwell, the third son, and Thomas, the youngest, with his beautiful wife Carys. Maxwell, or Max as he was known by most people, like his older brother Noel, did not appear to enjoy pleasantries, and said nothing as he shook her extended hand. Thomas said, 'How do you do?' in a companionable tone. Carys, tall, almost painfully thin, her blonde hair twisted into an expert chignon, and dressed in a silver and red dress which looked as if it cost more than a year's mortgage on Ailsa's old London flat, moved forward towards Ailsa with an amused look on her haughty face. Her eyes were the bluest Ailsa had seen, they were almost turquoise, and her pink smeared lips were set in a hard line.

'Well, Lady Hamilton-Dunbar, and how are you liking Storm Winds?' Without waiting for an answer, she rattled on, 'It's so nice to have neighbours again, but it must be daunting to have a title thrust upon you when previously you were just an ordinary person doing an ordinary job,' and she finished acidly, 'What exactly did you do in London anyway?'

Before it had dawned on Ailsa that Carys was being anything other than friendly, she answered amiably, 'I worked for an advertising agency.'

'How . . . how *practical*,' Carys retorted, and, turning to spot Denbeath at the open door, she announced to the group, 'Dinner is ready, shall we go through?' then rudely turned her back on Ailsa, gripped Thomas by the arm and walked out the door.

Ailsa felt herself flush again, this time in annoyance at this cold treatment which she was sure she had not merited, when the Colonel once again steered her, this time, in the direction of the dining room.

She found herself sitting between Max, the widower and doctor, and Thomas, the husband of the woman who had just insulted her. Across the table sat Malcolm and Belinda. The Colonel sat at one end and the other was left empty. The room became an instant flurry of activity as the staff brought in the first course, poured the wine and handed out bread to accompany the soup, which was delicious.

The Colonel liked to hold court, and boomed out questions and remarks to all of them, particularly Ailsa. 'So, Ailsa, what do you plan to do with Storm Winds, are you going to keep it as a family estate?'

Ailsa was a little taken aback at his directness, but she nodded. 'Yes, I think so. I am trying to find out all that goes on so that I can continue the good work Sir Angus did. I know there is a lot to learn, but I am hoping to employ an estate manager soon who will help.'

'Good estate managers are incredibly hard to find,' the Colonel barked. 'You may have heard that Stephen Millburn worked with Sir Angus on a kind of part-time arrangement, that was mainly because he couldn't find anyone suitable to take on the post full time. I will send him over so that he can advise you.'

Ailsa had not been in the house for more than an hour, but already she thought it would not be a good idea to refuse the Colonel anything, so she assented to this 'request'.

'Do you think you will like living in Scotland, Ailsa?' Thomas asked, with a genuine smile.

'Yes, I think I will,' Ailsa said, gulping down her wine to calm her nerves. 'I love the area, and the house is very large and old-fashioned, but I am going to add my own stamp to it, and hopefully it will feel more and more like home.' She looked up just in time to catch Carys giving a derisory sniff at this last, which made her feel angry and uncomfortable, especially when it was followed with a patronising remark.

'Oh? And do you think working for an advertising company will equip you with the skills to run an estate?'

'Well . . . I . . .'

'Oh, come now, Carys, don't be unkind, darling.' Thomas looked affronted at her remark. Ailsa's eyes sparkled with anger, but she chose to ignore Carys and took another mouthful of wine, which was immediately refilled.

Emboldened by the alcohol, she turned to Max who had been silently eating his soup. 'So, Maxwell, do you all work on the estate?' she ventured. Max shook his head.

'I work for a living, as the local doctor,' he said, implying openly that the others didn't, 'and it's Max.'

'Yes, Max is the brains of the family,' Thomas said, with a laugh. 'The rest of us work on the estate with father. Oh, and Noel does a bit of art dealing, here and there.' At this, the oldest member of the family cast a glance over to the youngest brother.

'Thomas, I do more on a weekday than you do in a whole week.'

Thomas laughed again in return. 'Yes, you do, Noel. Big bruv is always travelling to far flung countries, buying and selling art and making his own private fortune!'

'Do you like art, Lady Hamilton-Dunbar?' Carys piped up, again holding Ailsa's gaze with an acerbic expression on her face. 'Sir Angus built up quite a collection at Storm Winds, you haven't sold them all already have you?' and she gave a humourless laugh.

'Of course not.' Ailsa was beginning to get seriously irked by Carys' attitude towards her. Especially since Carys insisted on using her title when she spoke to her, despite her pleading with everyone to use her first name.

'There is that lovely painting of Sir Angus' old friend in the library which I have always so admired. What do you think of that?'

Ailsa looked astonished. Why had Carys made reference to the portrait of Hunter? She presumed this was the one Carys meant, but, before she could reply, the Colonel burst in to the conversation. 'That's enough, Carys,' he said, in his strident voice. 'Give Ailsa a chance to find her feet before you pester her with questions about paintings.' At this Carys subsided but did not look in the least subdued. She smiled with satisfaction, and turned to Noel to speak to him.

'We hear you are single, Ailsa.' Thomas was like a friendly puppy and didn't seem to feel any of the undertones of the previous conversations. 'Have you never been married?'

'For God's sake Thomas, don't be so blunt.' Noel again picked up the thread of the conversation from across the table.

Ailsa was beginning to feel a little lightheaded with the wine she had consumed so far and answered quickly. 'Oh, that's no problem,' she said, smiling at Thomas. 'I was married once, when I was much younger, but it didn't work out.' She drained her glass again, as the plates were cleared away and the next course appeared. There was a lot of conversation following about the estate, to which Ailsa could not contribute, so she ate the fish course and drank more wine, taking in the conversation from around her. Once or twice she caught Malcolm's eye across the table, and he was watching her with an amused expression on his face. He winked at her at one point, and as she was feeling the hostility from Carys, and to a lesser extent Noel and Max, she was relieved to find that someone appeared to be pleased to have her there. She smiled in return. When her glass was refilled again, and she put it to her lips, Max frowned in her direction. Ailsa was surprised at the look. The Colonel also noticed the expression on his third son's face and bellowed down the table.

'Enjoying our wine, Ailsa? It is from our very own vineyard in France, part of the MacKenzie export business.'

'It's lovely!' Ailsa said, slurring her words ever so slightly.

'And very strong,' Max snapped, acidly. 'Let me give you some water.'

Ailsa took his meaning, and her face flushed in annoyance. 'I am quite capable of pouring my own water, thank you,' and she almost snatched the decanter from his hand. It slipped, and he only just caught it, stopping it from crashing back on to the table.

He seemed non-plussed, and said, 'Well, make sure you drink it,' in an officious offhand manner which made Ailsa bristle with rage, but, before she could think of a suitable answer, the next course arrived.

The rest of the meal passed in a bit of a blur for Ailsa, and when the Colonel stood and declared that they would all retire to the drawing room for after dinner drinks, Ailsa stood up warily, conscious of the fact she had taken quite a lot of wine and was feeling more than a little tipsy.

'Feeling a bit lightheaded?' Max asked her sarcastically.

'Not at all, thank you.' Ailsa willed herself to think and talk coherently and took Malcolm's proffered arm thankfully. His face was very close to hers as he breathed,

'Let me escort you, Ailsa.' Ailsa just had time to notice Belinda's strange look as her husband sat on a two-seater sofa, pulling Ailsa down beside him. She was not too far gone to realise that there was a smug ambivalence to Belinda's expression which surprised her.

When the time came to leave, because she had had no more to drink for the rest of the evening, she managed to make her departure in a more dignified manner than she had displayed at the table. It had annoyed her though that Max seemed to have glanced over at her more than a few times as she sat with Malcolm. 'Probably watching what I'm drinking,' she thought.

Malcolm once again took Ailsa by the arm, to lead her out to the waiting car, and she made her unsteady way towards the back door of the vehicle, feeling Malcolm's arm around her waist. Then, as he lowered her in, she thought his hand brushed very lightly and almost imperceptibly against her thigh. She waved goodbye and slumped exhaustedly on the back seat as Jim drove her the six miles back to Storm Winds.

Chapter Six

Carys walked into the breakfast room at Trannoch dressed in an elegant cream suit with a blue blouse which brought out the turquoise of her eyes. She filled a plate from the platters on the sideboard and slipped into her chair. Everyone but Belinda, who was still in bed with a headache, was already seated and eating breakfast. The Colonel did not even look up from his paper as she joined them. She poured herself some tea, and lightly buttered some toast, looking thoughtfully round the group of people around her. 'So, what do we think of our aspiring Lady of the Manor?' she said, as she delicately sipped her tea.

Max shuffled in his seat but kept his eyes glued on his paper. Noel continued to shovel huge forkfuls of egg and bacon into his mouth, unheedingly. Malcolm grinned at her, then looked away, and Thomas looked startled by the question, began to say something, then shut up. The Colonel remained behind his upheld paper. She waited a minute and tried again. 'I do think it showed a remarkable lack of finesse getting drunk at our dinner party, especially since it was her first time at Trannoch and we had been good enough to invite her.'

The Colonel laid down his paper and eyed her appraisingly. 'Neither you nor any of the rest of you invited her, it was I who invited her,' he said, angrily. '*And,* I shall invite her again if I feel like it, I thought she was charming.'

'Really?' Carys said, in mock surprise. 'You shock me, Colonel.' She had a habit of calling him Colonel, as she wrongly assumed it annoyed him when actually he rather liked it. 'I think she showed her true colours. If Sir Angus had had another child, he would have left Ailsa in seedy old London where she belonged and not tried to turn her into something which she quite apparently is *not.*'

'Oh God, Carys, give it a rest,' Malcolm said, with a contrary grin. 'You're only annoyed that she is a little bit of competition looks-wise.'

'Oh, Malkie, you really crack me up,' Carys said, laughing shrilly. 'She is absolutely no competition for me. Her looks are manufactured, mine are real.'

'Darling, I do believe your doting husband paid nearly five grand for those boobs.' Noel was still hurling food into his mouth at breakneck speed and joined the conversation with bad-tempered relish.

'Noel, I will not have that kind of talk at the table!' the Colonel said, absently, not even looking up from his paper. His eldest son ignored him.

Thomas looked at his elder brother in surprise. 'How did you know how much I paid?' he asked, with a childish innocence which made Carys toss her head in disgust.

'Nothing false about Ailsa's figure,' Noel added, ignoring his brother's question, and he chuckled through his mouthful of scrambled eggs.

Carys eyed her brother-in-law with distaste, but, before she could say anything, Malcolm again piped up, 'But, you must admit, Father, she did make rather a fool of herself with the wine.'

Max looked up in amazement at this point. 'It certainly didn't stop you fawning over her all evening, Malcolm. Belinda must have been mortified.' But Malcolm just shrugged non-committally, and finished off his breakfast. 'Anyway, she was probably just nervous. Anyone would be, given the prospect of meeting a bunch of vultures for the first time.'

'Well, well! Are you sticking up for her now, Max? That's a surprise, since you openly chastised her at table for drinking too much!' Malcolm almost spat the words out.

'Certainly not. I could see she was gulping it down, and I was merely trying to get her to take some water to re-hydrate. She can drink as much as she likes for all I care!'

'Anyway, don't worry about Belinda.' Carys was not put out for long, 'She's used to Malkie's wayward behaviour, isn't she, darling?'

'Stop the bickering, all of you!' the Colonel suddenly thundered, 'and let me have my breakfast in peace!' At which they all subsided.

'My ears are ringing!' Ailsa said, to Eileen, as she sliced open her letters at the breakfast table. Eileen had brought in the plate of toast and scrambled eggs for her, and Ailsa had motioned her to take a seat beside her while she ate her breakfast. Eileen had refused in case Miss Cochrane should appear. Ailsa's comment was in response to her question about how her night at Trannoch had gone.

'Why, what happened? Was it horrible?' Eileen asked, expectantly.

Ailsa considered for a moment. She knew she was confiding more and more in Eileen, and there was a certain etiquette she needed to follow, and she didn't want to go too far. Eileen was in her employ, and she wanted to keep some dignity. She chose her words carefully, 'Well, it was more about the personalities of the MacKenzies. I mean, Carys, who is Noel's wife, is very blunt, and she said a few things that made me feel I should not have been there. I did find the whole evening a bit of a strain, if I'm honest, and I had a wee bit too much wine . . . although don't think I made a fool of myself,' she finished, uncertainly.

'I am sure you didn't,' Eileen said comfortingly. Anyway, it's . . .' she got no further as Miss Cochrane came in at this point and asked her pointedly if she didn't have any work to do, rather than idling about, and Eileen fled.

Ailsa took a walk, her favourite one, up to the headland and down to the beach. The weather was warm for spring, the primroses were out all over the side of the banks, and the sea was turquoise and beautiful. She had received a letter from the local committee which organised various events, asking her to take over her late father's position on the board, and participate in the next meeting to organise the Arnasaid Highland Games. She felt that it was one of the 'duty things' she wanted to undertake as part of the running of the estate, but things like Highland Games were so far removed from what had been her life in London that she did not see what value she could bring to the discussions. Sir Angus had been an integral part of the community in the same way that the Colonel still was. What did she know about tossing the caber or Highland dancing? Such was her consternation about these things that she did not hear the footfall of someone approaching, and she jumped involuntarily when Stephen Millburn put his hand on her elbow and took her out of her reverie.

'Morning!' he said, with a grin, 'I see I am disturbing your thoughts!' She had seen him a few times from a distance since that night when she had met him for the first time just yards away from where he was standing now, but somehow he looked more handsome in the bright sunshine than he had done previously. His dark hair curled out from the base of his cap, and in the bright light she noticed that his face was more rugged than she had first thought. Tanned from working outdoors, his hazel eyes danced in the early morning light. He had a slightly unkempt look which only added to the overall attractiveness, and as he smiled, he showed a row of teeth any Hollywood star would have been proud to own. 'The Colonel said you might need some help finding an estate manager?'

'I ... er ... yes, he did mention that maybe you could help out with that.' She suddenly felt that he had been reading her thoughts and reverted to an aloofness of manner at which he raised his eyebrows. 'I want to do as much as I can myself, but I understand my limitations and would like help from someone who knows about the land and managing an estate.' She stuck her chin up a bit further than was warranted. She had no idea at the time why she was acting this way.

'Okay,' he said, finally. 'I have a friend who was an estate manager in Aberdeen for the last eight years. The property was sold recently to Americans who want to turn it into an hotel and golf course and Roddy wants to come back to this area. It's where he was born and brought up. They offered him a post helping to plan out and maintain the new golf course, but that's not Roddy's cup of tea.'

'I see.' Ailsa was continuing her coolness towards Stephen. 'When could he come for an interview?'

'He doesn't arrive back in Arnasaid until next week, but I could ask him to come over, say, Wednesday?'

'That sounds fine. As long as that suits you, of course.' She couldn't keep the sarcasm from her voice. 'Say three o'clock?' Ailsa was crisply business-like, and Stephen began to get a little frustrated at her attitude.

'Look, I was only trying to help out,' he said, not unreasonably. 'If you want to go and find other candidates or advertise, or whatever you want to do, it's no skin off my nose!'

Ailsa looked a little ashamed of herself, but kept up the front as she answered, 'No, I am willing to see your friend, and thank you for bringing him to my attention.' And, with this, she turned and walked away from Stephen leaving him with his mouth open in surprise.

'Now, what did I do to deserve *that?*' he mused, as she walked up the hill away from him.

Ailsa continued up to the house and her library, ready to take up her writing for the day. She sat herself at the table in front of her laptop, all manner of feelings jumbling up inside her. As she booted up the PC she noticed Stephen standing talking to Jim Hutton and the two then walked together across the lawn, deep in conversation. 'Why did I speak to him like that?' she asked herself. 'He was only trying to be friendly and offer me a candidate for estate manager, and I just about took his nose off!' She tried to put her mind to her story, a historical romance set in 17th century Scotland, but she could only bring herself to write a few pages then she gave up. Her characters seemed wooden and unnatural, and the words did not flow as they normally did. Her thoughts turned to the MacKenzies and dinner the evening before. Carys, she decided, was a bitch of the first order, but there was no denying she was an attractive bitch, beautiful even, and so elegant and sure of herself. Ailsa felt that Carys was the only one who would stand up to the Colonel, certainly none of the sons seemed to. Noel was a buffoon, Thomas was a silly man who acted years younger than he was, Max was a sanctimonious pain in the neck and Malcolm, what did she think of Malcolm? She knew she was attracted to him, but he was married. She thought he seemed attracted to her too, after all, he winked at her across the table, and commandeered her attention for most of the evening, especially when they decanted to the drawing room. She couldn't quite remember the conversation with him though, which was a worry, but she could remember him patting her hand as they sat together on the sofa. Belinda – she kept forgetting about Belinda, she was such an insipid nondescript character compared to Carys. Belinda was in awe of Malcolm, that much was certain, but he brushed her aside at every turn, and not one of the others seemed to stick up for her. 'I suppose they are all just used to her being in the background!' she thought.

Miss Cochrane interrupted her thoughts as she brought in Ailsa's mid-morning cup of tea and a slice of chocolate cake. 'Thank you,' Ailsa said, smiling up at the stern face before her, and decided to take her into her confidence. 'I wanted to ask you something. As you know I am looking for an estate manager and the Colonel suggested I talk to Stephen Millburn for help. I met him this morning and he has a friend, a guy called Roddy from Aberdeen who he is recommending.'

'And you want me to say whether I think Stephen Millburn is reliable or not?' Miss Cochrane returned.

'Yes, I suppose so.'

'Then I would say he is very reliable. If he thinks this friend of his, Roddy, did you say? Is suitable, then I would take him at his word. In fact, now that you mention it, I wonder if it's Roddy McLean he is talking about? He comes from Arnasaid, and I know his mother very well. A very nice family.'

'Oh!' Ailsa said, lamely. 'Well if I have your seal of approval too, then the least I can do is interview him!'

'Oh, I don't think you really need my seal of approval,' Miss Cochrane said, sarcastically, and turned on her heel and walked from the room.

'I wish she would lighten up!' Ailsa said to herself, and bit into the chocolate cake.

Early the following week, Ailsa attended the meeting of the Round Table. The meeting was in Arnasaid village hall, and the main agenda item was the Highland Games to be held in July, as normal. The committee were very welcoming and assured her that they were delighted to have her as part of their team, and she had a very enjoyable meeting. She was asked to open the Highland Games, in her capacity as Lady Hamilton-Dunbar, which she said she would be pleased to do. Further meetings were arranged in the run-up to the games, and Ailsa left the village hall with a feeling that she had at least accomplished something which was part of the overall duties attached to her inheritance, and this made her feel wanted for the first time.

She pottered about the few small shops in the village, picking up a magazine, some chew sticks for Bluebell and Rosie, who were growing fast, and through the store window she noticed Stephen talking to a woman on the other side of the street. It was not someone she had met before: she was slim and about the same height as Ailsa, with cropped dark brown hair which gave her a very striking appearance with her well-cut lips, large dark eyes and high arched eyebrows. Her cheekbones were high, and she wore a warm smile as she stood conversing with Stephen. Ailsa felt a pang of jealousy. A girlfriend? Partner? Sister? As Ailsa turned over these thoughts the woman suddenly looked up and caught her eye through the shop window. Ailsa turned quickly to pay for her purchases, a flush creeping over her face. When she left the shop, the woman had disappeared, and she could see the back of Stephen striding down the village street, his two spaniels at his side.

'Well, hello!' a familiar voice said behind her, and she turned to face Malcolm smiling at her. For the second time that day she felt disconcerted to meet someone she had not planned to meet, and who, in just as forceful a fashion threw her off-balance.

'Hi!' she managed. 'What brings you into Arnasaid?'

'I was just about to go for a quiet drink after a long day on the estate,' he said, smiling. 'Care to join me?'

'Oh, I don't think so, it's a bit early,' Ailsa said, reluctantly, and looked at her watch for confirmation.

'Early!' he laughed. 'It's five o'clock! Come on, just one, and I would really like some company instead of the usual crashing bores one finds in the pub at this time.' His easy manner and good looks again had a disarming effect on her, and she accepted with a smile and a nod.

The Wee Dram was the local pub where Ailsa and Connie had enjoyed lunch on that first trip to Arnasaid, and on this occasion it was virtually empty except for a few locals and four people who looked like hillwalkers. She picked a secluded table near the back of the pub, silent in the shadows and away from the main window where the sun still streamed through. Malcolm came back to the table with a pint for him and a large glass of red wine for Ailsa. She had an excited feeling of anticipation, and when the thought that he was married and she should not be doing this entered her head, she pushed it wilfully away, telling herself that this was a harmless drink with a family friend.

'So, what did you think of the MacKenzies?' he said, as he sat on the dark wood settle beside her.

'Well, I must admit I was really nervous to meet you all. I am not used to all this pomp and circumstance you know,' and she took a sip of her wine.

'Yes, I don't blame you, we can be an intimidating bunch at times. For what it's worth though, I think you did really well.' He seemed to say it genuinely, and Ailsa smiled.

'Thanks. I think your brothers are quite . . . difficult,' she searched for the right word, 'to get to know. Although you all seem completely different.'

He laughed good naturedly. 'Yes, I suppose we are all really different. We have our own lives although we spend time together as a family.'

'But you all live in the same house. How do you avoid living as a family?'

'We don't try and avoid each other really, we all have our separate suites in Trannoch, although we always try to meet together for breakfast and dinner. Three of us work on the estate, but we rarely spend more than a few hours a week together, as we all have our separate jobs to do. Noel travels a lot anyway, with the art business, and Max works from the surgery just a short walk away from here.'

'What about the wives?' Ailsa couldn't resist asking, 'Do they work?'

'Carys is kind of in partnership with Noel in his art business and sometimes helps him out with the administration of the website and occasionally accompanies him on his trips. As you can probably imagine, she is a far better sales person than Noel.'

Ailsa laughed. 'I can imagine. She is a beautiful woman.'

'I think she was a bit jealous of you, Ailsa,' he said, smiling warmly, then, when he saw she started at this remark he continued in an offhand way, 'you're not so bad yourself, you know.'

'What about Belinda?' Ailsa asked pointedly about his wife. 'Does she work in the art business too?' He shook his head, drained his pint then stood up abruptly, excusing himself, and walking towards the gents. Ailsa had felt the tension of this question and drained the remainder of her wine. Should she just leave while his back was turned? She knew that would be the best and proper thing to do, but she felt strangely compelled to remain there waiting for him, and as she did so the door opened and in walked Stephen, complete with spaniels. He spotted her sitting on her own and approached the table.

'Hello!' he said warily, as if he was unsure of the reception he was going to get from her following their meeting earlier.

'Hi!' Ailsa retorted.

'All alone?' he asked, cheerfully expecting her to answer in the affirmative, then just as he spotted the empty pint glass a voice beside him answered.

'No, Lady Hamilton-Dunbar is with me, Stephen,' said Malcolm, in a curt voice, and Ailsa noticed Stephen's whole body going rigid, before turning to face the other man.

The look which passed between the two men was unmistakeably hostile, and Ailsa was astonished at the vibe which emanated from them. They stared at each other for what seemed like a very long time but was in fact only 30 seconds, when Stephen turned and walked over to the bar. Malcolm lifted the two empty glasses. 'Let's have another,' he said, in an overly cheerful voice, but Ailsa declined.

'I'm sorry Malcolm, I need to get back. Thanks so much for the wine,' she said, as she slid out from behind the table and picked up her bag. As she walked from the pub, two men watched her go.

Ailsa was relaxing in her favourite blue sitting room later that evening, with Bluebell and Rosie beside her on the sofa. The log fire crackled in the grate, as the evening was chilly, and, as she had found out, the house was draughty when a wind was blowing as it was this evening. She was reading and sipping a glass of wine when Miss Cochrane came in to the room.

'Excuse me, Madam,' she said, much to Ailsa's chagrin. No matter how many times she asked the housekeeper to call her Ailsa, she would not comply. 'Mr Millburn is here to see you. Shall I send him in?'

'Here we go,' thought Ailsa to herself, as she assented, and Stephen stepped into the sitting room.

'Hi! Have a seat,' she said, as the puppies frolicked around his ankles. He crouched down to pet them.

'They smell Sheila and Sandy,' he said, talking about his two spaniels. He sat down, and she looked at him expectantly.

'Would you like a drink?' she asked him, but he shook his head in reply.

'I'm sorry to bother you,' he said, and, as she didn't answer, he forged on. 'I have been in touch with Roddy and he is able to attend an interview next Wednesday for the estate manager's job.'

'Great,' Ailsa said. 'Thanks for arranging that.' There was a silence, and Ailsa knew he had come for something other than telling her this. 'Did you come over just to tell me that, at half past nine at night?' And she saw a look pass over his handsome face before he answered.

'No, not really, but I am not sure you will be happy with what I am about to say,' he said.

Ailsa took a gulp of her wine as she eyed him, willing him to get it over with. 'It's just that I don't want Malcolm MacKenzie to try to take advantage of you.'

Ailsa was astounded and looked at him a long moment before she answered.

'Stephen, I am not a child,' she said. 'I am a grown woman with responsibilities,' and she waved her hand around her indicating that the estate was one of them.

'Of course, I realise that, but . . . it's just that he's got form,' he blurted out.

'Form?' she answered, in a cold voice. 'You mean he has been with other women when he is married, before?' And as he nodded, she went on. 'That's all very interesting, but what makes you think he was trying to seduce me, if that is indeed what you thought? I was having a quiet drink with him after I met him unexpectedly in the village. What's wrong with that?'

'People will talk,' Stephen insisted, urgently. 'I'm sorry if you think I am interfering, but this is a small community, it's not London you know. Everyone knows everyone else's business, and you have just taken over the estate and the title. I don't want anything to blemish your reputation. If it had been anyone but Malcolm . . .'

'Yes, you two didn't look as if you were all that fond of one another,' she said, sarcastically. 'What is it, have you been at daggers drawn over some woman in the past?'

'Don't be ridiculous,' said Stephen, heatedly, and rose to his feet, the puppies still dancing around his ankles. 'I just thought I would give you a friendly warning, but I shouldn't have bothered. Sorry I butted-in.' And, before Ailsa could come up with a suitably withering response, he flung himself from the room, banging the door behind him, and leaving Ailsa seething behind.

Chapter Seven

Spring edged its way into summer, and over the next six weeks Ailsa threw herself into the running of the estate. Roddy McLean proved to be an asset and taught her many things about managing the land. Stephen Millburn had agreed to carry on as part-time manager, while Roddy settled in, and to offer assistance and expertise, but he studiously avoided Ailsa. Gennina continued to manage the events and busy social diary of the estate, and Ailsa thought many times how she had misjudged Gennina owing to her 'dumb blonde' appearance and mannerisms, not realising that she was very adept at what she did and a supreme organiser, which Ailsa most definitely was *not*.

She attended the Round Table meetings helping to prepare for the Arnasaid Highland Games which were always staged in the big field, overlooking the sea, in the village. It was one of the main events in the social calendar, that and the Ghillies' Ball which was held alternately at Trannoch and Storm Winds. This year it was Storm Winds' turn to host the event, and Ailsa was looking forward to it. She was not, however, looking forward to being the centre of attention as she opened the Highland Games, but she had taken on the commitment and she was determined to see it through. Her new life and her vow to herself was that she would carry on the duties that Sir Angus had bequeathed her. Although it was so far removed from her whirlwind of a life in London, she was feeling the benefit of the fresh air and exercise she was taking on a daily basis. In London, she had been flat-packed in a tube twice or three times a day, whereas here she opened the door of Storm Winds and the fresh breeze and smell of the sea greeted her. She was noticing things like landscape, wild flowers and gurgling streams, or 'burns' as they are called in Scotland, and appreciating the simple things like shelling peas from the garden, and long walks across the headland – her headland, with her two lovely puppies, who were growing bigger and stronger and could walk farther each day. Bluebell followed Rosie's lead everywhere, and the two could not have been more different in their doggie personalities. Rosie scampered about the hills and beach, running headlong into peat bogs and little burns without a second thought; Bluebell skirted round these. Rosie jumped between the rocks, slipping into rock pools and chasing crabs across the beach; Bluebell stopped and seemed to assess each jump before she tried it. Rosie ran into the sea barking madly at the waves as the gentle surf broke around her; Bluebell tottered sensibly at the edge giving a warning bark to her sister as she saw the waves approach. The weather was pleasantly warm when the sun was out, but as is evidenced in this part of the country it rains a lot, and the high winds sweep the coastline whether it is mid-winter or mid-summer.

On one such day, Ailsa had taken a walk into Arnasaid, her jacket pulled tightly around her and her hood up against the lashing rain. She had noticed a small gallery the last day she had been there, just off the main road in the village, and she wanted to have a look. She had been busy papering and painting her bedroom to freshen it up, and was looking for a painting of the area, and especially with the sea, if she could find one, to finish off her room.

'Morning!' came a voice from the tiny upstairs room where the rickety outside stairs had led her, and she peered through the dim light to see a figure approaching from the back room.

'Hi!' Ailsa returned, as she saw the woman with the short chestnut hair and hippy appearance she had seen talking to Stephen Millburn in the village. 'I, er . . . I was looking for a painting.'

'Well, you've come to a gallery, so that's a good start,' the woman grinned. 'You are Lady Hamilton-Dunbar.' It was a statement of fact more than a question, and Ailsa nodded.

'Yes, can't hide in this neck of the woods! But, please call me Ailsa.'

'It's a pretty name, Ailsa. My name is Clem, short for Clementine, would you believe, but no one has ever dared call me that since I was at school,' and she laughed a musical laugh. The penny suddenly dropped, and Ailsa nodded.

'Oh, yes, you are Clem MacKenzie then? I . . . I've . . . ' but here she faltered, and her words ran out.

Clem laughed again. 'I think you were probably going to say you've heard about me? All bad I hope! I have no doubt the MacKenzies speak regularly about me. I did a rare thing you know, going against them and leaving my husband. Noel and I are divorced, as you are probably aware. In fact, I have as little to do with the family as possible. I usually go for dinner at Christmas and other holidays, as Melody is home from Uni. then. Melody is our daughter, she's studying medicine like her Uncle Max,' she offered, as further explanation. 'Would you like a cup of tea, Ailsa? I've just boiled the kettle.'

Ailsa nodded, then wandered round the tiny gallery admiring the lovely paintings which she determined were 'real' paintings and not modern art which she loathed. One caught her eye, with the edge of a house just visible through the trees to the left, high on a cliff, overlooking a stormy sea. It was a dramatic scene, the sky almost black and the sea reflecting the gloomy colours, with the edges of the waves a bright white contrast. Ailsa felt that she could almost smell the waves and feel the rain pouring from the heavens. 'Storm Winds,' she said, softly.

'Yes, it is Storm Winds,' Clem said, reappearing with two mugs of steaming tea and a plate of biscuits on a tray. She put them down on the counter and brought two stools round to the front. 'I painted it last year during one of the many storms we have around here. I took a picture at the height of the storm and copied the painting from there. The light wasn't good enough to do a first-hand copy. Do you like it?'

'I love it,' Ailsa said, dragging herself away from the picture. 'I've just decorated my bedroom, and the painting is perfect to finish it off. I'll take it.'

'Great!' Clem said, with pleasure. 'Now come and have some tea and some of my own special chocolate chip cookies.'

The two of them sat and drained two cups of tea and five cookies between them, chatting like old friends.

'It must have been a shock to inherit Storm Winds,' Clem said, biting into her second cookie.

'I admit it was quite decidedly a shock,' Ailsa returned. 'I had no idea Sir Angus was my father until he tried to find me through his lawyers and send for me from London. My friend Connie came up here with me, and we stayed for a week. He managed to tell me about my past and my inheritance before he passed away that same week. The weird thing was I felt no connection to him.'

'Well, why would you? He was a stranger to you!' Clem retorted.

'Yes, I know, but I always thought that if I met my real parents I would somehow feel something. He seemed so old, more like a grandfather than a father, and I was not like him in any way.'

'Well, it seems to me you have tried to take the bull by the horns and carry on the old traditions of running the estate, joining the Round Table etc, and that's commendable.'

'You know about all that? Well, news certainly travels fast!'

'Nothing escapes the good people of Arnasaid,' said Clem, sardonically. 'Everyone knows everyone's business. When I was breaking up with Noel, Kevin and Judy Watt asked me if I wanted to buy this place before I had announced I was leaving!' She chuckled at the memory. 'I did want to stay near, for Melody's sake, so that I would be around when she came back for the holidays from school. Now she's at Uni and has a flat in Glasgow and comes up for the holidays to Trannoch. We do a lot together, we have such a good relationship, but she stays with the MacKenzies. I don't have a spare room here.' There was an almost imperceptible defensiveness to her tone.

'I see,' Ailsa said, not really seeing at all. Something in her tone made Clem explain further.

'The MacKenzies are very controlling,' Clem sighed. 'They paid all Melody's school fees and bought her the flat in Glasgow. I could never afford to do that for her, so the control lies with them. If it means a better life for Melody, then I am happy to go along with it, as long as she's happy.'

'And is she?'

'Oh yes, she loves the Colonel and her Uncle Max. She's also very fond of Belinda,' said Clem, surprisingly. 'But, like the rest of us, and unless you tell me any different I include you in this, she hates Carys.'

'I'm not surprised at her hating Carys,' Ailsa pulled a face at the memory of the dinner party and all the insults from her, 'what I am surprised about is that she likes Belinda. She didn't speak one word at the table when I was there for dinner and seemed so down-trodden somehow!'

'Yes, she does come across like that,' Clem said, thoughtfully. 'But, as you will probably find out, there is more to Belinda than meets the eye.'

Clem wrapped the picture for Ailsa, and, when the transaction was complete, she turned to go. 'I live in the flat under the gallery,' Clem said, as she held the door. 'Why don't you come over on Saturday, if you are free, I'll cook supper and we can have lots of wine and have a good old natter?'

'Sounds great, thanks, I will!' and Ailsa made her way down the steep outside stairway thinking happily that, in Clem, she had found a friend.

When Ailsa got back to Storm Winds, Miss Cochrane met her in the hallway, looking slightly flustered. 'Colonel MacKenzie is waiting for you in the library. I tried to tell him I didn't know how long you would be, but he insisted he wait for you.'

Ailsa looked surprised. 'Okay, thanks, how long has he been waiting? Did you give him some tea?'

'About an hour, he helped himself to a book and has been reading whilst he was waiting. I did take him in some tea. I'll bring some in fresh.'

Forgetting that she was clutching the painting, Ailsa made her way to her library. The Colonel, who had been sitting in one of the wing-backed chairs by the fire, put down his book and rose to greet her. 'Colonel MacKenzie! This is a surprise!' she said, and tossed her wet coat over a nearby table. 'Miss Cochrane is just bringing in some fresh tea.'

'Ailsa! My dear, how are you?' was the booming reply, which made Ailsa wonder momentarily if he ever spoke quietly at all. She sat in the seat opposite him and put the wrapped painting at the side of her chair.

'What's that you've got there?' he asked, affably.

'Oh, just a painting I picked up in Arnasaid. I was decorating . . .' she got no further and was surprised to see his shaggy brows come together in a dark scowl.

'So, you have met my ex daughter-in-law Clementine?' he said, his mood seeming to change at once. 'I say that as there is only one shop which sells paintings in Arnasaid.'

'Yes, as a matter of fact, I did meet Clem,' she said, calmly. 'I thought she was a lovely person, and,' she paused for effect before she finished with, 'I think she and I are going to be great friends.' She noticed, with satisfaction, that the Colonel's face had turned a dark red at this. The conversation halted temporarily as Miss Cochrane brought in a trolley with a huge teapot, two matching china cups with saucers, and a tiered cake stand laden with luscious cakes.

'My goodness, Miss Cochrane, do you think you are feeding an army?' Ailsa laughed.

'The Colonel likes his cakes!' retorted Miss Cochrane with a snap, and taking away the other tray, stalked out of the room. By the time she had left, the Colonel's colour had returned to normal. Ailsa poured the steaming tea, and they filled their plates.

'Your cook was always a better baker than mine at Trannoch,' he said, gruffly, as he finished an éclair in two short mouthfuls, and proceeded to demolish a cream bun.

'Then you must come for tea more often!' she said, with dancing eyes, and the Colonel smiled.

'Are you settling in, Ailsa?' He changed tack at this point. 'I mean, this is a hell of a lot to take on, and you are so young . . .'

She smiled, 'It does seem like a huge task, but I am enjoying it so far. It is so beautiful up here and I feel . . . well, I feel like this is where I belong.'

'Well, you were born here, generations of your ancestors hail from this area, and Angus lived here all his life.'

'And my mother?' Ailsa held the Colonel in her gaze.

'Your mother?' The Colonel looked non-plussed, and sloshed his tea out on the saucer.

'You knew her, didn't you, my real mother, Hunter?' Ailsa asked directly, and the Colonel seemed to flop back into the seat in resignation. The fire crackled and a log moved noisily in the grate as they both summoned their defences.

'Yes, I knew her,' he said, in the quietest voice Ailsa had heard from him. 'I had no idea Angus would tell you who your real mother was, I presumed he would tell you it was his late wife, Elizabeth Douglas.'

'Why would you think he would lie to me?' said Ailsa, astonished. 'This isn't the nineteenth century, Colonel, people have affairs all the time.'

The Colonel looked decidedly uncomfortable and stammered his answer into his old-fashioned moustache. 'I am aware of the fact, but our old families have a duty to uphold our values and reputations. Angus was one of the 'old school'.'

'Yes, that's why he gave me up for adoption, to maintain his reputation,' Ailsa said, dryly. 'What was she like?' She followed his eyes up to the painting of Hunter on the wall.

'She was beautiful, of course,' the Colonel said. 'She had every man in the district and anywhere she travelled running after her. But, it was more than that. She was full of spirit and vitality. Her personality filled a room. She was blunt to a point, smart, funny and fiercely independent. I don't know you very well yet, Ailsa, but I think you have a lot of Hunter in you.'

Ailsa held his gaze thoughtfully for a few minutes, then continued, 'Anyway, to get back to the original subject, I really want to carry on the old traditions, but the values and virtues may just elude me.'

'Oh, don't say that.' The Colonel was glad of the diversion. 'I think you will do splendidly, on all accounts.' Ailsa filled the teapot with more boiling water from the water pot and poured some more tea.

'So, what about you, Colonel? Has there been anyone since your wife died?'

He hesitated a fraction too long to be believable. 'No. I am seventy-two and not likely to meet anyone else now. Anyway, I have my wayward family to take care of!'

She smiled and finished off the last piece of her cake. Miss Cochrane came in to clear away the tea things, asking if she could get them anything else.

'Yes!' Ailsa said, suddenly and brightly. 'I would like a glass of red wine please, Miss Cochrane. Colonel will you have one?' Miss Cochrane looked mildly outraged at the mere suggestion of having alcohol at four o'clock in the afternoon.

'No, thank you,' the Colonel said, just as brightly, and with his booming voice back in gear. 'I'll have a whisky please, Miss Cochrane!'

When the Colonel had gone, Ailsa found it hard to settle. Thoughts of Hunter and her late father went through and through her mind, upsetting her and filling her head with doubts about her own competence in taking over the estate. She took the dogs out for a walk around 8 p.m. but went in the opposite direction this time in case she met Stephen with his two spaniels. He was the last person she wanted to see that evening.

The cliff path was steeper going the other way, but she kept assiduously to the rocky path, enjoying the sound of the waves crashing against the rocks. She could see the Small Isles much better from this path than from the house, and Eigg, Rhum and Muck looked splendid in the early evening light. The sun was beginning to sink to the west and it shone its golden and red lights over the islands. It was a beautiful sight.

Rosie and Bluebell scampered about happily by her side, enjoying the new pathway with the different smells. Her thoughts returned to the Colonel. He was really an old sweetie. He was a controlling man, who liked his own way, and had quite probably been a very strict parent when the boys were growing up, but, apart from this, he was a doting father. He did seem to have been friendly with Sir Angus too. It seemed that he really wanted her to do well in this new venture, unlike Carys, and, she suspected, a few more of the MacKenzies. She was certain that she could go to the Colonel for help at any time, and he would be more than happy to give it.

A series of yelps interrupted her thoughts, and she looked around quickly for her two pups. Bluebell was sitting at the edge of the cliff path, barking continually. Rosie was nowhere to be seen. She ran to the cliff edge and looked over. It was not sheer to the sea at this particular spot, but a steep slope of scree led from the path down to a clutch of rocks which stuck out from the side. In the middle of those sat Rosie, wagging her tail and yelping upwards.

'Rosie!' she shouted. 'Come back up here at once!' But, even as she said it, she knew that the slope was much too steep, and the little dog would never manage to scale it back to the top. She looked frantically around her for inspiration but found none. The path was deserted, and she could not see another soul anywhere around. A search of her jacket and jeans pockets revealed that she had forgotten her mobile, so there was no way she could phone ahead for help. She shouted again to the dog who studiously ignored her pleas, so she decided that the only thing to do was to try and reach Rosie herself. After taking a recce of the slope, she thought that the only way to negotiate it would be to sit down and slide towards Rosie. She sat and gingerly edged towards the slope. It was steep but not non-negotiable. If she fell, she would land either on the rocks on which Rosie currently stood, or further down on the grassy ledge which led to the rocky shore. There was no danger of falling into the sea at this point. She put her hand down onto the wet stones, a mixture of small and larger rocks which made up the scree, and pushed off. Unfortunately, she pushed a little too hard, and she began to career downhill as if she was on a ski slope. The scree was as slippery as ice. To stop her progress, she decided quickly to throw herself onto her front to have a better grip on the land, and, as she did so, her left foot caught on a rock, twisted and was held there fast, while her whole body did a 180 degree turn and she landed upside down with her foot entrapped in the rock. Her head was inches away from Rosie on the rocky outcrop, and the little dog jumped for joy up towards her. It was as much as she could do to stop herself screaming in pain, but she held Rosie in her arms as the pup licked away her salty tears.

'Oh God, Rosie, we've really done it now!' she said, as she cuddled her pet into her neck. She could hear Bluebell yelping forlornly at the edge, but thankfully, the other dog didn't try and follow suit and scramble down the hillside. Ailsa tried to move her trapped foot, but the pain seared up her leg, and she felt sick. After about ten minutes of hanging there, she decided to try and crawl back round to an upright position. There were one or two biggish rocks she might be able to clutch onto to help her circle back round at least to an upright position. She tucked Rosie under her left arm, and, with her right, pushed a painful inch at a time back and up to the left. She felt for and managed to grab a rock sticking out from the scree and used this to pivot herself slowly up so that her back was resting on rock, but her foot was still snagged. She very gradually wriggled her right leg under her left one and managed to get herself, miraculously, into a lying position across the slope with her head on the big rock, her left foot stuck fast in the other rock, and Rosie sitting happily on her stomach. She began to cry again, just from sheer relief of being upright, 'Oh Rosie, you bad, bad dog!' she said, half-laughing half-crying as the dog again licked her face. 'You think this is all a game!' Rosie agreed with a companionable 'Woof!' And, looking up, she could just see Bluebell's little face peering over the side as if wondering what this game was all about.

After she realised she had been lying there for almost an hour, she began to seriously panic. What if no one came and she was stranded here all night? It was starting to get colder, the weather had been mild but in the evenings the temperature had plummeted as quickly as her spirits were now doing. What if her dogs got hypothermia? 'I'd never forgive myself if anything happened to you and Bluebell!' she said out loud, with a voice tinged with hysteria. She had no thought for herself at this point, such was the pain in her foot that her senses began to get muddled, and her body began to shake involuntarily with the cold and damp which was seeping into her very bones. 'It's okay, Bluebell, we'll be up soon, just taking a wee rest!' she shouted, and dissolved into hysterical giggles. Bluebell suddenly became distracted and jumped up. She could hear her barking furiously, and then a voice came to her from the cliff top. 'Hello, you, what are you doing here? Are you lost? You look like one of Ailsa's wee dogs. How did you get here, eh?' Ailsa realised at once that someone had found them, and summoning all her strength she shouted, 'Hi!! I'm down here . . . I'm down heeee . . .' and promptly lost consciousness.

Chapter Eight

When Ailsa came to, there was a man leaning over her foot. She still felt the searing pain, but her foot had been freed and she could move it at least. Rosie was lying full out on top of her, staring into her eyes enquiringly, and as she gasped as the pain shot up her left leg, the man looked round.

'Well, you're with us again then, are you?' Max MacKenzie said, in an ironic voice. 'Don't try and move, I've phoned for help, they'll be here in about five minutes. It's not broken, but it will be badly sprained at best.' She shot a quick look to the top of the cliff, and he continued, 'Your other dog is sitting patiently at the top waiting for you.' Ailsa did what any self-respecting dog rescuer would do, turned her head to the side and was violently sick. She reached into her pocket for a tissue and wiped her mouth as he surveyed her grimly. 'What possessed you to try and climb down here?' His tone was incredulous and far from friendly. It did the trick in terms of bringing her to her senses.

'I can assure you, I am not in the habit of climbing down cliff faces.' She summoned up as much energy as she could to sound as cutting as he was being. 'Rosie got stuck and she wouldn't come up when I shouted, so I came down after her.'

'Well, it was a stupid thing to attempt,' he snapped. 'Why didn't you ring for help, or did you leave your mobile at home?'

'Yes, actually, I did. I didn't know that Rosie would think of exploring over the edge, or I would have made sure I brought it with me,' she returned, equally sarcastically.

'Well, it was a daft thing to do anyway.' He was determined to add insult to injury. 'These cliffs are dangerous, and you're not even wearing proper walking boots. Of course, being a 'townie', you wouldn't have thought about that now, would you?'

'Look, I'm sorry if I'm interrupting your evening stroll . . . ' She got no further as a shout in the distance was hailing them, and even as he unceremoniously told her to shut up, he whistled loudly to draw them to the rescuer's attention. She heard the purr of an engine, and two men got out and peered down. It was Jim Hutton and Stephen Millburn.

'Now my evening is complete,' Ailsa groaned to herself, as she saw the latter.

They lowered a rope down, and Max helped her to strap it round her so that it wouldn't pull an arm out of a socket as they pulled her up. Stephen shouted down that they were securing the rope to the back of the quad bike, which had been the engine Ailsa had heard, and in no time at all had her hoisted safely up to the edge. Max lifted Rosie and agilely scaled the slope behind her.

'Stephen, we'll walk back with the dogs,' Max said, nodding to Jim. 'I'll call in home and get my bag then come over and have a look at her.' All this was said over Ailsa's head, and she seethed angrily.

'I am still here, you know,' she began, but Stephen had started up the engine of the quad and, trying not to jolt her, slowly made his way back to the house. Ailsa glanced back to see the two men carrying a pup each, walking quickly in their wake. There was no conversation with Stephen on the way back, and, as she got to the door, Miss Cochrane met them, and she and Stephen helped her hobble into the house. It was well after ten o'clock by this time, but Ailsa insisted on going to her sitting room, there was no way she could negotiate the stair, and she was damned if she would give Stephen Millburn the chance to carry her up to her room. Her foot was badly swollen, and as Stephen made his excuses and left, Miss Cochrane loosened and pulled off her light trainers, pulling over a pouffe on which to prop it up. 'I'll get you some painkillers,' Miss Cochrane said, turning to leave, and Ailsa glanced at her housekeeper realising, with mild surprise, that the older woman had a worried expression on her face.

'Could you get me a glass of red wine too, please?' Ailsa asked.

'Do you think you should be . . .' the housekeeper began, but got no further.

'Yes, I absolutely do think I should.'

When she returned with the painkillers, a glass of water and a large glass of red wine on a tray, she set them down on a small table at Ailsa's side. 'Jim Hutton has just brought back the dogs. They are in the kitchen having some dinner,' she said with a gentle voice, which Ailsa had not heard her use before.

'Thanks!' she said, and swallowed the tablets just as the front door clattered, and swift footsteps were to be heard coming up the hall.

'Typical arrogant doctor,' Ailsa thought to herself. 'Doesn't even bother to knock!' Miss Cochrane opened the door, and Max strode in.

With a curt 'Good evening,' to Miss Cochrane, he knelt down in front of the foot, and deftly examined it, whilst Ailsa sipped her wine. His abrupt bedside manner, or lack of it, suddenly struck her as funny, and she said, 'Don't mind me, I'm just joined-on to the foot.' What she expected was for him to answer her with his usual sarcasm, but he stopped bandaging, sat back on his heels and smiled at her.

'Sorry,' he said, 'I'm afraid I'm no good at small talk,' and continued to strap up the ankle.

When he was finished, he stood and surveyed her grimly as she cradled her wine glass and eyed him with a defiant expression. 'That should do it. It will be sore for a week or two. Try and sit with it up as much as possible for the first three or four days. I can't see you managing the stairs for the foreseeable future though. Do you have a bedroom downstairs?'

'I'll get Jim to put a camp bed up in here if you want.' Miss Cochrane had been hovering about and now sprang into action, glad to be doing something practical.

'Good idea,' Max said, snapping shut his bag. 'I'll pop in and see you in a couple of days, and don't drink too much wine. Alcohol lowers your temperature, and you've had a shock tonight.' He made his way to the door and turned back. 'Miss Cochrane, try and see she doesn't do anything daft.' And, before Ailsa could think of a suitably crushing response, he had gone.

During the night Ailsa developed a fever. Every time she tried to move, she cried out in pain as her ankle throbbed mercilessly. Miss Cochrane appeared around 3 a.m. with another two painkillers. She slept fitfully for the rest of the night and woke exhausted at 9 a.m., with Miss Cochrane arriving with a breakfast tray. Eileen had been in earlier, and on the housekeeper's instruction had made up the fire which took away the gloom of the misty morning. Ailsa sat up and pulled her cardigan around her shoulders. She felt drained with her escapade and the pain in her foot. There was a downstairs toilet and shower room, the next room but one to her sitting room, and even in her delirious state she had managed to hobble there at around five in the morning, although she was worn out with fever and pain as she had returned to her camp bed. She drank her tea and took two mouthfuls of boiled egg and a piece of toast before she pushed the tray away. Miss Cochrane had suggested she stay in bed, at least for the morning; she was beginning to get to know Ailsa a little and didn't want to suggest staying there for the whole day or that would have had the opposite effect on her patient, who would then have insisted on getting up. When she took the tray away, Ailsa snuggled back down in her bed saying she would, 'Just rest for an hour or two,' but was sleeping like a baby before the housekeeper had left the room.

Ailsa was not a good patient. She did not like sleeping on a camp bed in her sitting room, and after four days had passed she managed to get up and down the stairs without too much difficulty. Max had attended her on the third day, and they had almost come to blows as he had been his usual surly self, and Ailsa, bored with being housebound, was not in the mood to humour him.

'Yes, looking much better,' he said, as he finished re-strapping the foot. 'Miss Cochrane said you had a fever that night. Are you ok now?'

'Nothing that I can't handle,' said Ailsa. 'I'm just fed up that I can't get outside for a walk.'

'Well you will do stupid things.' He snapped his bag shut, and a frown furrowed his brow. 'This isn't London, you know. You don't know the land around here, and it would have been sensible to have had the dogs on leads since that was a walk you were unfamiliar with.'

'You don't half rub things in, do you? I realise all that, and I've ordered a pair of walking shoes, for your information.' She thumbed her laptop which was on the sofa beside her indicating she had done this online.

'Hmmm. Well that's a start, I suppose,' he said grimly. 'Well, you could try a short walk in a few days, and in another week, you should be able to walk almost normally. As long as you rest, like I told you to, you should be okay.'

'Well thanks for nothing,' she returned, ungratefully. 'If it clears up later on I was planning on going for a short walk round the grounds this afternoon.'

'I'm sorry,' he was at his sarcastic best, 'am I somehow talking to myself rather than out loud? I've advised not for another few days, at least. Do you want to risk permanent damage?'

'Of course not, but I think I know myself how I feel, and, if I think I can walk on it . . .'

'Do you never listen to advice?' His voice became heated as he lifted his bag and jacket to leave. 'If you choose to ignore what I advise, you can just register with a doctor fifty-five miles away and serve you right.'

'Suits me!' she flung back at him, seriously riled by now. She noticed his incredulous look and picked up her laptop again and began to log on, rudely ignoring him until he swore under his breath and clumped out of the room, pulling the door none too quietly behind him.

'Stupid arrogant man!' Ailsa said out loud, annoyed with herself that she wasn't able to think of a better counter argument.

'I think he's lovely!' Eileen said, as she walked in with a lunch tray for Ailsa. She pulled over the small table and set it down. 'You just think that because he's ordering you about for your own good that he's arrogant.'

'Absolutely not! He *is* arrogant. All the MacKenzies are, to a certain extent, but he's just the limit. I'm going to do as he suggests and register with a doctor in Fort William.' And, with that, she began on her chicken soup.

Clem arrived to keep her company that night, as it was Saturday and the night when Ailsa was supposed to go to Clem's. 'If Mohammad won't come to the mountain . . .' Clem giggled, as she barged into the sitting room. She was carrying two bags, one with bottles of wine, and the other full of fresh ingredients. 'I remembered that this was Cookie's night off, so I brought stuff to cook for my wounded BFF. Can we decant to the kitchen?'

The kitchen was warm and dimly-lit, and, as usual, scrubbed within an inch of its life. Ailsa hobbled onto a tall stool at one of the counters while Clem opened the first bottle of wine. She then shoved a chopping board in front of her friend and found a knife from a drawer. 'Don't think that just because you are an invalid you can't chop!' Ailsa laughed and reached over to turn on the small radio, and tuned it to Classic FM. 'All this and a classy lassie to boot!' Clem laughed, as she found a huge frying pan and hauled in onto the top of the ancient range top. They sipped their delicious red wine, dark and full bodied and gloriously blackcurrant in flavour, as they chatted non-stop and cooked and chopped companionably. Clem put strong flour and water into a bowl and mixed it with her hands.

'What are you making?' Ailsa asked, as she chopped shallots and fresh tomatoes.

'Pizza of course, the world's favourite food,' Clem said, as she mixed the dough. 'I have Italian ancestors, you know, from a place called Cecina in Southern Tuscany. Nonna – my Italian grandmother – died just a few years back, and I only met her once, but she was an amazing cook and when I left she gave me a book of her hand-written recipes. That's really when I got interested in cooking, and I absolutely love it now.'

Ailsa looked at her in surprise. 'That's great. I've always liked cooking, mostly traditional food although I have dabbled in Italian food and would love to try real pasta rather than packet stuff. I've made pizza too, but always bought the shop bases, I've never made my own.' She watched as Clem turned out the dough onto a floured board, and with a series of three hand movements, produced a flat almost round pizza about 15 inches in diameter. Firstly, she hit the dough with the heel of her left hand, then stretched it out, then swung it up onto the clenched fist of her right hand where she twirled it quickly and it grew a few inches a time. She kept repeating this process until she was satisfied with the size of the dough base.

'I'm seriously impressed!' Ailsa said, laughing. 'You make it look so easy!'

'It's easy once you get the knack. Are those tomatoes chopped now?' She put the dough onto a greased and floured tray and added olive oil, fresh tomatoes, fresh herbs, onions and garlic to the pan. She then took a selection of Italian sausages and sliced them finely for the top, and buffalo mozzarella cheese which she cubed roughly. Clem spooned the tomato mixture onto the base then added the selection of sliced sausage and scattered over the mozzarella. Finally, she added more fresh herbs and olive oil and slid it into the great oven which was burning furiously and heating the big cosy kitchen. Clem tidied round then joined Ailsa on a stool at the counter, re-filling their glasses.

'The villa I inherited with this estate is in Tuscany somewhere, although, to be honest, with so much going on, I haven't even had a chance to look at the papers yet and find out exactly where it is.'

'Well, Tuscany is a huge area.' Clem wiped spilled flour from her jeans. 'Nonna had a small holding near the sea, with a vegetable patch and chickens. She also made her own olive oil from her trees.'

'Sounds lovely,' Ailsa said, dreamily. 'One of the downsides of this beautiful place is that we don't get much sun, unlike Tuscany. Maybe I'll go for a wee break and check out the villa, once I find out where it is!'

'So, what do you think of Doctor MacKenzie?' Clem asked, as she took a deep gulp of her wine and ran her fingers through her spiked brown hair.

'I think he's an arrogant, spoiled man used to getting his own way. He's pushy and bad-tempered and basically a right royal pain in the ass.' Clem looked surprised at the ferocity of her friend's reaction.

'I admit he is quite surly at times but then again he's had a lot to contend with. Elaine died of cancer around five years ago, and he's had Ryan and Aria to bring up on his own.'

'Bring up?' The wine was starting to kick in now, and Ailsa was not going to accept this last comment easily. 'They both go to boarding school, don't they? Not only that, I am sure they had a nanny like the rest of the MacKenzie kids, so what 'bringing up' did he have to do?'

'To be fair, Ryan was only seven and Aria five when their mother died. That's young enough for them to remember all their lives exactly what and how it happened and need their Daddy badly.'

'So?' Ailsa said. 'That doesn't give him the licence to be a moron and treat people badly.'

'No, it doesn't,' Clem agreed, 'but most folk tip-toed round him for years, and maybe he's just not used to someone treating him like a normal guy again.'

'Well that's a shame,' Ailsa returned, sarcastically. 'I feel sorry for the kids, of course I do, but life goes on, and if that's the way he treats all his other patients too, then I am sorry for the Arnasaid community!'

The pizza was delicious, the best one Ailsa had tasted as she readily told her friend. 'I hate it when the base is thick and spongy,' she said, munching the food hungrily. 'This is just amazing, you can't half cook Clem!'

'Glad you're enjoying it, Mrs Lady of the Manor! Thanks, Nonna!!' She pointed the pizza cutter heaven-ward then jumped up and opened another bottle of wine.

'So, what about you Clem?' Ailsa ever so slightly slurred her words.

'What about me?'

'Well, is there a man in your life? Is it Max?' she suddenly thought out loud. Clem had after all been very defensive about the doctor, and Ailsa thought she had inadvertently hit the nail on the head.

'No, it's not Max, and, at the moment, there is no one special.' Clem's face was slightly flushed, and Ailsa suspected that it could be due to more than the red wine and the heat of the kitchen. 'I like Max, but he's not my type. Plus the fact I would need my head examined to take on another MacKenzie. Isn't one failed marriage enough?'

'Well, from what you have told me of Noel he is nothing like his younger brother, but I see what you mean about more than one MacKenzie. I couldn't live in Trannoch with all that lot, it would drive me up the wall!' They both dissolved into school girlish giggles. 'Hey, wait a minute. You said, "no one special" does that mean there is someone who might not be special *yet*?' she asked, shrewdly. Then she suddenly remembered that the first time she saw Clem she was having a long conversation with Stephen Millburn, and she wondered with a little inward quake if Stephen was indeed the one who had made her friend flush. As Clem refused to give her any more information, Ailsa was left with this thought.

They tidied up the kitchen, grabbed the bottle of wine and, in Ailsa's case, hobbled back to her sitting room. The big windows showed the sun setting over the Cullin range of mountains on the Isle of Skye, and they both watched it reverently. Clem threw another log on the fire, as the night was chilly, and they sat, each with a dog on their lap, as they chatted like old long-lost friends. It was the best night Ailsa had experienced since she had come to live at Storm Winds. When the day wore on to night and the darkness finally came at around 11.30 p.m., Clem left with the promise of getting together again very soon.

For the first time since the accident, Ailsa hobbled her way upstairs to her own bedroom. The fire had been lit and she turned down her bed, finding the electric blanket was on. Miss Cochrane had the night off, but as Ailsa had come to know her habits, she guessed that she would still be at home in her own 'apartment' as she liked to call it. Sir Angus had had it modelled for the housekeeper from three old servants' bedrooms. There was a small kitchen, comfortable sitting room, and bathroom, all decorated in her own simple taste. There was an outside entrance right beside her sitting room, and the housekeeper used this when she wanted to entertain her own friends and relatives. The fact that she had put on Ailsa's electric blanket and lit the fire was no surprise to Ailsa, they often passed in the house or around the grounds when it was Miss Cochrane's day off. She was very grateful to the housekeeper for the care which she was showing to her and wondered fleetingly if they had tidied the kitchen properly. The last thing she wanted to do was get in Cocky's bad books, after all she had done for her.

Sunday was wet and windy, and Ailsa decided to sit in her library and read for a while after breakfast. Eileen made up the fire for her, and she curled up in her favourite chair, her foot extended out on the matching stool, and her book chosen from the extensive collection. *Pride and Prejudice* was still her favourite Austen book, although *Emma* made a close second. The rain streamed down the tall sash windows, and the wind rattled them, producing drafts all over the room. She pulled her throw closely around her and stared for a minute into the mesmerising flames of the open fire. She thought about what a brilliant night she had shared the previous night with Clem and hugged herself with glee to think that she had a real friend in Scotland. It would be good to introduce Connie and Jan to Clem. She knew they would all get on like a house on fire, they all had the same sense of humour, and, it appeared to Ailsa, were on the same wavelength as each other.

'A visitor, Ailsa,' Miss Cochrane interrupted her thoughts. She had managed to drop the 'Madam' after much persuasion by Ailsa, but this only worked when she was in a good mood.

Ailsa looked up in surprise, as she had not even heard the library door. Before she could ask who it was, the housekeeper stood aside and none other than Belinda came into the room.

Chapter Nine

Belinda sat opposite her, with a blank look on her face. Ailsa could read nothing from her expression and wondered how to begin a conversation. When she had been to Trannoch for dinner that eventful evening, months ago, she couldn't remember Belinda talking at all, and she felt very awkward as she sat there looking at her visitor.

'Sir Angus and I were friends.' Whatever Ailsa may have expected to be Belinda's opening gambit, this certainly was not it. 'I used to come over on a Sunday and we would talk for hours about books and politics and anything really. He sat just where you are sitting, with the fire on and his whisky on the little table by his side. He loved this room.'

When Ailsa got her breath back, she answered. 'The only time I met him was in this room, and he was sitting here, on this chair, as you say. Unfortunately, I didn't get the chance to get to know him.'

'He and the Colonel were not friends, despite the assertions that they were. They both wanted similar things in life but were more like lifelong adversaries than friends.' Again, Ailsa was surprised at the turn of conversation. Was Belinda trying to tell her something? 'What are you doing here, Ailsa?' she asked quietly and suddenly.

'Doing here?' Ailsa was robbed of her breath again. 'What do you mean? I live here of course.'

Belinda's face was immobile, although her eyes flickered with emotion. 'It's a strange thing to do, move from London up here when you are young and have your whole life in front of you.' Ailsa looked at her long and hard before answering.

'You're here, aren't you? You live at Trannoch and spend your life here. Why is it so difficult to believe someone else would want to live here?' Belinda looked away and didn't answer her. The door opened, and Miss Cochrane brought in the small trolley with tea and cake and set it between them on the hearth rug. Ailsa poured her a cup and handed it over. They sat in silence for a few minutes, eating and drinking, Ailsa trying to make sense of what Belinda had said.

'Malcolm and I don't get on.' Belinda again spoke with surprising frankness, as she nibbled her cake daintily. 'We sleep in separate rooms, and basically live separate lives.'

'Why are you telling me this?' Ailsa felt the colour flush her cheeks.

'Because, I think he is interested in you.' Belinda's steely eyes bored into hers. Belinda got up from her chair and fingered some books on a nearby bookshelf. 'It won't be the first time he's had a, a . . . dalliance.' She smiled a humourless smile. 'In fact, he is a perpetual womaniser.' She spoke matter-of-factly, although the air was taught with emotion.

'I can assure you Belinda, there is nothing going on . . . ' Ailsa got no further.

'I wasn't asking you that.' Belinda returned to her seat and fixed the other with a stony gaze. 'You see, I don't care whether he strays or not. I have no feelings left for him at all.'

'Why do you stay?' Ailsa asked, quietly.

'Because of David and Melissa, my children,' she said, simply. 'They are still at school and while they are, I will be at Trannoch when they arrive back.' Ailsa nodded understandingly.

'I hate the MacKenzies.' Again, Belinda took Ailsa's breath away with her candidness. 'Every one of them, excepting, of course, the unfortunate children of the house, although they are only there in holiday time. The only time I am with the family is at mealtimes, and even then I try to skip as many as I can or have a tray in my room.'

Ailsa looked at her wonderingly. Why was she telling her this? Ailsa, with whom she hadn't even bothered to make conversation the one and only time they had met.

'You seem to have a really difficult time, Belinda.' Ailsa was genuinely concerned for the woman opposite her. 'If there is anything I can do . . .' She let the cliché hang in the air as was customary when this phrase was used.

'There is nothing anyone can do. The situation and the family are what it is. Nothing will ever change as long as there are MacKenzies at Trannoch.'

Ailsa felt that she was a player in some corny soap opera, and, before she could respond to this last astonishing assertion from Belinda, her guest had got up, said goodbye and left as quickly as she had arrived, leaving Ailsa feeling literally drained in her wake.

'What was all that about?' she said, out loud.

When Miss Cochrane came in to clear away the tea things Ailsa decided to question her.

'What do you know about Belinda MacKenzie?' She decided the direct approach was the best idea, but Miss Cochrane looked startled at the question.

'What do you want to know?' the housekeeper asked cautiously.

'I don't know, she's really strange.' Ailsa decided to open up. 'When I went to dinner with the MacKenzies, weeks and weeks ago, she never opened her mouth. Then suddenly she visits, with no warning, and talks about how much she hates the other MacKenzies. I didn't know whether she really wanted to talk to me or whether she wanted to test me. I actually think she's a bit mad.'

'In my opinion, Belinda is best avoided. There is something badly wrong with her and I wouldn't be doing my job as housekeeper to you if I didn't take the time to warn you off. All is not what it seems with Belinda,' was the sufficiently startling revelation.

Ailsa looked at her squarely. 'I'm not sure what you mean,' she said, in a steady voice. 'It's not about being gossipy or anything like that, it's just that she chose to come here today and talk to me about God knows what, and I need to have some perspective on her. I need to know if there is some agenda with Belinda.'

'There is always some agenda with Belinda,' said Miss Cochrane sourly. 'My only advice, if you asked for it, is to be very, very careful, as in my opinion she has a dangerous slant to her personality.'

Ailsa looked at the other woman with a mixture of scepticism and amusement. 'Great,' she said, sarcastically. 'All this and the mad MacKenzies too. Happy days.'

Ailsa knew that she would get nothing more from Miss Cochrane, so left it at that and settled down to read her book, but she felt disturbed, and she read pages over and over again, without taking them in, until she eventually gave it up.

It was almost a month before Ailsa saw Belinda again, and that was at the Highland Games in Arnasaid, in early July. Connie and Jan had come up to Scotland a week before the games. They had taken holidays from work and were looking forward to a great time at Storm Winds.

The nights were lighter now, the sea a gentle lapping turquoise, with the white sand shining beneath, reflecting through the clear waters. The days grew warmer, but still with the cold north wind bringing a nip to the air. The flowers and shrubs which grew up the banks and in the gardens of Storm Winds danced in the breeze tripping off the waves. It seemed to Ailsa like the land around her had grown up and flowered as she watched, blossoming and blooming like a great colourful palate shaking itself awake and splashing its colour all around. This was what she wanted, this land, this house, the sea and islands beyond, and the achingly fresh air which seemed to breathe its way all through her body. She had never felt so alive.

Clem came over on the Thursday evening before the games to meet Connie and Jan. Miss Cochrane had the night off, and they sat outside in the bright evening sunshine, at a patio table set which Ailsa had bought recently, much to Miss Cochrane's despair. The housekeeper said it made the back of the house look like a pub beer garden, which had amused Ailsa greatly. Dishes filled the table, stacked with fresh salmon, locally cured ham and cheese, rice and pasta, with garden peas, fresh chillies and newly cut spring onions. The bread was baked that morning and was torn off in chunks and drizzled with green olive oil. Glasses were filled with chilled white wine and a large jug of water chinked musically with ice cubes. The back of the house sloped steeply to the sea, with a lawn just in front of the high terrace. The naturally rocky landscape surrounding the lawns had been used to best advantage with mature plants and flowers planted around and between, making the whole picture look natural, and not manicured. The ancient terrace which folded out from the house had a wall with crenulations, and a semi-circular sweep of stone steps led down to the lawn and on to where the forest stretched down from the mountainside. There were cliffs on the other side where she walked each day, the path winding round the landscape to Arnasaid. The table sat on the terrace, which overlooked the grounds, the tops of the trees and the sea. The Small Isles beyond sparkled in the dazzling sunshine and would later be bathed in the fiery light of the sun smelting in all its hot redness, out to the west.

'My God, Ailsa, you couldn't buy a view like this.' Connie held up her wine glass in appreciation, flicking back her red hair. 'It's bloody gorgeous! I've travelled all over Europe and America, and this place can beat most for spectacular scenery!'

Ailsa pulled apart her bread, spread it with cream cheese and a slice of salmon and bit into it with relish. 'Yes, and if you want to take home a keepsake, visit Clem's gallery in Arnasaid, she paints it all for posterity!'

'I intend to!' Connie said. 'That picture you have of Storm Winds is beautiful, but I would love a bit of a view of the scenery of the islands, like this,' and she drew her hand from left to right in front of her to indicate the surroundings.

'Oh, I've got plenty to choose from!' Clem said airily. 'The folk round here are a wee bit tight fisted, and I have to rely on tourists to make a living!'

Jan spooned out some salad and a piece of chicken. Her blonde hair glinted in the sun, and she looked tanned and fit. 'Well, this will be the first Highland Games for three of us! What are we to expect Clem?'

Clem ran her fingers through her short hair, which sprang back into exactly the same position as before. 'Well, it's just a family day out. Things for all ages to do, Highland dancing competitions, good old-fashioned games, like tug o' war and tossing the caber, and stalls, plenty of eating, barbeques and homemade cakes and lots and lots of booze – for the grown-ups of course!' she laughed, and the others joined in. 'And – this will be the first year that Lady Ailsa will be opening it, so she's sure to draw a larger crowd than normal.'

'Shut up.' Ailsa glared at her. 'You know I'm dreading that.'

'Oh, lighten up!' Connie laughed. 'What can be so difficult about it? You'll be marvellous, I mean, you look spectacular, you speak well, you are young-ish, free and single, and you are rich to boot! There must be lots of eligible guys lusting after you!'

'Change the record, why don't you!' Ailsa laughed, sarcastically.

'Is there someone on the radar?' Connie was nothing if not direct.

Ailsa was exasperated to feel a flush creep slowly up her neck and face, much to the amusement of everyone else. 'No,' she said, unconvincingly. 'No! Stop it you lot! We were supposed to be talking about the games and suddenly we are now all interested in my love life!'

'Oh, so you have a love life then?' Jan was swift to pick her up on this. 'I have to say men are a lot more interesting to talk about than the Highland Games!'

'Well, I'm sorry, but there is nothing to talk about,' Ailsa said, with finality. 'More wine?'

After the dishes had been cleared away, and the sun had been drawn downwards into the Atlantic, they dispensed to Ailsa's pretty sitting room with their wine. Miss Cochrane had shut the windows and lit the fire, as the nights were still chilly, despite the warm sun during the day. Ailsa began to relate the episode with Belinda.

'Sounds like she's a bit of a fruitcake,' Connie said, with a chuckle. 'This place seems to harbour a few secrets!

'Like what?' Ailsa asked quickly.

'I don't know, it's just that in this day and age you don't stay with a family you detest just for the sake of your children coming home from boarding school in the holidays. Do they have some kind of pull over her, d'you think?'

Clem had been silent during this conversation, but she got up at this point and stared out of the long sash windows towards the darkening sea. 'It's not that easy.' She turned abruptly to say, 'The MacKenzies are a powerful family, in every sense of the word, steeped in tradition and old conservative values. I got out, but not without going through a terrible time, when I was threatened with losing my children, almost stopped from getting my little flat and studio, and only just managed to get a fearfully reduced divorce settlement from Daddy MacKenzie's favourite family lawyer.'

'Oh my God, that's terrible,' Ailsa said, with feeling. 'How did you cope?'

'I didn't really,' Clem sighed resignedly. 'I took a breakdown and was hospitalised for two months before I was able to come back here and start again. As a matter of fact, I stayed here for a further two months, and Sir Angus was the one who helped me get well again and fit to fight the MacKenzies!'

There was a startled silence at this last revelation.

'Then Belinda was right!' Ailsa said, almost under her breath.

'Yes, well, she was right that Sir Angus and the Colonel were not the best of friends, but she was instrumental in causing a lot of problems for me too. Although I don't particularly want to go into all that now.' She looked round, with a watery-eyed grin.

'Let's top up the glasses and drink to Ailsa's first Highland Games!' Jan jumped up and did the honours, while Ailsa watched Clem quietly and thoughtfully.

The next day was dull to begin with, but brightened up before twelve noon, when the games were to open. The committee had sent a classic thirties-style Rolls Royce to pick up Ailsa and her friends from Storm Winds. Ailsa had on a lemon calf-length flowing muslin dress, with a bow at the back and a black pashmina round her shoulders. Jan had expertly tied her blonde hair, which was now growing longer, into an elegant chignon, and a line of tiny yellow buttercup hair clasps adorned the back of her head. Her lemon shoes and handbag completed the picture, and her friends, who were dressed much more casually in jeans or trousers and summer tops, all declared she looked like a million dollars.

'He'll be mad about you,' Jan whispered, as they made their way across a make-shift walkway on the field towards the podium.

'Who will?' Ailsa asked, astonished, stopping in her tracks.

'Whoever,' laughed Jan, irritatingly. 'What does it matter who? They're all gorgeous!'

The field was full of tents, set around the perimeter, selling different wares, homemade baking, jams, chutneys and the usual local produce. There were arts and crafts areas for adults and children to try their hands at making instead of buying, and having a good time doing it. There were areas cleared for the actual games competitions, stages for the Highland dancing, a bandstand for a brass band made up of local folk, including some very aspiring youngsters. The beer tent, which incidentally stored much more in the way of alcoholic drinks than just beer, was one of the biggest areas, and had competitions running throughout the day for the best homemade cider, wine and sloe gin, to name but a few. A lone piper was hailing the crowds to the opening ceremony, and a stage stood to the left of the field for this purpose.

Ailsa was led up onto the stage, where sat the committee, and Donald Campbell, local councillor, came forward like an old friend, kissed her formally on both cheeks and led her to the centre seat. Clem arrived and joined Jan and Connie in the middle of the swelling crowd. People were drifting across the field in groups towards the stage, the children dressed in Highland garb, and tracksuits for the more athletic games, people carrying picnic baskets and folding chairs, and men dressed in white vests and kilts with biceps larger than Ailsa's waist.

'Tossers of the caber,' Donald Campbell helpfully pointed out these men to Ailsa, and she only just managed to contain herself from bursting out laughing at the description. He didn't seem to notice his faux pas, and the moment passed. Champagne was on a table at the side of the stage, and a microphone was in the centre which made Ailsa quake just looking at it. The lone piper had ceased playing when the time had come for the games to commence, and his expert playing was replaced with some indecipherable music which was playing through an AV system which had seen better days. Finally, amongst a flurry of interest and activity, the MacKenzie clan arrived, fashionably late and in style, in three large cars, carrying the family, including a bevy of children whom Ailsa had not seen previously. The crowds parted in a strangely deferential way to let the family through to the front. Carys, tall and beautiful, her blonde hair pinned up, was wearing a white linen dress with red Italian shoes and a matching bag. Her small red jacket, fifties-style, with three quarter length sleeves and large buttons, made a startling contrast. Led in by the Colonel, she nodded frostily at the people either side of her, looking the picture of the Queen of the games. The Colonel cut a dashing figure in plus fours, jacket and deer stalker, and looked very much the part of the Scottish country Laird. Thomas was just behind the two, in tweed trousers and jacket, and looking, thought Ailsa, quite ridiculous. Noel, Malcolm and Belinda were in a row next, with Max bringing up the rear, surrounded by the MacKenzie children. The Colonel, being one of the most important dignitaries in the area, was welcomed onto the stage, and took a seat beside Ailsa, after kissing her formally on both cheeks.

At exactly 12 o'clock, Donald Campbell, who also doubled up as Master of the Ceremonies, resplendent in a mayoral styled pendant and newly applied white gloves, stood to deliver a short speech, which included safety instructions and timings. Ailsa mused that she could be back in London at a conference to hear his speech. At last, when everyone was starting to visibly appear bored, he turned to introduce her.

'It is my pleasure to invite up to the microphone, for her first ever Highland Games, Lady Ailsa Hamilton-Dunbar, Baroness of Strathkinnieford, and Marchioness of Dunlivietor and Arnasaid!' He ended with a flourish of his white-gloved hand, and for a terrible moment, Ailsa was stage struck, and seemed rooted to her seat. The Colonel glanced at her, and seeming to realise her predicament, took her gallantly by the hand and led her skilfully up towards the microphone, almost as if this had been a rehearsed move. She smiled at him weakly, and, catching sight of her friends in the middle of the crowd who enthusiastically led the clapping, garnered her courage and spoke. It was a short and simple speech, delivered with the right mix of professionalism and style. There was hearty clapping afterwards, and a little girl in a Highland costume of red tartan kilt, white frilly shirt and red sash, was led forth to the podium with a large bouquet of flowers for Ailsa. The crowd applauded again, then dispersed to their various activities and pursuits in the field.

'Well done, Ailsa, my dear!' The Colonel boomed, giving her a bear hug. 'Very well done! Well you don't need to do anything formal now until you present the prizes, so why don't you join your . . . ahem, friends,' this last as he caught sight of Clem standing near, with Jan and Connie. 'I'll find my own cronies.'

'Thanks Colonel, for rescuing me,' Ailsa said, appreciatively. The Colonel beamed as he grabbed her a glass of champagne, pressed it into her hand with a huge grin and moved off.

Clem, Jan and Connie had just been joined by a girl who looked about twenty and had the most beautiful hair Ailsa had ever seen. It was naturally auburn, thick and dark and hung in a wavy mass, well below her shoulders. Her eyes were a dark emerald green, and this colouring would pre-suppose a white, freckled complexion, but her skin was tanned and unblemished, with dark lashes and dark eyebrows. Her well-cut lips were devoid of lipstick and as she looked straight into Ailsa's eyes, with an honest, straightforward gaze, it was apparent that, despite the difference in colouring, this was Clem's daughter, Melody.

'Hello,' she said simply, as Ailsa returned her gaze, 'I'm Melody MacKenzie.'

'Of course you are!' Ailsa laughed. 'I would have picked you out in this whole crowd as Clem's daughter. You are very like your Mum.'

Melody nodded, and gave her mother a squeeze, glancing at her with an expression which was close to hero-worship.

They moved round in a little group, Melody linking arms with her mother, with Ailsa, Jan and Connie in tow, their glasses of champagne held aloft. Soon they reached a platform decorated in bunting and with a healthy crowd cheering on the beautifully dressed boys and girls in their Highland dance uniforms. They all wore varying colours of tartan kilts, white blouses, sashes, and some with gorgeous velvet waistcoats. Ailsa glanced around and caught the gaze of Stephen Millburn, standing several feet away, dressed in jeans and open-neck granddad shirt, with a tweed cap on his head. He held a plastic beaker of beer, and, as Ailsa caught his look, he lifted the beer in salute, then abruptly turned away. Ailsa felt a flush cross her face at his temerity, he was obviously making a point of turning his back on her, and she felt slighted and annoyed in equal measure. She did not admit to herself what her innermost thoughts were, that he looked gorgeous with the sun on his hair, and his sleeves rolled up to display a very tanned and muscular physique; it was his brusque treatment which irritated her. Just as she was telling herself that she was being completely stupid and naïve for even allowing him to bother her, a lovely dark-haired woman, much younger than herself, sidled up to him and handed him another beaker of beer, placing her hand on his arm. As Ailsa watched, he took the beer, said something which made the woman laugh cheerfully, then he quickly looked back round to catch Ailsa staring at them. He grinned, and Ailsa raged, mortified that she should have been so caught out. At this point, the three girls, who had been dancing round swords on the platform, came forward and formally bowed to mark the end of their performance, and Ailsa was swept up in the clapping and comments that the girls were all great. She refused, after that, to let herself look over anywhere in Stephen's direction, downing her champagne, and allowing herself to be led by Jan and Connie over to the drinks tent nearby to replenish the plastic flutes.

The games were a great success. The sun was hot, the breeze cooling an otherwise inclement heat for the participants, and Ailsa found that people sought her out to congratulate her both on her moving to Storm Winds, and her speech. She knew and had met a good many of them by this time, recognising most of them as residents of Arnasaid. The MacKenzies didn't appear to mix as well with the crowd as she herself did, most of them keeping an aloof profile, although Malcolm was conspicuous by his over-frequent attendance at the beer tent, and Noel and Thomas stood together for most of the day, not mingling, but acknowledging Ailsa and her London friends. The various MacKenzie children either hung around their Uncle Max or were to be seen here and there with local kids throughout the day. Max and Melody were together a lot. It seemed that Melody was very close to her uncle.

Later on in the afternoon, Ailsa, feeling a little claustrophobic in the drinks tent, where the volume of noise competed with the raucous socialising done by some of the people over-drinking, she murmured her excuses to her friends, and slipped out the back behind the tent, to clear her head in readiness for the prize giving event which was to happen shortly. She sat on a nearby rock overlooking the beautifully and unusually calm sea over to the Isle of Skye. No one could see her here from the games field, she gave a sigh of relief as her shoulders began to relax for the first time that day. The sun blasted its vitamin-rich rays into her, as she held up her face to meet its glare, thinking about the day, and its demands and pleasures. It was great to have Jan and Connie here with her for her first formal public appearance, and she was growing more and more fond of Clem too. As she luxuriated in her time alone in the warm sun and scenery, she was brought up short by a footstep beside her, and she squinted upwards to see Malcolm MacKenzie standing over her.

'Good afternoon, Ailsa,' he said, with a grin. 'How is my favourite Lady of the Manor? I saw you come out behind the tent and wondered if you were feeling all right?'

As he spoke, Ailsa got to her feet, and, seeing that Malcolm was a few pints on the overload, she decided to avoid any potential scene and head back in to the tent. She said, with as much friendliness as she could muster, 'Of course, I am fine, thank you,' but her words came out abrupt and stilted. 'I was just on my way back to the tent . . . 'and began to move away. She had gone just a few steps when Malcolm caught her arm and pulled her towards him. Before she could even form a word of protest, he pulled her into his strong arms, and with a hand on the back of her neck, drew her roughly into a kiss which was anything but gentle. She tried to pull away, but he held her fast, his mouth, stale with the smell of bitter beer, covered her own, in an urgent, seeking and abandoned crunch of lips and teeth. She felt her lip start to swell, and in a state of sheer panic, managed to pull herself away, her eyes flashing with fear and anger, the back of her hand automatically finding the spot of blood on her upper lip.

'I knew you wanted me to do that since the first time we met,' he snarled, and she looked at him in undisguised disgust. There was nothing passionate or caring about the encounter, it was raw, unfeeling and sullied. Ailsa drew back her hand and slapped him soundly on the cheek, and such was his level of intoxication that he didn't see it coming, nor was he able to prepare for the blow as his mind was several steps behind. He stumbled backwards, his hand clutching at his left cheek, and his eyes holding a bewildered expression which turned very quickly to anger.

'You little bitch . . .' he started to say, but this time she was ready for him.

'Don't ever do that again, or I'll have you charged with assault, and don't flatter yourself with the idea that this is what I wanted. You, Malcolm, are the very last person I want.' With this, she walked swiftly back into the beer tent.

As she arrived back into the drinks area, Stephen Millburn, who seemed to have been waiting and watching for her arrival back in, looked at her slightly dishevelled appearance, and immediately cornered her.

'Ailsa, are you okay?' His handsome face showed real concern as Ailsa approached the bar, but she could not at this juncture look at any man, far less Mr Millburn. She picked up a glass of ready-filled champagne from the counter, and obtusely turned her back on him and walked off to seek her friends.

'He *What?*' Connie gasped incredulously, when she heard what had happened. She happened to be on her own in a corner, just outside the beer tent catching up on her texts, the others having gone to watch a tug of war game. Ailsa reached into her bag for make up to disguise the small cut on her lip, and nodded at her friend.

'Oh, don't worry, Malcolm doesn't bother me, and I am more angry than anything that he managed to catch me out alone in a quiet spot. I think he is a lecherous bastard, but harmless.'

'I wouldn't be too sure, here give me that foundation and I'll just . . . there, that's better, all fixed.'

'Hiya! Have we missed anything?' Clem laughed, as she and Jan joined the other two, Melody having gone off somewhere else. 'I got us fresh champers,' and she handed out two plastic flutes. Connie filled them in on the encounter with Malcolm.

'I mean, he is a really good looking guy,' Jan said, as she gulped her champagne, 'but who does he think he is?

'Typical guy, thinks that he is the only bloody fish in the sea,' Connie added. Clem was silent, with a strange look on her face which Ailsa noticed, but merely said,

'Well, heigh ho, I'd better make my way back to the stage for the prize giving. I'll see you girls later.' She gave a forced half-smile, and vanished.

Chapter Ten

The after-games barbeque was to take place at Trannoch. It was part of the duty, community-mindedness and traditions of both Trannoch and Storm Winds to throw open their doors at various times to the people of Arnasaid. Not everyone would make their way to the great estate from the games field, many of the people attending the games had travelled far, some had young families or elderly parents whom they wanted to get home.

The perfectly manicured lawn at Trannoch had been set up with an assortment of tables and chairs, and the barbeque itself stood at the side of the house, with another long table laden with food and drink. A few of the estate Ghillies had been commandeered to help out with grilling burgers and sausages. 'It's a man thing, to barbeque,' Clem had said, when she saw the estate workers, much to the amusement of her new friends.

Belinda walked past, looking bemused. Malcolm could be seen out of the corner of Ailsa's eye, he was with a different woman now, and he wore a sickeningly superficial grin every time their eyes met. Ailsa studiously avoided him, the hackles on the back of her neck going up at the very sight of him. 'How does Belinda put up with it?' she thought.

The MacKenzie children all looked pleasant enough, Melody was a beautiful young woman, and often to be seen with her arm through either the Colonel, or Max's arms. Ryan and Ariadne, or Aria as she was known, were nice children of 12 and 10 respectively, and quite obviously adored Max, their father, the way they interacted with him and brought laughter to his boyish face, hitherto unseen by Ailsa. David 16, and Melissa 15, the very grown up looking children of the salacious Malcolm and the bewildering Belinda, looked strangely respectable despite their dysfunctional parents. They both had an air of responsibility about them, and quite obviously looked after their younger cousins, especially Melissa who could be seen mothering both Ryan and Aria throughout the evening, playing the various games which had been set out on the lower lawn for children and adults alike. Carys and Thomas had no children, it seemed that Carys had no room in her self-absorbed life for them, and Thomas was too weak to contemplate arguing with his beautiful wife, whom he worshipped, but who quite apparently was at best indifferent and at worst despising towards him.

Ailsa felt that it was her place to mingle with the guests, which she did, with great success, getting to know the people of Arnasaid. She quickly made her mind up whom she liked and who she most definitely wanted to stay away from. Some were only anxious to know her because she was rich and titled. 'You need to be able to sort out the genuine ones from the social climbers,' Donald Campbell said, as one of the latter breed moved away quickly when Ailsa's face showed she could take the gushing flow of sycophantic speech no longer.

'Sorry, I think I was quite rude to Mrs Patterson-Howe,' Ailsa sighed, as the plump woman who looked as if she had been stuffed into a shell-pink dress flounced away, her large nose skyward.

'Well she did come across as over-bearing. I knew she was going to ask you to go to Blue Gables for one of her speciality afternoon teas, but I also moved over to warn you she would try to manipulate you into one of her dreadful committees and 'society dinners' as she calls them. She only asks the ones she considers to be good enough and by that I mean either has money or is titled. You were an obvious target!'

'Getting to know your flock?' A warm voice came from just beside her right ear, and she turned to see Stephen Millburn holding two paper plates with cheeseburgers, one of which he handed to her. 'I didn't know if you wanted sauce, so I put tomato on the side,' he grinned. 'I did notice you hadn't eaten.'

She hesitated before she answered, still having the vision of Stephen with the woman in the games field. She shrugged. 'Watching out for me then, were you?' she replied with a sardonic smile. She had already had enough of mixing with people by this time, enough of being the new Lady of the Manor, and she sat down with relief on the nearby chair Stephen pulled out for her and began to eat her burger. She eyed him surreptitiously as she chewed. He was really handsome. Tall and rugged, he had a smile that made her stomach flip. She felt tired and emotional and a little lightheaded, which had nothing to do with the burger.

'So, have you forgiven me?' he asked suddenly, edging his seat closer to her. 'I mean, for interfering and giving you advice?'

'Well, as it happens, the advice was unwelcome to begin with, but sound, as I later found out,' she replied cryptically.

'Why, what did he do?' A thunderous look passed over his well-cut features, the light changing in his eyes.

'Oh, nothing I couldn't handle,' she said, suddenly regretting her comment. 'Malcolm seems to be having some sort of mid-life crisis.' As she spoke, she saw him in a far corner of the garden and taking the hand of the woman he was with, led her down a small woodland path out of sight. Stephen followed her eyes and shook his head abruptly, anger now apparent on his face. He wiped his mouth with a napkin and drew a gulp from his bottle of beer.

'Problem is, Malcolm has been having his so-called mid-life crisis since he was a boy. Excuse me, I'm going for another burger – would you like one?'

But Ailsa had suddenly gone off her food. She felt extraordinarily tired. She walked up towards Connie and the others who were congregating on a small stone wall at the side of the lawn.

Carys walked past, holding aloft a glass of champagne in a glass flute, everyone else had plastic beakers, and Ailsa tried to fashion a smile as she stood in front of her.

'Your speech was . . . interesting,' Carys deigned to say, and Ailsa answered her in mock appreciation.

'Thank you, it's been an interesting day.'

'I suppose these are your London friends?' She cast her gaze upon Connie and Jan, and then her stare landed on Clem. Her expression, however, did not change from the disdainful one she had worn from the start.

'Yes, they are. Would you like to meet them?' Ailsa said, and instantly regretted the question as she watched Carys' gaze return to Clem.

'Thank you . . . no,' she said, with what she probably thought was a fetching smile. 'I am in the middle of something.' She turned abruptly and walked away.

'What a bitch she is,' Clem said, with undisguised hatred. She had heard this last remark from Carys. 'I can assure you, you don't want to meet her anyway,' and Jan and Connie laughed.

'We saw you talking to the gorgeous Stephen,' Connie said, laughingly.

'Not many like him in a pound,' Jan said, with a twinkle in her eye and raised her glass in salute.

'No, you're right, he's a really nice man,' Ailsa nodded in agreement, a warm glow covering her cheeks, all thoughts of previous problems with Stephen vanishing into a distant memory. She sat down on the wall beside them, not noticing Clem's colour had risen in tandem with her own. She could not help but think about the woman Stephen had been with in the field at the games. Who was she? And where had she gone?

Later, Ailsa gathered her things together and looked for Jim Hutton to drive them home.

'I'll meet you out on the drive in five minutes,' she said, to Connie and Jan. 'I just need to pop inside to go to the ladies.' The house was relatively quiet, as the party was still going on outside, and finding the downstairs cloakroom engaged, she decided to go up to the first floor and use one of the many bathrooms up there which she had seen on previous visits. The first floor was deserted. Ailsa pulled off her shoes, which were killing her feet by this time, luxuriating in the feel of the deep pile carpets which covered the middle section of the first floor galleried corridor; the ancient wooden floors framed the edges, brought to a dark high polish by centuries of hard work by Trannoch staff. The darkness of the wood and the height of the ceilings added a coolness after the heat of the afternoon, and the dishes and vases of beautiful garden flowers provided a light perfume to the atmosphere. Pictures of Trannoch ancestors adorned the walls, along with landscapes of Scottish battles of yore which Ailsa still didn't really understand but really wanted to learn about, along with her own ancestral lineage. The doors on this landing were more than eight feet high, and Ailsa pushed one open into the bathroom. On her way back out she was just closing the bathroom door behind her when she heard what she thought was crying nearby.

'Oh God, this is quite surreal, like one of these B-rated movies,' Ailsa said, quietly to herself, as she pivoted, trying to hear where the crying was coming from. It was a sprawling house, and this particular corridor was long, with many rooms adjoining. She moved down a small corridor off the main one and saw a door slightly ajar. The sobbing – as this is what it was – was coming from this room. The person was definitely female, but Ailsa couldn't tell beyond that whether they were young or old. She gingerly touched the door, and it swung open to reveal a bedroom, lit by a table lamp. The figure on the bed was lying in the foetal position, a bottle of wine with a glass stood on the bedside table. Ailsa slid into the room, her gut wrenching at the tragic sounds of the sobs, and as she got to the foot of the bed, she must have made a noise, as the figure on the bed suddenly stopped sobbing, and slowly lifted her head.

Her dark hair tumbled around her thin shoulders, and as she lifted an oval face, lips well-cut and large dark eyes blinking little pools of mascara down her olive-skinned cheeks, Ailsa realised that this was the young woman she had seen at the games with Stephen.

'I . . . I heard . . . I heard you cry, and . . .'

'You are the Lady Ailsa, yes?' The voice was unmistakably Italian, matching the dark olive complexion, as the tragic expression through the beautiful large eyes held Ailsa's gaze.

'Yes, I am. Who are you?'

'Olivia,' she answered, with a pronounced Italian accent.

'Are you all right, Olivia? I saw you at the games, with . . .' She got no further.

''He molested me,' she spat, her lovely face changing as the anger frothed in her snarling mouth. Ailsa froze, her whole body rigidly galvanising against the words of this stranger, a taste of bile rising in her throat. She steeled herself before she was able to frame any words.

'He *what*?' Ailsa could not quite believe what she was hearing, and actually thought the woman must be drunk.

'He molested me,' she said, again, this time stronger, and, wiping her face with the back of her hand, straightened herself up to a sitting position.

'Are you . . . are you sure?' Ailsa was gradually starting to feel the blood return to her face after the shock had wiped it out. 'I mean, that's quite an accusation . . .'

'Yes, I thought you all say that. Never mind, I go now,' and she scrambled up off the bed to leave.

'No, wait a minute, I'm sorry, it's just that I didn't expect you to say anything like . . . are you hurt? Do you want to call the police, or get medical help?'

The woman stared back at her. Finally, she began to cry, quietly this time, her silent tears cascading down the already smeared cheeks. Ailsa felt more moved than when the young woman had been sobbing, there was something tragic about this new reaction. 'I no want medical help, I no want the politzi, I no want anything from you people.' She turned her back on Ailsa and with a quiet dignity, pulled on her shoes and left.

Ailsa felt that she had been hit by a thunderbolt. Her stomach was churning as she watched her disappear through the door, and it was several minutes before she could steel herself to follow her. As she closed the bedroom door behind her, she caught sight of a figure to her right on the wide corridor standing silently in the shadows, and, as she heard herself catch her breath, she watched Belinda smile a tight-lipped smile, and walk away.

Back at Storm Winds, the party was hilarious apart from Ailsa, who, despite having drunk several glasses of champagne throughout the day, was sobriety itself. She knew she had to play hostess to her friends though, and as she had previously asked Clem to stay the night with them too, they made their way into the larger, more formal sitting room which she had decorated recently and kept good for such occasions. Miss Cochrane had lit the fire and laid out a light supper on a side table.

'Ailsa, Cocky is amazing!' Jan slurred her words slightly as she filled a plate with bread and cheese, smoked salmon and pickles. Ailsa laughed lightly, trying to join in the party atmosphere, but, as she looked up and caught Clem's knowing gaze, she knew she had been rumbled. Clem said, in that look, that she knew something had happened. Ailsa poured herself a large glass of red wine, and, kicking off her shoes, curled up on one of the new pristine white damask settees which were placed either side of the huge ornate fireplace, and pulled the clips from her hair, shaking it loose.

'Ailsa, darling, are you all right?' Connie asked suddenly, stuffing herself with delicious cold vegetable quiche. 'You've been very quiet since we came back from the barbie!' At once the others turned and looked at Ailsa, watching intently until the hot colour rose up her cheeks.

'I'm fine!' Ailsa answered, too brightly. 'I'm just absolutely shattered. If you don't mind, you three, I'm going to take my wine up to bed with me and turn in.'

'Of course we don't mind, honey, you go up, we'll be sure to finish this lot. Don't want to disgrace you on the food and drink front you know!' Jan laughed, as she bit into a cold chicken leg with relish.

As Ailsa lifted her glass in salute to her friends she locked eyes with Clem, who was smiling both reassuringly and worriedly.

Ailsa stood for a long time in her pyjama shorts and tee shirt, on the Juliet balcony overlooking the sea. She could see the lights of Skye blinking in the distance and the lighthouse on the promontory of the island. The saltiness floated on the light breeze, and she could hear her favourite sound since she had arrived at Storm Winds, the lapping of the sea on the shore. Moths buzzed in the light from the room behind her, and she wrapped her arms around her as she thought about the events of the day. She thought about Stephen with another woman's hand on his arm in the games field. She thought about Malcolm with his beer-filled breath, his urgent lips covering her mouth, and his obvious anger as she slapped him. She thought of Belinda, hiding in the shadows of Trannoch's upper corridor as she had that unforgettable exchange with the strange young Italian woman. How much had Belinda heard? Did she know the woman? What was she doing lurking outside the bedroom? Olivia herself, her obvious grief, and her accusation. Would Stephen be capable of molestation? Had the word lost something in the translation from Italian to English? What had Olivia meant by it, had Stephen kissed her in much the same way Malcolm had kissed her this afternoon, or had he been more intrusive in his advances, or worse, had he raped her? The thoughts steamrollered through her mind like a train hurtling through the darkness, and she could make sense of nothing. She didn't want to make sense of it. She wanted to blot it out and not think of it again, but she knew that this would not be possible.

Shivering, she closed the French doors to the balcony, and after bumping her pillows with ferocious punches, she climbed into bed with her wine, sipping thoughtfully until the glass was drained, then sliding down the bed and into a sleep from which she did not stir until nine the next morning.

Chapter Eleven

Connie and Jan left at the end of the week to go back to London. Ailsa was not sorry to see them go, as following the barbeque they continually questioned her as to why she seemed so withdrawn. She felt she couldn't confide in her friends, a rare thing for her but one which Ailsa couldn't help. She had been on such a high since coming to Storm Winds that it was inevitable that she would have a bit of a 'downer' at some point when things settled down. This was that point. So, Connie and Jan returned to London in high spirits after their holiday, but none the wiser as to what was the matter with Ailsa. It was somehow worse with Clem though, who seemed to sense that Ailsa was hiding something significant and not just that she had been overly tired and a bit quiet, which was what Jan and Connie believed. Clem had cornered her at breakfast the next morning, Jan and Connie were still in their beds, and it was only the two of them.

'Is there something you want to talk about, honey?' Clem asked her friend as she bit into bacon and toast. Ailsa lifted eyes full of an emotion her friend could not decipher and shook her head.

'No, sorry about last night, I was just really worn out and feeling a bit emotional,' she managed to say.

'Well, if you're sure that was all it was.' Clem knew she couldn't press the point, after all there are only so many times you can ask the question, and, if Ailsa wanted to keep her worries to herself, there was really not a lot Clem could do.

Ailsa was trying to learn all she could about the affairs of her estate and had called upon her late father's lawyer more than a few times to get a grip of the way things were tied up financially. After the Colonel, she was the biggest landowner in the North West of Scotland, and the prospect daunted her. Her diary was becoming full, with engagements across the area. Gennina became her full time personal assistant, making appointments and handling Ailsa's extensive portfolio of charity events. The Ghillies' Ball was a key event in her calendar, and this year was to be hosted by Ailsa at Storm Winds. When Ailsa asked about the traditions of a Ghillies' Ball, Gennina was only too happy to 'fill her in.'

'It used to be a Ball for all the servants, but the gentry – that's you' she added helpfully, 'would be allowed to come along and they would dance with the lower classes.' Gennina chewed her lip thoughtfully. 'In all the years that I have worked here,' she had been working at Storm Winds for around four years, 'there haven't been very many servants, not like my gran said were here in the old days, so lots of people from the village and round about were invited to increase the numbers. It's always a good night, everyone seems to enjoy themselves,' she ended, with a smile, and continued to tap on her laptop keyboard.

'I'll just be in here, I want to read through some papers,' Ailsa said, walking towards her open office door.

'I'll get you tea,' Gennina bounced into sudden action and made for the tiny kitchen. Ailsa bent down with her back to the door to get a file from the bottom drawer of the cabinet.

'Nice view!' came a sultry voice from the open door. She straightened, blushed, and turned slowly.

The appreciative grin on his face galvanised her into action. 'What do you want, Stephen?' she asked, curtly.

'Sorry, that was a bit sexist,' he answered, sheepishly, although he looked mildly surprised at her tone. 'Well, I just wondered if you had anything you wanted me to do today? The tree-felling is complete, and the casuals are tidying up, and . . .'

'Yes, I want you to leave,' she said, quietly, but with a tremor to her voice.

'Leave? What do you mean leave?' he said, in astonishment, 'I've only just got here! There's plenty to do, I just wondered if you had anything specific you wanted me to tackle. What do you mean leave?' he asked again, as if it had only just got through.

'I want you to go. I don't want you to work here any longer.'

He looked incredulous. 'You're sacking me? Now wait a minute . . .' He came closer, just a few feet away. Ailsa felt herself grow in panic.

'Is this in some way about Saturday and the games? If so, I can't believe you could be so shallow. That girl I was with was coming on to me big time, but aside from watching the games with her and buying her a few drinks, I had nothing to do with her.'

'I have no interest in your extra-curricular dalliances.' Ailsa was all 'Lady of the Manor' now.

'So, it is to do with that then?' he asked, his voice a mixture of confusion and anger. 'I could say it has nothing to do with you, even if there was something in it, but do you know what? I can't even be bothered.'

'I want you out now,' Ailsa said, again. 'Pack up your things and leave. I don't want you near my property again.'

'God you are so bloody dramatic,' he said, disgustedly, 'And as for "packing up" I hasten to remind you I live at Trannoch, not here, and, thanks to both the Colonel's and my generosity of spirit and hospitality, I was helping you out on a part-time basis. Of course, you still have Roddy, but you need more than one estate worker. You're lucky to have Roddy,' he said, pointedly.

'She told me what happened,' Ailsa spat out.

'What? Who told you what?'

'I think you know that already, you are not going to make me say it.'

'Are you talking about the girl at the games? Olivia?'

'Oh well, at least you remember her name.'

He took a deep breath and gave her a hard look. 'I think this estate and title and money are all going to your head. I have no idea what you are talking about and can only presume you think that money can buy you whatever you want, including people. So, Miss Marple, I'm off, and good luck, I hope you find what you're looking for.'

'Oh, Morning Stephen!' Gennina's timing was legendary, and she swung into the office with two cups of steaming tea. 'Would you like a cuppa?'

With a grunt, Stephen bumped past her and slammed the front door of the estate office with such force that the windows rattled, and a potted plant suddenly found itself upturned on the floor.

'You know, he gets worse every day,' Gennina sighed, with total insensitivity and seeming oblivion to the previously raised voices and slammed door. Ailsa sank down wearily onto a chair.

She went for a long walk that afternoon with Rosie and Bluebell, the dogs scampering about joyously along the cliffside and coastline. It was possible to walk along the coast at low tide, from the small beach beneath the cliff at Storm Winds. She had not taken this path very often before, as she never seemed to time the tides right. It was a gorgeous day in early August, the sun was warm but not hot, and a fresh wind was blowing, tossing her blond hair about her face as she strode out with a pent-up frustration borne of the conversation she had held with Stephen. She knew she was attracted to him, and it had been like a knife in her heart when she had discovered the Italian girl at Trannoch and her subsequent revelation. She thought again why she seemed to be the one who always fell for the wrong men. Her life was beginning to become a lot more complicated than when she had arrived in Scotland.

'Hello there!' a voice hailed her, as she came up the grassy bank straight onto the road which boasted the name 'Main Street', and which seemed incongruous in this little village on the seafront, with its cluster of houses and shops mixed together. A parking area held a few cars and a touring campervan, pointing towards the view of the Small Isles and Skye, and on the grassy bank stood some large boxes of flowers, and a few wooden picnic tables. Arnasaid's small coastline was rocky, and boats bobbed in the harbour which had been extended over the years. More than the harbour had been extended, originally there had only been a row of fishermen's cottages which grew over the years in size and complexity of architecture, some turning into shops. The pub and the rest of the village grew up the hill behind, to make quite a community. Clem's gallery was in one of the small side streets off the Main Street. A new restaurant was opening at the other end of the village, with a decking area built on the front with the optimistic idea of having outdoor eating; the view being the most enviable part of this piece of entrepreneurship by a couple from the South of England where the summers were significantly better than in the North West of Scotland.

Ailsa turned to see the Colonel, who was walking along the street, a paper under his arm and a huge smile on his face.

'Ailsa, my dear, how are you?' he boomed, with obvious pleasure at seeing her. He gave her a bear-like hug and suggested they try the new hotel for a spot of lunch.

'It's very good of you, Colonel, but I don't really feel hungry,' and, as she said this, the smile went from her face and the sparkle from her eye.

'Well, let me take you for a glass of wine then. Maybe we could share a packet of crisps or nuts?' he said, with a conspiratorial chuckle. She sighed, laughed and agreed, fastening the leads on the two dogs, and followed him over the street to *The Wee Dram*.

'My doctor has advised I get more exercise, which is why you see me strolling along the street in Arnasaid today, Ailsa!' he said, when they were settled with glasses of red wine and a selection of savoury nibbles. The dogs sat quite happily on the wooden settle, one on each side of her.

'You mean Max?' Ailsa said, with a dryness to her tone which made the Colonel raise an eyebrow in surprise.

He shifted in his seat and took a gulp of his wine before he answered. 'I fear you and my son Maxwell do not see eye to eye. I wonder why that is?' he said, almost as if he was talking to himself.

Ailsa felt and looked uncomfortable. 'I don't know. I have my opinion of him, and he obviously has his own opinion of me. I think we got off on the wrong foot.' As she said this she smiled at her own pun with a thought to the rescue on the cliffside.

'Yes, yes, I think we all have our own opinions of each other, some of them may be correct and some may be grossly unfair. I mean, take my own opinion of you, Ailsa. When I heard that a young London socialite was taking over a hugely important neighbouring estate, one which had simultaneously been part of our own existence at Trannoch for centuries; with no training, no apparent roots in either the function of the estate or Scotland itself, I met the news with a great deal of trepidation, and, if I am honest, wholehearted cynicism. I mean, there has never been a time in Storm Wind's history where there wasn't an immediate heir whom everyone knew at the helm, far less someone who was ultimately a stranger to the family and the area.'

'Or a woman.'

'Yes, or a woman, but my point with all this is that I couldn't have been more wrong about you. You obviously inherited a great deal of skills and attributes from Angus, but you have brought here your own brand of determination, freshness and creativity which we have not seen for a very long time.'

Ailsa took some time to digest what the Colonel had just said. She felt a warm glow pass over her cheeks, not altogether brought on by the wine she was drinking. 'Thank you,' she said, simply. 'It has been challenging at times, but I love it here, and, as you say, I am determined to make it work. When I made the decision to move here it was as much a surprise to me as it was to everyone who knew me. Storm Winds intrigued me. It's history and it's place here in the North West. I don't want to sound jingoistic, but I felt that this change in my life gave me the opportunity to make a real difference, and I want much more than just being a nominal head of the estate. I know this will sound corny, but I feel almost that this is like a 'calling', and I am so lucky to be here.' She felt tears in her eyes as she spoke the words which had been longing to escape, but no one had made her face her reality in the same way that the Colonel had just done, and she felt very emotional.

'I hear too, that you and Stephen Millburn have had a clash of sorts?' He said it in his forthright manner, not trying to soften the words. 'I am sorry about that, as my opinion of Stephen is very high.'

'I think we'll agree to disagree on that point, Colonel.' Ailsa felt an inner rage begin to boil even at the mention of his name.

'Very well, I know you have Roddy MacLean working full time, but he needs Stephen's guidance. I think letting him go, even although he was only part-time, working alongside Roddy, may leave you in a bit of a spot. Storm Winds is a huge estate, and there is a lot of work which needs to be done. May I make a suggestion?'

'Of course.'

'Well, we have had a good lad working alongside Stephen at Trannoch for the last month or so, called Joshua. He seems to be shaping up well. Just moved here on a visa or whatever you call them, from New Zealand or Australia, or somewhere. Would you like me to send him over for an interview?'

'Great idea,' Ailsa smiled, appreciatively, and was glad that the problem of the lack of an additional estate worker at least was being addressed, if not solved.

He took her hand across the table and squeezed it. 'I was right about you, Ailsa, you are the best thing to happen to both Storm Winds and this area in a long, long time. But you must watch out. There are some who don't like it that you have just taken over a huge estate and inheritance and would like to see you fail.'

'Anyone in particular?'

'I'm not going to say anything, as you need to size up people yourself. What I will say is that of the people I suspect who are not happy about you moving here, my son Maxwell is not one of them.'

On the way home, Ailsa mused over the Colonel's comments. She was flattered and felt a strong sense of comfort and belonging after his words. He was a father figure who she thought she would be able to rely on, amongst the long list of characters whom she just could not fathom. Her thoughts turned to Stephen. How could he betray the MacKenzies, and her own trust with his actions? Why had he ruined everything by assaulting Olivia? She had felt an urge to talk to the Colonel about it, but he seemed to have Stephen up on a pedestal, and she was not going to be the one to knock him down. Stephen had stirred an emotion inside her which made her feel less like an heiress and more like a desirable woman again, but she could not, and would not, allow herself to think of him in that way again.

The invitation had come from Trannoch for Ailsa to have dinner with the family and talk about the Ghillies' Ball with a view to helping her with any preparations and 'give a few tips', to quote the Colonel, as to what people have come to expect. She had not been for dinner at Trannoch since that first night when she had newly moved to Storm Winds, and she expected her game plan would be to stick to the Colonel as far as she was able, and keep away from the other MacKenzies.

'What dress are you going to wear?' Eileen was in Ailsa's bedroom pulling out options from the growing wardrobe. 'I really like this deep purple one . . .'

'I'm going to wear my black skinny jeans and my black sparkly top,' Ailsa said, with finality. She looked up and caught Eileen's surprised look.

'I think for dinner at Trannoch . . .'

'Yes, I know what you think Eileen, as do half the populations of Strathkinnieford, Dunlivetor and Arnasaid think the same thing, but I am not in the mood to wear a dress, and I'm going to wear my jeans and top.' Ailsa swept past, across to her en suite where the bubble bath was running, and the glass of chilled white wine was on the side.

'Random!' Eileen said, with a chuckle, and turned to the wardrobe again.

Jim Hutton was ready with the car at 7 p.m. and transported Ailsa to Trannoch. She had dressed in her jeans and top and had put her hair up in a very attractive and flattering roll, with wisps which framed her face. She knew that her choice of clothing would not be palatable to some in the company, but she was growing in confidence and just did not care. Her top was simply cut, expensive for Ailsa and hung well, flattering her figure. She had inherited jewellery from her late step-mother, Elizabeth Douglas and she took it out from the safe in the library and selected a simple emerald necklace and bracelet, to match, which suited her outfit completely.

Denbeath met her at the door, and, with a dignified and guarded glance at her attire, led her into the Great Room where the family were gathered. If the Colonel thought anything untoward in her choice of apparel he certainly did not voice his opinion nor show it in his expression, as he welcomed her heartily with a kiss on both cheeks and handed her a glass of champagne.

Carys was looming in the near distance with her champagne flute held as high as her attitude, and Thomas her husband was quietly talking to Max in a corner of the room. Noel sat alone nursing a large whisky, and Belinda was nowhere to be seen. The Colonel had ushered her to one of the sofas on either side of the magnificent fire, and Malcolm, from the corner of the room, joined them sitting opposite. Carys stood behind him, her disdainful look saying she felt it would be beneath her to join them by sitting on the sofas, her pose looking like a still for 'Hello' magazine. She very pointedly looked Ailsa up and down then said, 'Well, the favoured heiress again! I can give you the address of an excellent dress shop in Fort William if you are interested. I don't suppose you have had much time to do some proper shopping, what with all your engagements and meetings,' she said acidly, yet with a sweet smile on her face. Ailsa fumed.

She in turn looked Carys up and down, and as all the eyes in the room were on her, following Carys' loud remark, she answered with equable smoothness, 'Is that where you shop?

I think I'll pass,' and she was rewarded with a few sniggers around the room.

'Now then ladies!' Malcolm sneered. 'No cat fighting, unless of course you would like to mud-wrestle which would be highly amusing to watch . . .'

'Shut up, Malcolm,' Max said, and sprung up to his feet. 'Dad, shall we go through? I think I hear Denbeath coming,' as the butler duly appeared at the door. As Ailsa rose again to her feet, a figure came from behind Denbeath and into the room.

'Colonel, so sorry I'm late, a calf was stuck on the fence and it took me a bit of time to get her loose.' Stephen Millburn came right up to the Colonel and shook his hand. Ailsa felt her face go bright red with anger, and her eyes flashed as he turned to her with a curt, 'Lady Ailsa, I hope you are well?'

'Everyone through now!' the Colonel boomed at them, like they were a class of primary school children, and Ailsa suddenly felt ashamed of herself for rising to Carys' bait. He saw her discomfort and took her arm immediately, before she could do anything but nod at Stephen's greeting, and led her through to the dining room.

'Lady Ailsa indeed! Who is he trying to kid?' she thought, as she took her place at the table where the Colonel led, and the others sat down, Stephen diagonally in front of her. When she glanced at him as she took a sip of champagne, he wore a troubled, perplexed expression on his face, which slightly surprised her. 'He obviously doesn't know that I 'know' and is hiding behind that,' she thought. Max was on her left and Thomas on her right, with the Colonel at the head, and Carys at the foot of the table. Malcolm sat opposite Ailsa, and on the other side of Thomas, Noel faced an empty chair, presumably set for Belinda. Ailsa pointedly ignored both Stephen and Max as she tried to make light conversation with Thomas, thinking, 'God, this is going to be one of those bloody nights.'

As the soup was being served, the Colonel shouted Denbeath over to him. 'Send someone up to my daughter-in-law and fetch her down here,' he said, angrily, and continued, as Denbeath departed, 'I am sick to death of her missing out on family meals. You need to make sure she attends, Malcolm, especially since we have guests tonight. It is downright rude, and I won't have it!' He crashed his glass on the table, the wine spilling over the side, as Malcolm looked completely unmoved, shrugging his shoulders in resignation.

Ailsa felt Stephen's eyes upon her, and sensing he was going to speak, she immediately turned to Thomas, asking about the estate management and how the Colonel had mentioned Joshua may be interested in working for her.

'Oh, you need to ask Stephen about him,' Thomas smiled, in his simple friendly way. 'I really am more office-based, but Stephen is the one who does most of the hard graft out on the land.'

Stephen looked startled. 'So, that's my replacement is it?' His voice was low, and, as the others were engaged in conversation, was only picked up by Thomas and Ailsa herself.

'I need to interview him first, but yes, the Colonel has suggested it, and I am happy to speak with him.' Her tone was not lost on Stephen.

'Oh, are you coming back to work with us full time then Stephen? That is really good news.' Thomas innocently asked the question, completely mis-reading the situation.

'Yes, I believe I am,' was the curt reply, and before Ailsa or Thomas could answer, the door opened and Denbeath appeared and quickly made his way to the side of the Colonel.

'I am sorry to interrupt, Colonel.' His voice was the deepest one Ailsa had heard, even deeper than that of the Colonel.

'Where is she?'

'Erm, Sir, Debbie was sent up, and said that Mistress Belinda is not in her quarters. A further search of the house alluded to the fact that she is not in the house at this present moment.' Ailsa smiled at the butler's formality, but before the Colonel could respond, the door was thrown open and a young man of around Ailsa's age came tumbling into the room to a volley of gasps and exclamations from its occupants. He was tall, with dirty fair hair, and a very muscular tanned body.

'Joshua!' Both the Colonel and Stephen spoke at once.

'What the hell do you think you are doing, breaking in on my dinner party?' The Colonel threw his napkin on the table and stood up in a rage.

'Colonel, I am really sorry!' He spoke with an unmistakeable twang. 'I . . . I . . . don't know how to say this, Sir.'

'What's happened?' Max too, rose to his feet, and at the same time Stephen spoke.

'Is it the calf again? Has something happened to her? Spit it bloody out!'

'No, it's not the calf, Stephen.' Joshua suddenly looked as if the air had been sucked from him, so deflated was his expression as he turned to the Colonel.

'It's Belinda.' The colour drained from the Colonel's face as he waited for the rest. 'I found her lying on the bench on one of the back lawns, with a bottle of pills beside her.'

'I'll come at once. I'll just get my bag.' Max was moving to the door when Joshua swung round on him.

'I'm afraid you won't need your bag, Sir. Belinda's dead.'

Chapter Twelve

Belinda's funeral, like most funerals, was an extremely sad affair, held in the small church in Arnasaid where the family had their own small pew. To Ailsa's astonishment, she too had her own pew, which had been in the Hamilton-Dunbar family since the church was built in 1839. It was a beautiful building, with colourful stained-glass windows depicting some of the great biblical stories. The golden oak interior seemed to glisten in the afternoon sunshine, and the bright blue carpet, which ran the full width of the aisle down to the transept, added more colour and warmth to the interior.

The church was not full. The family were all present, with the workers from both Trannoch and Storm Winds in attendance, but even that was not enough to fill the small church. Ailsa noticed Clem coming in and sitting near the back, which was surprising as her own children were there with Noel. The children had all been brought back from boarding school and sat beside their respective parents. David and Melissa sat at the front with their father, Malcolm.

The Minister, Rev. Doctor Ian McPhearson, was warm and pleasantly spoken with a musical Highland lilt. He was in his sixties and obviously knew the family; he spoke about Belinda in descriptive and knowing terms. Ailsa, although she didn't feel a deep sense of loss for the complicated and destructive Belinda, felt saddened to see the weeping children, and strangely more sad to see that Malcolm was dry-eyed and expressionless.

The wake was held at Trannoch in the Great Room where Ailsa had been weeks and weeks ago, shortly before they had all learned of the tragedy. The death of Belinda had been investigated fully, and the result was that it was unmistakeably suicide, as a result of ingesting a huge number of pills washed down with straight vodka. It had affected the Colonel more than probably anyone ever imagined it would, and Malcolm less than everyone would have hoped or wished to witness.

The Colonel seemed to have shrunk suddenly, his voice was not so booming, and he was not his usual hospitable self. Carys, as ever, thought it was all about her. She wore a black Hermes dress and jacket and had on a little hat, perched on her beautifully rolled up hair, with a veil which did nothing to conceal her heavy make up and bright lipstick. 'Understated' was not a word used ever in the same sentence as Carys. She was strutting about the room, not deigning to talk to anyone, and if someone approached her with condolences, she squashed them with her icy disdain.

Thomas sat in the corner, with Max, and Melissa, who looked distraught. Her white tearstained face, black dress and black patent flat shoes making her look much younger than her 15 years. Her older brother, David, was sitting with his father, Malcolm, who again seemed to be consuming whisky at three times the rate of anyone else. Noel and Carys were carrying out a conversation, 'Grief bringing them together for once?' Ailsa wondered, and their only child, Melody, sat near to them, sipping a glass of wine. She had come home from Uni but would travel back on the train the next day.

The sound of a pager went off, and Max stood up, went over to his father and excused himself, obviously being called to attend to a patient. Looking over, Ailsa saw that Melissa had started to cry again, and watched as the teenager left the room unobtrusively via a French window onto the lawn outside. No one else appeared to see her go. Thomas, very sweet and simple, did not notice she had gone from his side, and Ailsa wondered what to do. Melissa was still a child, and seemingly a very heartbroken one at that, now left without a mother and a grandmother, and only a selfish self-centred aunt in Carys, to provide a female role model. 'God help her,' Ailsa thought, as she got to her feet and followed Melissa outside.

She took the path which led to a walled rose garden with late roses blooming in the October sunshine, their scents filling the air. She noticed Melissa going through a tiny wooden door, set in the far wall, which must have been there since Trannoch was built and people were smaller.

Soon she was standing on the other side of the door which led to a huge arboretum, filled with trees, exotic and indigenous, stretching out before her and up the hillside beyond. Melissa had her back to a tree, her left foot perched behind her on the tree's trunk, and a cigarette in her hand which she defiantly sucked, blowing rings in the air. 'Oh, it's you,' she said, wiping away her tears with the back of her hand.

'I saw you go out, and I just wanted to make sure you were okay.' Ailsa felt her heart go out to the thin white-faced girl before her, stuck between childhood and womanhood. It struck Ailsa how like Belinda she looked, but in a much more attractive way. Her mousey brown hair was highlighted to a light blonde and cut so that her fringe framed her small-featured face.

'I'm okay, thanks, so you can go now. I don't want you here.'

'You must feel very lonely,' Ailsa ventured, 'I know how it is to feel lonely.'

'You know nothing about me,' Melissa sneered, with a venom which surprised Ailsa.

'I would like to get to know you though,' Ailsa tried again. 'You still have your father, and the rest of the fam . . .' she got no further as Melissa broke in.

'My father!' she spat out, with incredible force. 'That whoring bastard, you mean! I'll never talk to him again.'

Ailsa was taken aback by the strength of feeling, and for a moment was thrown off guard. Before she could speak, Melissa started again, 'You have no idea what this family is like. He drove my mother to take her own life. He practically *made* her do it. I wouldn't be surprised if he had put the bottle of pills into her hand.'

'Look, Melissa, I know you are extremely upset, who wouldn't be, but your father . . .'

Again, the younger girl chipped in, 'Please don't try to tell me how I feel or anything about my father. You're a stranger here, what the hell do you know about us and how we are? I *saw* him, time and time again, I *saw* him. So did David, but he's too weak to ever say anything, he *worships* my father, and ignores what an utter bastard he was to Mum. Now go away and leave me alone – you know *nothing*.'

Ailsa was blown away by the tirade, and decided she wasn't going to get through to Melissa at all. She turned to go.

'Wait!' Ailsa turned back to her. 'You're not going to tell the Colonel, are you, about this?' and she held the cigarette up. In that moment she had demonstrated just how young she really was, despite the accusations, all Melissa was really worried about was that her grandfather shouldn't know she'd been smoking.

Ailsa smiled grimly, 'No, I won't say a word.'

All she could think about after that was what Melissa had meant when she said, 'I *saw* him, time and time again, I *saw* him.'

Do what?

The following week, Ailsa interviewed Joshua and found him to be charming and willing to work hard. She offered to take him on to work alongside Roddy. He had been given digs when he worked at Trannoch, as Roddy had, in what had always been the servants' quarters in the old days. She summoned Miss Cochrane to sort him out with a tiny apartment in the rooms beyond the kitchen. He was delighted at having his own space, and even more delighted when Miss Cochrane said they would have a local plumber and joiner to work on the 'kitchen' the following week, installing some cupboards, a cooker, sink and other necessary accoutrements. An old sofa was brought down from the attics for his bigger room, so that he had a kind of bedsit arrangement.

The Ghillies' Ball had been put back for quite a few weeks due to Belinda's death, and the arrangements now needed to be picked back up again. It was a cold sunny day near the end of October when the three of them, Ailsa, Gennina and Miss Cochrane put their heads together to discuss.

'I mean, the problem is, we usually begin the arrangements and preparations for the Christmas Party for the children at the end of October, and here we are still trying to get the Ghillies' Ball out of the way!' said Miss Cochrane, her voice tinged with stress.

'Well, I haven't been at or been involved in either of them, Cocky, but, if we all pull together, we should be able to produce something not half bad,' Ailsa smiled at her housekeeper, encouragingly. Much had changed between the two of them since her early days at Storm Winds, though Ailsa had not been sure how the starchy Miss Cochrane would take to being called 'Cocky'. She had tried it out a few weeks ago, shortly after Belinda's funeral, and it seemed that the tight lips had loosened a little, and there was a brightening of her eyes and a softening of her hard face. None of the other staff dared to copy her, needless to say, they still referred to her by her formal title, and only in private would they call her 'Cocky', with a surreptitious look over their shoulders first.

'The caterers we used the last time let us down, so I suggest we use either MacMillan's or Browns, both of Fort William,' Miss Cochrane said, as she looked at her list.

Gennina nodded vehemently, 'I agree, Co . . . er, Miss Cochrane.'

Ailsa laughed, 'Ok, why don't you have them both here to do a bit of a sample testing and looking at menus etc.? You and Gennina could do that, Cocky. We'll order the champagne from the usual warehouse, and, Gennina, did you say you had sourced a few event management companies to do staging and lighting, music and so on? Well, I suggest you have a day when you ask all the suppliers here with their proposals and see what you think fits best with the old traditions. Would that work?'

'I think that's a very good suggestion, Ailsa,' the housekeeper said, taking notes, 'and, would you still want Abigail Apple to come along and bring some dress designs for you?'

'Love her name!' Gennina said, gushily, 'I mean, what a brill name for a dress designer! If she has any children she could call them Adam, you know Adam Apple? And, Red for a little girl! That would be pure totes amusing!' Ailsa fell about laughing at this, and even the grim Miss Cochrane smiled at the joke.

'Yes, I think I would like that,' Ailsa agreed. 'I would love to have a dress made up with a big Hamilton-Dunbar tartan sash – you said most people wear tartan in some shape or form? If you could ask her to come over on Friday morning, I could see her before I have the Round Table meeting in the afternoon.'

That afternoon, Ailsa pulled on a cream mac over her jeans and cream jumper and took Rosie and Bluebell across the cliff top walk towards Arnasaid. The summer visitors had mostly left, but, there were still signs of people on holiday, a caravan was parked on the front and walkers with backpacks coming out of the new hotel. Ailsa was going to visit Clem, who had promised to make her a boozy afternoon tea which Ailsa was looking forward to very much indeed. She had not seen much of Clem since the barbeque. She felt that things had not been absolutely right between the two of them, and she was unsure why. Then, when her friend had phoned and asked her to come over today, she had readily accepted.

'Come in, Ailsa!' the greeting was cheery, as Clem gave her a hug and drew her into the cosy flat, with a fire already lit in the grate, a small table laden with sandwiches, scones and cakes, and a bottle of Prosecco chilling in a wine bucket.

'Have a seat by the fire, I'm just going to get the teapot, if you could pour us a glass of wine each?'

'Of course!' Ailsa suddenly felt that Clem was not altogether at ease, and she seemed to be disguising this by bustling about, 'But, I could be completely wrong, it's not the first time I've read too much into the way people act, and it won't be the last,' she thought.

Clem poured the tea from an old china teapot, and they filled their plates. The crackling of the fire after the cold wind outside had made Ailsa's cheeks glow. Clem had made everything herself, and the chocolate cake and cream fingers were especially good.

'Absolutely gorgeous,' Ailsa said, biting into a little French fancy which, again, Clem had made, and Clem said nothing, but gave a small smile and sipped her wine.

After much eating and some talk, which included the sad subject of Belinda's funeral, Ailsa still felt the discussion was full of undercurrents. Clem refilled the glasses and sat back in her seat.

'I wondered what there was between you and Stephen Millburn?' Clem said, steadily, as if she had been practising this question for a long time.

There was a silence filled only with the noise from the fire shifting and sparking, and logs falling.

Ailsa, for some reason, felt trapped. 'I don't think I know what you mean, Clem.'

'I think you do.'

'What is this? I thought you had asked me here for a nice afternoon of food and wine, not that you had your own agenda.'

'Ailsa, I know you now. You are astute enough to know that there was a reason I asked you here today, especially since we have not exactly been friendly over the last few months. You knew something was wrong with me, but you didn't bother to try and find out what it was.'

'Hey, wait a minute. I did actually think there was a bit of tension between us, but I've not the first clue what that's about. If it's something that I'm supposed to have done, then I don't know what that is. I would have asked *you* over to explain and to make up, if so, but please don't try and push whatever is bothering you onto me, when I don't even know what I am supposed to have done.'

Clem got up abruptly at this and vanished into the kitchen. She reappeared a few minutes later with another bottle of Prosecco, opened it, poured and sat back down again to look at her friend.

'I've been seeing Stephen Millburn.' Whatever Ailsa expected her to say, it was not this. She felt a deep blow to her gut as if she had been punched, and her mind flitted back to their first meeting in Arnasaid when she had spotted Clem talking to Stephen. 'I see you are surprised. I thought you would be, as I know that you like him too. Oh, I know you have had your run-ins, but I think there is a strong attraction between the two of you. I was not seeing Stephen during the Highland Games, we'd had a huge argument and grown apart, but we got back together again shortly after the games.'

Ailsa didn't know how she felt, her emotions were in a turmoil, she hated Stephen and was attracted to him in equal measure, but her friend Clem had really put her in a position with this revelation, and she was upset and put out. 'He's an attractive man,' she said, lamely. 'I was more frustrated with his attitude than I was attracted to him, though,' she wound up, and wondered to herself if this sounded convincing.

Clem nodded understandingly. 'Okay, I thought you would say something like that, and I am absolutely fine with it. But, there is a bit of a problem. Stephen has told me that you have accused him of something, he didn't say what, but it definitely involved another woman.'

Ailsa felt the hot colour flush her cheeks. She thought back to the games and the barbeque at Trannoch, where Stephen had made it plain he liked her – was that all for show in front of Clem as some kind of ruse to make her jealous? She thought about Clem having been part of their group while Stephen brought her a burger and sat beside her, cheerfully forgetting the woman he had been with at the games, Olivia, who had accused him of molesting her. How could she tell Clem this?'

The fire burned cheerily in the grate, a deep contrast to the atmosphere between the two women, and Clem got up and threw on another log. She sat back down and eyed Ailsa with an expression which said she was not going to let her off without an explanation.

'I'm going to be frank, as I really value your friendship and would not want to lose it,' Ailsa said. 'I was attracted to Stephen, at the beginning, but the fact that he was with that woman at the games, then tried to come on to me at the barbeque, I thought he was a bit of a womaniser, and I backed off. I had no idea there was anything between you two except perhaps a casual friendship, or I would never have even entertained him.'

Clem nodded, 'Sorry, Ailsa. I really didn't mean to put you on the spot, it is just something that Stephen said the other night about you accusing him of something, but he wouldn't say what,' she explained again. 'I think he is probably just annoyed that he got turned down by Lady Hamilton-Dunbar!'

'Well, I don't know about that, but let's just let bygones be bygones.' Ailsa felt such a coward. She was also just beginning to let Clem's news sink in and see what the future consequences might be for her friend.

Clem nodded and raised her glass in a half-hearted salute.

Ailsa felt completely dumped the next morning. She walked into her breakfast room, which she had recently painted pale yellow and where she had also changed the old wine velvet curtains, which seemed to hang all over the house, and the seats of the chairs to duck egg blue brocade. The furniture was dark Scottish oak, like most of the furniture in the house, which she retained as she thought it was so beautiful. The French doors, which opened onto the east side of the house, looked on to the lawn which was ringed with Scots pines in a dramatic mountainous backdrop. Ailsa loved this view. On this late October morning the mist was holding the near surroundings in a damp white shrug, shut out by the warmth of the room. Ailsa stood staring out of the window for a long time until she heard Eileen come into the room looking for her request for breakfast.

'Orange juice, porridge, brown toast and poached eggs, coffee and croissants with black cherry jam,' Ailsa reeled off the order, almost as if she were in a restaurant and not in her own home.

'You must be hungry this morning!' Eileen said cheerily, but Ailsa was not in the mood to converse, and gave her short shrift.

'That's all, thank you, Eileen. Oh, and I will be in my library writing for most of the morning, please see that someone walks Rosie and Bluebell, and I will have coffee at eleven.'

Eileen looked astonished. This was not like the cheery friendly Ailsa she had been used to, and she opened her mouth to say something teasing, and shut it firmly as she saw Ailsa's expression.

'Yes, Ma'am,' she felt compelled to say, and scurried from the room before Ailsa realised she was making fun of her.

When Ailsa walked into her library it was like coming home. A fire was lit in the grate against the gloom of the day – Cocky, Ailsa was sure. She sat in her favourite chair, the one which her father had occupied the first and last time she saw him, and looked around the splendid old room with its half-vaulted ceiling and carved wood surroundings. She thought about that first meeting and how her life had changed extraordinarily in the last few months.

She had gone from a working London social animal to a Lady, with a long title, and a heap of responsibilities she would never have thought possible. She loved the house. She loved the scenery and the bracing sea air and the haar from the sea, the companionship of her friends and yes, the dysfunctional relationships with the MacKenzies of Trannoch. This place was what she was made for. She thought about her aversion to Max, her attraction to both Stephen and Malcolm, her feelings of hate for Carys, her pity for Melissa and lastly her deep understanding and friendship with Clem. She loved the time to write in inspiring surroundings which really got the creative juices going. Her duties, which included being part of the Round Table and organising charity events and making appearances, was probably the biggest surprise of all – she was amazed at how she had managed to slip naturally into the role. If anyone had mentioned 'Round Table' in her London days, she would have fallen about laughing at the mere idea.

Then there was Belinda. What had gone so horribly wrong with her life that she decided she couldn't live anymore? She thought back to that day when Belinda had visited her, as she sat reading in this chair. There had been a warning about Malcolm, and also a veiled threat? She wasn't sure what it was. Belinda had asked her what she was doing here in the North of Scotland as if she was amazed that anyone would want to live alongside the MacKenzies. Was she trying to tell her something? About Malcolm, or one of the other MacKenzies? No one would know what had driven her to take her own life. And what about Melissa's statements of the treatment meted out by Malcolm, and her assertions that she 'saw it'. Saw what? His womanising ways? Everyone saw that side of Malcolm. It was a sad reminder that money can't buy happiness, and Belinda herself had been far from happy.

On the Friday, Abigail Apple was shown into the library to discuss possible dresses with Ailsa for the Ghillies' Ball. She was a lovely dark-haired girl of around twenty-three, with dark almond shaped eyes and a clear, tanned complexion. She was very professional too, for all her young years, and took Ailsa through samples of white materials for the dress, which was what Ailsa had requested, and then the drawings of potential dress designs. Cocky brought in refreshments, and they set to work, finally deciding on a white dress, with a really wide neckline which sat on the top of her shoulders, a tight bodice in a low fitting basque style with a very fine, full and layered gossamer skirt floating down from the bodice. The tartan sash made a colourful splash, with an over the shoulder piece held with a brooch.

'I hope you can come to the Ghillies' Ball?' Ailsa said, when the sketches were all put away and Abigail was making her way to the door of the library.

'Are you kidding? Oh, Lady Hamilton-Dunbar, I would absolutely love it!'

'Please, call me Ailsa,' and as the younger woman began to protest she added, 'everyone does, and it makes me feel so much more comfortable.'

'Of course, then I will call you Ailsa! I am so happy you like my design for your dress, and it will be ready in a fortnight for a final fitting.' Ailsa nodded her approval at this plan. She continued, 'Great, and thanks so much for giving me this opportunity.' Abigail left with a huge smile on her face.

Chapter Thirteen

It was to be an evening to remember, and not only for Ailsa. Most people were to remember this day for many years to come, for various reasons and not all positive ones.

The weather had stayed unseasonably sunny and dry, although the mornings and the evenings were cold and frosty. The frenzied preparations of the last few weeks had paid off, and the date for the Ghillies' Ball had been set for 5th November, again a departure from the normal date. This was due to Belinda's funeral, and everyone understood that it was a necessary change in plan, and, in fact, far enough from Christmas for it not to really matter what the date was. The idea Gennina had put forward was that they would finish the Ball on the headland, with a massive firework display to mark Guy Fawkes Night, and this had met with distinct approval from both Ailsa, and Miss Cochrane.

The actual Ball was to be held in the ballroom at Storm Winds, which Ailsa had had decorated in a fresh style, while still keeping the traditional lines. It was nothing to compare with Trannoch's splendour, but she was delighted with the result. The house was so huge that she was doing a few rooms at a time. She still had no grand plan as to what she would do with the rest of the house – although a few ideas about writing weekends were floating in the outskirts of her brain. The East Wing had been largely untouched for years, and she meant to talk to Cocky and Gennina about possibilities for this very soon.

The walls of the ballroom were of oak panelling, there was a huge, almost walk-in, fireplace with a fire which still worked but had not been used in over a year, and the whole of one side of the room had a series of French doors which opened onto a side garden. A tent had been erected, complete with heaters, which led straight from two of the French doors, and here food was served, buffet style, a bar was set up, and a local, and very young string quartet were to play throughout the evening. In the main room the music was traditionally Scottish, with bagpipes, fiddles, clàrsaches, flutes and accordion, played enthusiastically to accompany the Scottish dances. Ailsa had been all at sea with the dancing, and for the last six weeks had attended a Scottish country dance class in Fort William once a week to learn. She had enjoyed herself so much that she decided she would keep going with the classes. There was a barbeque planned and set out on the headland, the food to be consumed after midnight; the fireworks would begin at midnight when the Ball would wind up.

Ailsa had tried not to be too ostentatious. She knew that the Ball was held alternately at Storm Winds and Trannoch, and she had no wish to compete, so there was simplicity too in the arrangements. The hall had been decorated with garlands made from the foliage and berries from the Storm Winds gardens, fresh berries, boughs and heaps of fresh flowers, especially Ailsa's favourite yellow roses. She had heard tales of food being imported from other countries in previous years, including caviar and other delicacies; this didn't interest Ailsa, she wanted it to be completely Scottish with plain fare. There were huge pans of homemade Scotch broth and pea and ham soup, an abundance of fish, for which this part of the country is renowned, including shellfish of every description, smoked salmon with local cheeses, freshly baked bread and oatcakes with paté. Sandwiches were made with fresh Aberdeenshire steak, sliced thinly, eggs from free range hens from a farm outside Arnasaid were used to make quiches, sandwiches and Scotch eggs. There were chicken pies, beer-battered haddock and chips, and piles of cakes, scones, jams and chutneys, all made locally. For the barbeque, it was simply a choice of burger or chicken kebab, with a vegetarian quorn kebab for the non-meat eaters. Many people commended Ailsa for not trying to out-do the MacKenzies, and she patted herself on the back for her efforts.

Her dress had arrived a week ago, and she was delighted with it. The white brocade bodice was beautifully classy, with a pointed, low hem at the front and a full skirt of spider-web layered gossamer material forming the skirt. The sash was attached to a cummerbund of the same turquoise tartan, draping across the front of the bodice and secured with a brooch, letting a long piece hang naturally from the shoulder. Her white dance shoes had been modelled on actual dancing shoes, with a tie round the ankle, and the height of the heel being quite small in comparison to the high heels Ailsa used to wear when she was going out on the town dancing. She wanted to be able to dance properly after all her practice.

Stephen Millburn was one of the first to arrive. He looked like a dashing figure from days of yore in his kilt, complete with scabbard, his frilly necked shirt opened at the neck to reveal a chest so strong and muscular that any man half his age would have been proud of it. He wore a velvet, loosely tied waistcoat and a huge shawl-like contraption which reminded Ailsa of Braveheart. She almost expected him to draw his sword, and felt a deep pang of something – confusion? dismay, fear, longing? She had no idea how she now felt about Stephen Millburn. She could not escape the fact that she knew what he had done, that fact steadfastly remained, but it was clouded with the issue that deep down she was still drawn to him.

Cocky had protested when she wanted to take him off the invitation lists, her housekeeper obviously had no idea what had happened to make Ailsa let him go and take Joshua in his place, and she argued that staff and workers were the mainstay of the Ghillies' Ball tradition. Being a Ghillie was part of their work, 'for God's sake', she had said, and Ailsa saw no way around it but to invite him along with the others. She had determined, though, to stay away from him at all costs, this last vow taken out of her hands as he was one of the first to appear.

'You look stunning, Ailsa,' was the first thing he said, and, using his costume almost as reinforcement, he bowed in a gallant fashion, taking her hand before she could protest and putting it to his lips. She pulled it fiercely away. He looked astonished. Turning to one of the young hosts Gennina had secured along with the catering company, she beckoned the spotty youth over, and requested him to get a drink for 'Mr Millburn' and moved swiftly away. Mr Millburn's face rapidly changed from bewilderment and hurt to anger at this brusque treatment but made his order and said no more.

The MacKenzies arrived amongst their usual flurry of pomp and circumstance, led by the Colonel, who seemed to have regained his usual stature and confidence since the death of his daughter-in-law. They all wore tartan of some description, the Colonel himself wearing a kilt, shirt and bow tie, and tweed jacket. Needless to mention, Carys was stunning. Her dress was deep turquoise, to match her magnificent eyes, low at the back, and fitting tightly to her slim body. A thin tartan sash was sewn onto the dress, obviously specially made for the occasion. Her blonde hair was curled and held up at one side with a jewelled clasp, and she wore long white gloves. Tainting this aesthetically pleasing picture was her supercilious air which dripped from her perfectly made-up face.

'How will she ever dance in that dress?' Ailsa asked Clem, who had just joined her to watch the parade of the MacKenzies.

'Ailsa, Carys doesn't dance,' Clem said, in a mockingly shocked voice, 'she poses.'

The hall filled up rapidly after that, and Stephen was caught up in dancing with all and sundry, especially with Clem. Carys watched Clem with the estate manager, a sneer spoiling her beautiful face as she turned to the ever-loyal Thomas who had brought her a flute of champagne. 'It's absolutely disgusting to see how low she has stooped,' she said to her husband, looking across at the pair as they flew round the room to The Dashing White Sergeant. 'I mean, to think she was once part of our family, and now she is going out with a Ghillie!'

Thomas stared at her sincerely. 'Well, a Ghillie is not so low,' he made the mistake of pointing out, 'and Stephen is a good chap.'

Carys eyed her husband with a mixture of anger and pity. 'Shut up if you can't say something sensible – good chap indeed, he's a bloody luddite.' And, she drew up her chin and walked off. Thomas, non-plussed, took a swig of champagne and sought out Ailsa to ask for a dance. Malcolm, as usual, was dancing with every woman in sight. He was getting steadily more drunk, swilling champagne like there was no tomorrow, and beginning to make mistakes in the dancing steps which was providing some people with additional entertainment. As the night wore on, he became more and more inebriated, and less funny, but still fascinating to watch.

Ailsa was enjoying herself. She kept pinching herself that this house and this beautiful ballroom were hers, and the fact that she was able to pull together an evening like this one in her own house, was a strange yet fantastic and exhilarating feeling. She was loving the dancing and could not have imagined a year ago, when she lived in London, that she would be any part of, or even enjoy, Scottish country dancing and any form of Ceilidh, a word she had heard but knew nothing about until she came to Scotland. She danced lots of dances and had held her head up high as she accomplished what lots of Scots people fail to do, to embrace their heritage through dance.

Since the earlier conversations, she had studiously avoided both Clem and Stephen, for obvious reasons. Where Clem was, Stephen was usually there or thereabouts, and Ailsa wanted to avoid a scene.

Cocky waved across the room to Ailsa, at one point, beckoning her to follow. Wondering what the matter was and hoping that there would be no dramas, she moved through the crowds to get to her housekeeper, out to the hall, and there, in the front lobby by the great front door, stood

Jan and Connie. Resplendent in kilts of Hamilton-Dunbar tartan, they stood with outstretched arms.

'Oh my God! You are both here!' she said, the tears choking her as she ran to hug her two best friends. 'You said you couldn't come!'

'Nor could we, to start with, but we wangled some work shit to be here, darling, and so glad we did too!' Connie said laughingly.

'Hey, Ailsa darling, the old cottage looks fab, I know you have done so much work for the Ball and I can't wait to see all the guys in their swords and scabbards! You look absolutely beautiful, Ailsa, your dress is amazing. Have you got food? We're starving, just come five hours from London and had lots to drink on the plane but not a lot of food.' Jan threw all this at her friend as she hugged her.

'Of course, I have food, I have a whole tent-full! Come on through to the ballroom, leave your cases and I'll get someone to take them upstairs.'

Jan and Connie were almost immediately swept up in the dancing, and although they didn't know the steps, they learned quickly and had a brilliant laugh trying. Ailsa watched them for a while, then showed them through to the tent, where the other band was playing soothingly, and the food and drink were flowing. There were some tables to sit and eat, but most folk wandered about, with their paper plates laden with food, watching the dancing and soaking up the atmosphere. The young hospitality people, employed to wait on the guests, were doing a sterling job, as they wandered in and out of the groups of people, bringing them drinks and taking away empty glasses.

An hour after her two friends had arrived, the three sat at a table in the tent with their food and wine and caught up with recent events.

'This smoked salmon is delicious,' Connie said, her red hair dancing in curls about her face. 'So, what's happening with you and Stephen . . . Millburn, is it? I thought that you and he really hit it off and would probably be married or something the next time we came up to Scotland.'

Ailsa was silent for a moment, then she gave them a short, edited version of what had happened between herself and Stephen. She did not tell them what she knew about him, firstly, it would have made no difference to them, and secondly, she could not be certain that Connie especially would not go and clobber him if she did.

'Pulling the wool over your eyes, you'd better watch him!' Jan said, biting into a chunk of bread. 'Men! Unbelievable, they just think the world was made for them. I hate the lot of them. Oh, by the way, Malcolm MacKenzie looks a bit of alright, doesn't he? And, not too distraught since his wife's death, eh?'

'What an outrageous double standard!'

'Well, Ailsa, you can't blame me, with all this talent I see before me!

'Let's have cocktails!' Ailsa suggested, to change the subject. She motioned over one of the waitresses who was hovering nearby. The young woman came over and spoke to them in a pointed Italian accent.

'Yes, Ma'am, what can I get you?' she asked, looking directly into the eyes of Ailsa. Ailsa started in surprise. For what seemed like about five minutes but was nearer to one, she didn't say anything. Jan and Connie looked at her in amazement.

'Ailsa, what's wrong?' Jan asked in a low voice, as she noticed the colour drain from her friend's face, while the girl stood stony-faced, watching. 'Ailsa?'

'Yes, oh, sorry, please bring us three Marguerita cocktails.' Ailsa snapped out of her reverie, then sharply turned her back on the girl.

Olivia.

'What was that about? You look as if you've seen a ghost! Do you know her?' Connie asked.

'No, not really, funnily enough I came upon her crying at Trannoch during the barbeque, that's all.'

'Oh, right, so her crying at the barbeque affected you so much that you went into a spasm when she approached? Come on Ailsa, get real, we're your friends, what the hell happened there?'

Before Ailsa could answer, Malcolm approached with an outstretched hand towards her. 'May I have this dance, Lady Hamilton-Dunbar?' he said, with all the charm he could muster through an alcohol-induced slur of whisky-breathed speech. Ailsa was looking for an escape at this point, and with the eyes of her two friends upon her, she decided to grin and bear it. When Olivia approached with three cocktails, Ailsa had gone.

Ailsa's two friends followed her, about ten minutes later, carrying fresh drinks into the ballroom, and were accosted in a friendly manner by two local guys: Jan with a fisherman, who was actually extremely wealthy and eligible, and Connie with another lawyer who had come to the Ball at the invitation of the Colonel. Gregory was a perfect gentleman, and Jan was bowled over by his simple manners, and modesty. Calum was more serious, but a perfect match for Connie's outgoing bubbly personality.

'Where do you live, Gregory?' Jan asked, after he had swept her back to a side table following the 'Gay Gordons', and poured out champagne into her glass, 'Is it near to here?'

'Yes, I live the other side of Arnasaid.' His lilting accent made Jan's knees go weak. 'Mum died a few years ago, and, as I was the only son, I inherited Erigh Mhor, our house,' he answered modestly, declining to mention that 'our house' was worth around £2m. 'What do you do, Jan?'

'Oh, I own a small traditional tea shop in London. I do all my own baking, and it is busy and . . . and …'

'And would you feel you always wanted to stay in London?' he asked simply.

'No, I suppose I would be happy to move, if I found love.'

Connie was having her own conversation with Calum, across the table from Jan and Gregory.

'Why don't you get the bloody weather up here?' she said.

'Oh, we do "get the weather" up here. But, if you mean nice weather, like you get down south, then I would agree we don't!' He moved his chair nearer to hers, looking directly into her eyes. 'I am working on it.'

'Working on what?'

'On more interesting things than the weather.'

When Ailsa managed to pull herself free of Malcolm, she went in search of Olivia, but couldn't find her anywhere. She had been absolutely knocked off kilter when the young woman had appeared, but it was not the fact that she was there, working as part of the catering staff, it was the sheer defiance in her look which had made her heart grow cold. It was almost a statement that she wanted Ailsa to do something about her predicament which had moved her so much. Had she failed this girl? She had shared the secret with no one, was that her fault? She had walked away from a serious accusation and although it had eaten into her, she had not done anything with the knowledge or accusation, that Stephen Millburn had molested Olivia.

But Olivia was nowhere to be seen.

Ailsa put on a huge wrap and walked outside and into the garden facing the sea. She loved this view, she would never tire of it, and at the moment there were couples and small groups dotted about, having come out for some air. She wandered, clutching her glass, to one of the picnic tables she had installed, much to Cocky's distain.

'Hello gorgeous, feeling a bit . . . hot?' The voice came from behind, the warm, sour breath on her neck. Ailsa stiffened, then turned to see who she already knew was behind her.

'Hi Malcolm.' She tried to sound natural. 'Have you finished dancing?'

'Dancing?' he said acidly. 'I am not interested in dancing, darling, you know what I want.'

'Malcolm, please don't do this . . .'

'I want you Ailsa. I so want you that it is hurting me . . .' his voice trailed away.

'You need to sober up.' She tried to sound matter of fact. 'Please, let's go in and . . .'

'I said I wanted you. You need to either say yes or no, there is no in-between.'

'Malcolm . . .'

'Say it!!' he shouted, so that some people near turned and looked in their direction.

'I think you have been under incredible stress. Belinda has gone and . . .'

'Belinda?' he sneered. '*Belinda?* She meant nothing to me, *nothing!* Don't even say her name, I despised her.'

'Malcolm, you don't know what you are saying, please don't say anything more. I won't be part of this. I am sorry, I need to go back.' She looked at him drunkenly hanging over her, and her heart went out to this attractive man who had completely lost it. She stood up, and he grabbed her. He put his hands round her back and pulled her into his body. She could not free herself. He put his lips to hers and kissed her so roughly that she felt her lips swell. He grabbed her hair, and forced her head next to his, driving his tongue inside her mouth. For several moments she was inert, her arms were effectively pinned to him and she was gasping for breath. She tried to think, though the bile was rising uncontrollably in her throat. She moved slightly more squarely onto his body so that he actually thought she was responding to him, and he relaxed his grip just a little, but enough for her to suddenly bring her right knee up sharply between his legs right into his crotch and knock him down like a nine pin.

She was shaking, as she left him there on the front lawn. Making her way back into the house and to her private bathroom, she thought she was going to throw up, but managed to hold it together enough to repair her make up, and, after around 15 minutes, return to the party. But, someone had seen her stumbling back over the grass, and, as Malcolm lifted himself up, he felt a strong arm turn him swiftly around and give him such a punch that he was propelled backwards into a flower bed, his lip streaming with blood and his senses gone. He was out cold.

The punch felt as if it had broken his finger, and he winced as he shook his hand in pain, trying to flex his fingers. He then went to look for help and got Jim Hutton and another man to lift Malcolm into the back of a jeep and drive him back home to Trannoch.

Jan and Connie were still with Gregory and Calum, and Ailsa was delighted about that.

'I need a drink!' she said, as she approached them again, looking better for her 'touch up' makeover, although she still had a slightly swollen lip.

'Ailsa, it is a fantastic night!' Jan said. 'You Scots know how to party!'

'Course we do! You must both come back for Hogmanay!' Gregory agreed.

'Yes, that's the biggest and best party of the year, with exception to your great party Ailsa,' Calum stuttered clumsily.

'It's almost time for the barbeque and fireworks,' Ailsa smiled shakily, looking round for Miss Cochrane who had organised this last bit of the festivities. The housekeeper walked towards her, but with a stricken look on her face. She uncharacteristically took Ailsa's hands, moved her away from her table, and started to steer her into a quieter corner but was stopped in her tracks by a tall beautiful, blonde and elegantly dressed woman entering the room. As Ailsa and her friends discussed later, it was like something out of a movie. The figure moved in, the swarm of people parted like the dead sea, the band stopped playing, and the silence was so great that you could hear each footstep as the woman walked up through the hall to the dais and the band. There was something about her which was spellbinding. She seemed to exude a certain graceful but determined confidence and, with her head held high and her beautiful features poised, she was like a wave, sweeping fluidly and seamlessly through the crowd. The microphone was snatched from the band member, who seemed to be under the same spell as the rest of the room, although they had no idea why, and they all waited with bated breath while the woman smiled and talked into the microphone.

'Good evening, everyone. I just thought I would introduce myself. As some of you already know, my name is Georgina Dillon, otherwise known as Hunter. I have just arrived from Australia, and I would like to extend an arm of friendship to my dear daughter, Lady Ailsa Hamilton-Dunbar. Hello, Ailsa, what a great Ball you are hosting. I am so looking forward to meeting everyone again. Now, if this wonderful band would care to begin again, I am sure you all would like to carry on dancing!' Some people clapped lamely, not really grasping the situation, but not really caring either.

Hunter stepped down from the stage and with eyes locked onto Ailsa's, she moved like a lynx towards her.

'Ailsa, I've come home.'

Chapter Fourteen

The relentless surge of waves and blackened skies brought rain lashing horizontally, stabbing the cliff-sides and the shore with merciless ferocity until the land was sodden and the houses in Arnasaid glistened black with moisture. The water seemed to rise to a new height in the bay. The trees lost their leaves in the stormy weather, which shut out all hope of a longer dry period, and winter drove through the mountains and forests, seeking out and destroying all remnants of autumn in the North West. Storm Winds seemed to rise to meet its fate, the grey turrets arching skyward, meeting the perennial onslaught. 'This is what I was made for,' it seemed to say to the elements, 'bring it on, for you won't knock me down.'

Hunter had come home. She had used those very words herself when she made the dramatic speech which led to the party being disbanded and the fireworks and barbeque boxed up for another day. She was not dead, she was very much alive, and Ailsa and the Colonel wanted an explanation. They ushered her to the library, drinks supplied by a stunned Miss Cochrane, who closed the library door on her departure, shutting out all explanations to herself and the guests, for the time being anyway.

'What the hell do you think you are playing at telling us all you were dead and then just reappearing in a puff of smoke? I bloody well nearly took a heart attack.' This from the Colonel, of course, as he sank into a chair by the newly lighted fire and gulped down a large whisky in one.

'Darling, you are far more likely to have a heart attack by knocking back the hard stuff than by seeing me.' Hunter's voice had a hard edge to it, strong and confident with an overlay of sarcasm.

'But why say you were dead? Why come here now? What's it all about?'

'So many questions!' she said, in a fake weary voice. She reached into her bag for a packet of cigarettes and made to light up.

'I'd rather you didn't,' Ailsa said quietly.

'Oh! There you are! I was beginning to think you had gone, but here you are and speaking out too!' Her sarcasm made Ailsa fizz, but the older woman put her cigarettes back in her bag, nonetheless, and, with a perfectly manicured hand, pushed back her bobbed blonde hair from her face which sported far fewer wrinkles than most women her age.

'Why say you were dead?' the Colonel persisted.

Hunter sat on the edge of a table and faced them. 'To cut off all ties. I had more than enough money of my own when I got to Australia. I was living with a man whom I adored,' she seemed to emphasise the word 'adored' just to annoy the Colonel, 'and he had pots of money too. I no longer needed any ties with this place, so Ricky and I made a go of the ranching business and made a fortune, and I walked away from my past. We had a son together, who disappeared when he was twenty, and I haven't seen or heard from him since.'

'You seem to make a habit of letting go of your children.' Ailsa wasn't going to let her away with this one.

Before Hunter could come up with a suitably crushing response, the Colonel chipped in.

'So, if you were having such a great life there, why come back here?' he asked.

'Because Ricky died six months ago and left me with huge debts, hundreds of thousands of dollars' worth of gambling debts and bad investments I knew nothing about. And, I wanted to track down my daughter.' She gave what she considered to be a winning smile, her expressions and reactions changing quicker than the conversation.

'Yeah, right,' Ailsa laughed scornfully. 'You came back because you're penniless and you want a piece of this!' waving her hand around her.

Hunter looked unmoved. 'Well, I am certainly not penniless, and I did also want to track you down, Ailsa,' she said. 'I can't say I regretted giving you up for adoption, it was the right thing to do at the time, but one gets so tired of the sun and I think I was happier than I have ever been when I was here living in Scotland.'

Ailsa was stunned into silence at her audacity. This woman was her mother, for God's sake, who hadn't set eyes on her since she had given her up for adoption and all she was talking about was coming back to Scotland because she was having too much sun! Ailsa felt less connection with her than with Sir Angus when she had met him. Granted, she was very similar in looks to Hunter, it was quite plain to see they were related, but her own personality, thankfully, lent more to her adoptive parents' upbringing than to genetics.

'I really wanted to be amongst friends, and the 'Aussies', as they call themselves, are so vulgar.'

'Well, what a bloody convenient time to leave, when your husband leaves you with debts and your son leaves too!' the Colonel almost shouted back, his face going dangerously red. 'This is quite unbelievable. That you would return here after all this time and expect everyone to welcome you back with open arms. Things have changed, Hunter. We've all changed.'

There was a remote flicker of emotion in Hunter's iceberg eyes which again quickly melted away into her depths as she gathered herself together.

'And as for staying here permanently at Storm Winds, you will over my dead body.' Ailsa's voice was beginning to rise at Hunter's apparently unflappable temerity. 'If you think you are going to come here and play 'Lady of the Manor', all of a sudden, you're in for a rude awakening.'

'Like you, you mean?' she said quietly, with a tight little smile, and Ailsa flushed.

'This was all a complete shock to me. I had no idea of your, or Sir Angus' existence until a few months ago. I made a choice to make this my life, and I have worked hard on the estate to put my stamp on it, but I certainly have no airs and graces about who I am and what I have inherited.'

'How very commendable of you, Ailsa. Now, of course I need to stay here, at least for a while. I have travelled all the way from Australia to see you, you can't just ask me to go?' She made this rhetorical question sound pleading.

'You can stay here until you find somewhere else, then you are going.' Ailsa got up and flung herself out of the room before the tears started to fall.

The next morning, Ailsa stood on her balcony looking across at the rapidly changing sky, feeling the cold wind on her face, and watching the mist lift from Skye's Cullin range of mountains which jagged up into the whiteness. The trees were bare of leaves now, but the evergreen mass still managed to colour the ever-changing landscape. The scenery was part of her now, what she had become since she moved here. She thought of everything which had happened in her short time at Storm Winds. She had moved here thinking it wouldn't be dull but wouldn't be exciting either. Most of what she had experienced here had been more challenging and life-changing than she would ever have experienced in London.

Eileen arrived to interrupt her reverie. 'Er . . . Mrs Dillon is in the breakfast room already.'

Ailsa was momentarily taken aback. 'Who?'

'Mrs Georgina Dillon,' Eileen said, looking embarrassed.

'Oh Hunter! Yes, I was trying to forget her! And what's she doing? Upsetting everyone, asking for quails' eggs instead of chickens'? Or Ceylonese tea instead of Scottish?' She couldn't keep the sarcasm from her voice.

'Not exactly, but she has been asking for you, so . . .'

'Yeah, well, I'll go down when I'm ready, as usual.' There was stiffness in Ailsa's tone.

Hunter was reading the papers at the top end of the table where Ailsa usually sat. She balked when she saw the older woman in her place, when she went into the room, but decided against saying anything. Hunter barely lifted her head when her daughter came in and looked very much in control of herself and the situation. She looked comfortable and easy in her position at the head of the breakfast table. Before Ailsa sat down, Jan and Connie came in, followed very quickly by Calum. Eileen came in to take the orders, as everything was cooked fresh.

'Is the bacon fatty?' Hunter asked Eileen, before she could ask anyone else for their orders.

'Sorry, what?' Eileen was confused.

Hunter studied her for a few minutes. 'What is it that you don't understand about that question?' she asked, as Eileen went red.

'Well . . . I . . . sorry, I . . . ' Eileen stammered, and Ailsa intervened.

'Is it streaky or our usual bacon, Eileen?' she tried to help the girl out.

'I . . . er . . . I think it is the usual, Ailsa, not streaky.'

'And you call your Mistress by her first name?' Hunter looked up and verbally pounced on Eileen, who looked incapable of answering.

'We don't stand on ceremony here,' Ailsa said firmly. 'Eileen, could you please just bring a plate of bacon and we can help ourselves.'

'Of course, Ailsa,' Eileen said, looking straight at Hunter. 'Shall I bring scrambled and poached eggs, cos that is what you all seem to want?'

Hunter looked at the girl coldly. 'Yes, I don't know why you need to talk about it rather than just bringing it.'

'I'm sorry, Hunter, it's just . . .' Eileen got no further.

The air was frozen by a stare.

'Call me Ma'am, or Mrs Dillon,' Hunter said shortly.

'Yes, of course, Ma'am, I do apologise,' Eileen said. She looked ready to burst into tears. Hunter looked down at her newspaper again with an air of indifference.

'Well, what a great night, Ailsa,' Connie said, with a sideways glance at Hunter.

'Totally brilliant, and so was the talent!' Jan said laughingly, with a sly look at Calum.

'Yes, I do admit it was a fabulous night,' Calum said with a laugh. 'I met the beautiful Connie and we hit it off – I think, did we, Connie? Please say we did!' he said smilingly, at Connie.

'Ailsa, I fear you have forgotten your manners!' Hunter said coldly, as she slowly lifted her head again and picked up her tea cup. 'Who are these?' She flipped her hand across at the others.

Ailsa and Jan both looked stormily at the older woman, and Connie burst into a snigger of laughter at the sheer theatrics displayed.

'These, Hunter, are my friends from London, Jan and Connie,' Ailsa said icily.

'And I'm Calum Andrews. I am a friend of the Colonel's, he invited me last night and I met them all for the first time.' He looked at Connie with a grin and a wink.

'Indeed?' Hunter returned acidly. 'Well, things happen very quickly around here! In my day, you had to woo a lady for some time before sleeping with her.'

'Shut up, Hunter, that was uncalled for,' Ailsa spat back, when the silence became ominous following this remark.

'We had separate rooms.' Calum looked mortified as he started to explain, but Hunter cut him off.

'Really, Ailsa, your language leaves a lot to be desired, and directed at your own mother too! Tut tut.' She lowered her head again to her paper.

'You are not, and will never be, my mother.' Ailsa was gritting her teeth in her anger. 'Why don't you just bloody well go back to Australia and take your venomous tongue with you?'

Eileen came in at that point and put the dishes on the sideboard, and Hunter looked up and began to speak as if nothing had happened. 'Oh, at last! I was beginning to think I was going to get this for lunch not breakfast!' Eileen went red again and left the room as quickly as she could.

Ailsa felt thoroughly fed up. She had waved goodbye to Jan and Connie as they got in the car to drive the four hours to Glasgow for the flight to Heathrow. Calum had left earlier to go back to Fort William. She felt more alone with Hunter staying with her than she had ever done on her own, and felt she was being usurped in her own house. Hunter had been given a room in the East Wing, as far away from Ailsa as possible, but had argued that she preferred the West Wing, as this was always where the family had slept, meaning of course, Sir Angus. Miss Cochrane's hackles were up, as she and Eileen had to re-do one of the vacant bedrooms in the West Wing, one with a balcony like Ailsa's so that she could look out on her 'favourite view'. Cocky was incensed at this, as Hunter had never stayed in Storm Winds as family. Her only stays were illicit ones when Sir Angus' wife Elizabeth had not been around to see her. Although they had been discreet, it was almost impossible for a housekeeper so relied upon as Miss Cochrane not to see his mistress, Hunter, creeping about, but she would have gone to her grave rather than impart this piece of information. As to the fact that she had mentioned her 'favourite view', it was commonly known that Hunter hated scenery, and the only outdoor pursuit she enjoyed was hunting and shooting as was testament to her name. Miss Cochrane had always thought that her hunting of men, not animals, lent itself more to her nickname, but as ever she dutifully kept this enjoyable notion to herself.

Ailsa was in the library, trying to do some writing, and, if truth be told, to keep away from Hunter, when the door opened and the lady herself appeared.

'What are you doing in here?' Hunter asked, in an amused voice. 'Playing games on your laptop?'

'No, I'm working.'

'Working?' It was almost like the concept was vaguely familiar to Hunter, but she couldn't quite put her finger on what it meant.

'Yes, working. I come in here to work as I prefer this room to the study.'

'I see,' Hunter made it plain by her expression that she didn't see at all, 'and what is the work that you are doing?'

'Sorry, I don't discuss that with anyone.'

'Gosh, top secret?!' Hunter gave a shrill laugh which lent nothing to humour. 'Never mind, I'm not really interested anyway, just asking out of politeness. Now where is that book I wanted to borrow?' This last was almost to herself. She perused a few shelves then picked out one, blew the dust from it, and sat down beside Ailsa at the table. Ailsa fumed, and looked at her with dislike.

'I like to work alone, I can't concentrate otherwise,' Ailsa said, through gritted teeth. Hunter looked up from the first page.

'Don't be silly, darling.' Her derisory tone infuriated Ailsa. 'I won't disturb you,' and she continued to read unperturbed.

'I'm sorry, but this is my house and my library, this is where I work, and I prefer to be alone. There are plenty of other rooms at your disposal, you don't need to come in here. Now please go.' Ailsa did not know how she managed to hold it together.

Hunter let out a loud sigh, then said in a patronising voice, 'I think you are being such a baby about me coming here, Ailsa.' Then in a much harder voice said, 'But, believe me, you won't get rid of me that easily,' and shutting her book with a bang, she threw it over the other side of the table onto the floor and flounced out.

'Bloody cow,' Ailsa said aloud.

Ten minutes later, Miss Cochrane tentatively opened the door and came in. 'Sorry to disturb you, Ailsa, but Mrs Dillon has requested to see the lunch and dinner menus for today so that she can be sure she will want what is on offer.'

Ailsa threw back her hands in resignation. She wasn't going to get any writing done today. 'What does she mean? Didn't you tell her I left the cooking up to Jean, and that she only works part-time anyway?'

'Of course I did, but she said . . . she said that she wanted a proper set of menus drafted out and brought to her today so that she could approve them.'

'How dare she? Cocky, Jean will not be able to cope with that. She's been here for donkey's years and the menus have always been left to her. Plus, her food is great!'

'Unfortunately, she got to Jean before I did, and I was only alerted to the kitchen by the shouting, and Jean telling her if she's not happy with the food she can go into Arnasaid and buy a bloody poke of chips!'

Ailsa hesitated, then they both burst into laughter. 'Good old Jean!' she said, wiping the tears from her eyes, 'But what happened next?'

'Jean threw down her pinny and left,' Miss Cochrane said sadly. 'I am not sure she will be back.'

Ailsa took the jeep and drove to Trannoch. The weather was terrible, storm clouds making the late afternoon darker than usual, and the rain driving into her windscreen as fast as the wipers could hope to clear. She had not phoned ahead to see if the Colonel was in, she just hoped that he was, but needed to get away from the house more than she needed to speak with him anyway.

Trannoch loomed up from the hills. Although it stood miles inland from Storm Winds, the two estates bordered each other which meant they were actually neighbours. The avenue of evergreen trees led her up to the front door, which she drove past and went around the back to use one of the side entrances, as was her wont and privilege as a neighbour and friend. She went straight in and hung up her coat. Denbeath heard her, and suddenly appeared in the hall, 'Honestly, that man seems to be hiding around every corner!' she thought, as she asked for the Colonel.

'No, Madam, he is not in, but Mr Maxwell MacKenzie is here and may help?'

Before she found time to say that Max was the last person she wanted to help her, Max himself came striding up the hallway in time to hear this last remark. 'Come in, Ailsa, what a day it is, do you want some tea, or a glass of wine perhaps to stave off the cold?' and, without waiting for her reply, he opened the door to a small sitting room where he had evidently been earlier, as the fire was on, and she could do nothing else but follow.

'What's up?' he asked, in that abrupt way of his, as Denbeath returned with two glasses of red wine.

'Well, I'm not sure that you can help . .' Ailsa said, as she took a sip and felt the heat from the fire return feeling to her fingers.

'Try me.' He got up and poked the fire, sending a crackling blaze up the chimney.

'Well, it's just Hunter.' He nodded as if he knew what she was going to say before she said it.

'Proving difficult to live with?' he said, lifting his glass to his lips with his left hand. Ailsa noticed his right hand had some sort of splint on it, and a bandage.

'What happened to your hand?'

'Oh, just a broken bone in my middle finger, nothing much,' he said with a frown. Ailsa got the feeling he was being guarded but said no more on the subject.

'I wondered about the Dower House at Storm Winds. It hasn't been used for years, I know, but Cocky says it's in great nick, and I would like to . . .'

'Shove her in there? Yes, why not?' he said, with a grin. I could get Stephen to go over it and see what's needed by way of decoration, and such like, if you want?'

This was the last thing she wanted. 'No, really, it's okay, Josh can do that, I just wondered what the Colonel's advice would be, that's all.'

'I imagine he would say first, "Ship her back to Australia" and then he would most likely think the Dower House would be a good substitute idea. How do you think she will take it?'

'Battles royal probably, but she has no choice. She may be my birth mother, but I owe her nothing, and she is turning my world upside down with her maliciousness.'

'She was always the same. I remember her as a boy, when she used to visit the Colonel, she was a very difficult person even then, throwing her weight about with the staff and upsetting all and sundry.'

'She used to visit the Colonel? Was she friends with him then?' she asked, innocently enough at first, then, as he started to answer, the penny dropped, and she sat back in her chair, her wine glass rocking dangerously near to spilling over.

'Let's just say she frequented Trannoch almost as consistently as she did Storm Winds.' Max uncrossed his legs and leaned forward, cradling his wine glass with an expression which showed that he knew he had already said too much. 'They were, ehm . . . very good friends, Ailsa.'

'You mean they were lovers?' Ailsa got up and started to pace. 'Hunter was seeing two men at the same time?'

'That was the talk at the time, but the Colonel had no idea any of us knew.'

'Great.' Then a thought cannon-balled through her mind, a thought she didn't want to give room or credence to, but one which she could not escape.

'Are you saying the Colonel might be my birth father instead of Sir Angus?' she spluttered.

'I am saying no such thing Ailsa. Don't start down that track.'

'But that is exactly what you're thinking.' She looked stricken, her stress levels rising to new peaks. 'Oh my God, I don't believe this.' She turned on Max, as she needed an outlet for her feelings. 'You didn't think I would have thought that when you told me? You didn't think to in some way soften the blow before you blurted this out?'

'Ailsa, I had no idea you would take two and two and make ten so quickly. I am not saying that I or anyone else thinks you may be the Colonel's daughter, my God, even their affair was only talk . . .'

'Yes, but talk which could be substantiated.' Her nose was in the air, then, as he raised his right palm in a gesture intended to silence her, she took it up a notch or two. 'And don't dare tell me to calm down! Do you know what this might mean? Have you any idea how this might impact on my life if I had to find out I wasn't Sir Angus' daughter after all? I've given everything up for this, living at Storm Winds and trying to make a go at running an estate . . .'

'Ailsa, sit down and have some wine. I apologise if I didn't think it through before I mentioned it.'

'No, you didn't. You just barge on in there with your non-existent bedside manner, telling me something like this which could AGAIN change my life around, then tell me to calm down . . .'

'Well I didn't exactly tell you . . .'

'Two feet at once, straight in there, missing the simple fact that I actually have a brain and can come up with my own answers without you or any of the rest of your family . . .'

'Now wait a minute . . .'

'Being part of this family is the LAST thing I would want. You're just like the Colonel. Arrogant, opinionated, controlling . . .'

'Sorry was that you, you just described?'

'. . . pig headed, forceful, demanding . . .'

'Ailsa, SIT DOWN, and stop this, you're working yourself up to fever-pitch. We need to talk about this rationally.'

'Don't tell me what to do – *Doctor* MacKenzie. I'm going, and I'm going to phone one of my *friends* to talk about it. Thanks very much for nothing.'

'Well, just don't jump to any conclusions . . .'

'Oh, shut up,' she said, rudely, and almost threw her wine down on the mantelpiece and stalked out. Max followed her.

'That's it, just stomp away, you seem to be really good at . . .' but the clattering side door drowned out any further remonstrations.

Denbeath morphed out of the wood panelling. 'Anything I can get you, Sir?'

'A whisky.'

Denbeath nodded and began to turn, the only expression on his face, a slightly raised eyebrow.

Chapter Fifteen

Ailsa felt she had to get away. After her discussion with Max a few nights ago, things had gone downhill rapidly at Storm Winds with Hunter, who was trying to 'rule the roost', as Cocky had said one day, and Ailsa felt that she was losing a grip on the household and its occupants. After much soothing and encouragement, Jean Morton the kitchen doyenne had agreed to return to work although she stipulated that 'that Mrs Dillon person' would not darken her kitchen again with her demands.

Ailsa had been overwhelmed by Max MacKenzie's statement. It opened a whole new chapter for her, concerning the mystery of her birth, and brought into question, grotesque though it was, that although it had been difficult to accept she was the daughter of Sir Angus, how much harder would it be to accept she was a MacKenzie? To imagine herself half-sister to the MacKenzie brothers. What would happen to Storm Winds with no heir? All this formed a perfectly horrible melee of unanswered questions, fears and doubts in her mind. Just as she was getting used to the idea of being Lady Ailsa Hamilton-Dunbar, she may have to change her whole way of thinking, and yes, her whole life, to become Ailsa MacKenzie. She couldn't cope with all of this thrust upon her. She felt as though her world was crumbling and she was losing her identity completely. She tried to call Connie but couldn't get her, so decided on another course of action.

Packing a bag and her two dogs into the jeep Ailsa told Miss Cochrane she was going to Skye for a two-night break, and to tell everyone she was going on business, but not to expand on this. She didn't want to let Hunter take control when she was gone, so informed Hunter herself, that it was just for a few nights and then she would be back. The discussion she had with her, as usual, was fraught with emotion, on her part, and patronising sarcasm, on Hunter's.

'I got Josh, our estate worker, to have a look at the Dower House, and it seems we can have it fixed up for you in the next week or two to use for a while,' Ailsa had said, making sure she was as vague as possible about the arrangements.

'Dower House? That little thing!' Hunter had turned away from her with a dismissive flick of her perfectly-cut and shiny bobbed hair. 'No, I shan't go there. It is very nice of you to offer me my own little place, darling, but I prefer it here. I am sure you will agree that you only want your mother to be happy?'

Ailsa ignored this last, and said, 'It has three bedrooms and two public rooms. You are on your own, what more do you want?' She was rapidly losing patience with Hunter. 'I have given you one of our employees to help you out. Olivia is new to us but knows the job well and will look after you.'

After the Ghillies' Ball, Ailsa had made enquiries at the hospitality agency and sought out Olivia, discovering that the young woman's job was temporary and poorly paid. Ailsa had felt desperately sad about how Stephen had mistreated the Italian and felt the right thing to do was to offer her a job at Storm Winds. She had half expected Olivia to refuse. Olivia had accepted without demur.

'That's all very well, darling, but I didn't come all the way from Australia to meet my daughter and be put out to grass in the Dower House. I really love Storm Winds and would prefer to stay here, where you are. I really think it is my due. I want you to think, Ailsa, about how you might alienate me if you ask me to stay anywhere but here.'

Ailsa looked at her with a mixture of incredulity and amusement at this false speech. 'Hunter, I have told you that I would put you up until you found something else, so that means just that – you keep looking, and, meantime, I'll put you up. You are a stranger to me, I certainly don't feel at this stage that I could ever look upon you as my mother. You have been rude and disrespectful to me and my friends and staff, and I see that the only way we can in any way be civil to each other is if we are apart. I think I am being really quite generous, doing up the Dower House for you, and it's either that or the local B&B. Take it or leave it.' Ailsa was seriously roused and strutted out of the room, her head held high.

She drove to Arnasaid Bheag, the port just to the north of Arnasaid, and got the ferry to Skye. She had booked into a small hotel there, and she drove the jeep off the boat, arriving at the hotel around an hour after landing. It was dark as she pulled into the car park, and off loaded her one bag and two dogs.

She was shown to a nice little room, touched up her make up and took the dogs down to the oak beamed lounge for a drink – she was not interested in food at this juncture, and just wanted to sit in the corner where no one knew her, with a glass of wine. The music was subtle, the real fire glowed in the grate, sending inviting shadows across the room, and the wine was amazing. She had her book with her, but, although it was opened in front of her, she didn't read a thing. Rosie and Bluebell cuddled into her on either side, and she enjoyed the anonymity and the excellent wine. After the second glass she began to relax. A random fiddler came in with a group and began to play. People began to sing softly to the music, and Ailsa began to feel maudlin. A few tears started to fall, and she brushed them fiercely away, telling herself that she would not get upset about the whole rotten scenario back at Storm Winds. She took a gulp of her wine and stroked Rosie.

'You look like you need another wine.' The voice came from her left and startled her out of her self-absorption. She looked up and saw a smart looking young guy, with dark curly hair and a wide smile, carrying a pint in his hand. 'What kind is it?'

'Kind?'

'Your wine.' He grinned again, and Ailsa felt warmth flood through her.

'Oh, er . . . Cabernet Sauvignon, thanks,' she heard herself say, before she allowed the thought to flit through her mind of how handsome he was.

He grinned and put his half-drunk pint on the table and went up to the bar.

He soon sat the wine down and shuffled in beside her. 'What's your name?' he asked, as he put his pint to his lips.

'Emily,' she said, with a smile, as she came up with the first name which came to her mind.

'Ah, nice to meet you, Emily. I'm Douglas. I work in a garage here.' Then, when he looked at her again, and, obviously wanting to impress her, he added in a slightly sheepish fashion, 'Well, I actually own the garage. It's not much, but it's mine, my own wee business.'

'That's great. I . . . er . . . I am up here on holiday from London.'

'London, eh? I've never been. I don't know if I fancy the rat race though, you know the tubes and all the crowds and stuff.'

'No, there is that,' she agreed.

'But I'd quite like to see the galleries and paintings though.'

Ailsa was surprised at this last. 'You like art?' It was the last thing she thought a mechanic from the Isle of Skye would slip into a conversation.

'Yeah, I actually did an art history course through the Open University, really loved it! Dave, my best pal, asked me what I was doing it for, did I want to change direction or sell my garage or shit like that, an I said, "Naw man, I just want to do it for fun," an he said, "Mate, you an me have different ideas of fun."'

Ailsa laughed. 'I think it sounds great, doing something totally different like that. Who do you like from the art world?'

Douglas had no hesitation in answering, 'Giotto, Durer and Caravaggio are top faves,' and he grinned widely. 'So, are you staying here, or just in for a drink?' he asked, as he looked at her two dogs on either side of her.

'Erm . . . I'm just staying here for two nights, on a bit of a tour, you know!'

He nodded. 'What's their names?'

'This is Rosie, and this little one is Bluebell.'

'Ok, pleased to meet you both. Gonnae move Bluebell over beside Rosie, then I can get a bit nearer to you?'

Ailsa looked at him and laughed. She couldn't help liking him, he seemed so genuinely straightforward and fun, and he didn't treat her with deference like most people she met, so it was a welcome change from the madness back at Storm Winds. He cuddled into her, and they listened to the fiddler, then a singer who sang Scottish songs along to a guy playing what were called the small pipes. These were a small version of the bagpipes, 'Dougie', as he insisted she call him, informed her. The atmosphere was so totally different from the pubs in London that she was drawn into the friendliness and comfort of good wine, good music, and, most of all, good company. In fact, he was great company. For the first time since Stephen Millburn, she felt instantly attracted to a man. She relaxed, trying to forget that Hunter had sabotaged her Ghillies' Ball, and the whole tumult of events and emotions which had gone after that. The wine took its toll, and when Dougie, much later, offered to walk her up to her room, she never batted an eye, but led him up the stair, the two dogs trailing meekly behind. They got to the door, and like two teenagers they stood in the hallway and snogged, the dogs lying at their feet, Bluebell comically sighing then turning her back towards them.

'Can I see you again before you go back?' he asked, as he hungrily sought her lips.

'Back?' she asked confusedly, then it dawned on her.

'Oh! Yes! Back to London! What about tomorrow? I'm only here for two nights.'

'Awesome, I'll meet you back here at the same time, around half seven?'

The next day Ailsa felt decidedly groggy as she went down to breakfast, which was laid out in the same lounge that she had been in the night before. There were two other tables with two people each, but Ailsa didn't recognise any of them from last night. They had either gone to bed early or made other arrangements for their entertainment. She ate eggs and toast with coffee and more toast with black cherry jam, her favourite, as she hugged herself with glee over the unexpected little 'holiday romance' of last evening. He was, she thought, about seven years younger than she was, in his late twenties, but he was gorgeous, and the chance meeting had done more to cheer her up than anything she would have imagined. She was looking forward so much to seeing Dougie again that night, but first, she would explore the town of Broadford where the hotel was situated.

She left the dogs with the hotel owner, who had a dog of his own, and was happy to dog-sit for the day for her. He said he would take them later when he walked his own dog. The path into a lovely forest led straight up from his back garden.

It was a beautiful day. The sun was shining, and it was dry and crisp. Ailsa pulled on a pair of jeans and black boots, a black ribbed polo neck sweater and a tartan shawl pulled around her. It was too late in the year now to go without a coat, and even now, in mid-November, the weather was dryer and sunnier than was usual, so she could get away with just a shawl. The street was buzzing. She saw a shop selling hand-crafted goods and bought lots of things she didn't need. She found a wood carving workshop, with huge carved pieces in the front garden of a side street and bought a wooden carved high-backed chair, which she asked to be delivered to Storm Winds. It would look great in her front hallway.

She found a restaurant for lunch, and ordered soup and lasagne, she figured she couldn't go wrong with the classics especially since it was an Italian restaurant. She also ordered a glass of white wine as she couldn't face red after over-indulging the previous evening. The meal was only average, and she thought guiltily of the garlic in the lasagne which she was sure she shouldn't have had, a) because too much garlic generally upset her and b) She didn't want a garlic breath when she was meeting Dougie that night. 'What am I like?' she thought and giggled to herself. She felt like a teenager on the first date.

She spotted a little boutique and bought some clothes to choose from to wear that evening. The hotel was not dressy, she didn't want to be overdressed, but she saw a few things she could match up with her jeans which wouldn't look too showy, so she bought them as well as a few dresses and a jacket she could wear at other times. She had only brought two tops with her to Skye; had she been asked she would have said that the chances of her meeting someone and hitting it off last night were virtually nil. It had been the last thing on her mind. She didn't get the chance to shop very often these days, and she had a ball. She asked the boutique owner about somewhere to get her nails done, and she found the shop, *Ellie Nails It* nearby, where she was given a walk-in appointment. When she got back to the hotel she went to fetch the dogs.

'Had a good day? You've hit it lucky these few days, lass, the weather has been bright and dry. Your two wee dogs were just champion, and loved their woodland walk.'

'Oh, I'm so glad, thanks very much, Bob, for looking after them. I wondered if I could have a glass of wine to take up to my room?'

'I think oor Dougie might be in again tonight – he plays with the wee band at the weekend, but he usually pops in for a pint in the evening anyway. He's my nephew.' He had a twinkle in his eye as he looked for a reaction.

'Oh! Yes, he said he might be in tonight.' Ailsa felt herself flush as she took the wine.

He was already at the same table when she came in, and he immediately sprang to his feet and kissed her as she approached. Bob had offered to keep Rosie and Bluebell in the back kitchen for a while seeing she had a, 'Hot Date,' he had teased her. He had noted the couple the previous evening.

Dougie had ordered a bottle of red wine, and they sat there talking and laughing for most of the evening. Around half past ten a crowd of musicians came in again, and they sat back to enjoy the music. One guy spotted them and came over. It turned out to be Dave, Dougie's pal that he had talked about.

'Hey mate, how's it goin?' They did that manly thing where they shake and bump their shoulder, that could not be construed as a hug, more of a man-hug, Ailsa thought.

'This is Emily. She's here on a kinda tour, from London no less,' he said, as Dave stopped and gave a little awkward wave across the table to her.

'Got to go, man, I'm getting in the first round,' and he made his way through the crowd.

The music was excellent, spontaneous and vibrant, and Ailsa was enjoying herself more than she had done since she came to Scotland. They got nibbles and munched these and sipped the wine until the bottle was finished then she got another one, and they started to drink their way through that too. People were singing, dancing up at the bar, sitting around the real log fire drinking pints and wine and whisky, and generally having a great time. When Dougie excused himself, she suddenly felt the urge to visit the Ladies. The toilets were situated in a kind of lean-to, which had a long corridor leading from the lounge. On the way back out, she heard Dougie's voice talking urgently, although she couldn't see him at this point.

'What do you mean, her name's not Emily?'

'Listen mate, I hate to burst your bubble, but she is Lady something or other, can't remember what. She lives in Arnasaid . . .'

'Yeah, right. You heard her accent,' Dougie had drunk quite a lot of beer and wine and was starting to slur his words. 'She's who she says she is, an she's fae London, no Arnasaid.'

'Look, Dougie, why would I lie to you, you daft bastard? I don't want you to get hurt again . . .'

'Shut up.' Dougie was getting angry now. 'She's no Lady so-an-so that you're talkin about, she's lovely an . . .'

'We played at her Ghillies' Ball. You couldn't play with us that night cos you were ill, so you didn't see her. Her name is Ailsa man, no Emily.'

Ailsa found him in the car park outside. He was standing against a wall. He looked up as she approached. 'Well hello, Ailsa,' he said, sarcastically.

'Dougie, I'm so sorry. I didn't mean to lie to you . . .'

'But you did. You lied to me and you didn't . . . don't . . . even know me. What would it be like if you did actually know me?'

'You don't know what it's been like for me, lots of things have happened in the last few weeks, and I just wanted to escape.'

'So, you thought you would have a wee plaything while you were recuperating?' He was starting to grow angry again.

'It was not like that . . .'

'No? Well, you know what, Mrs Ailsa Lady of the Lake or whoever the hell you are, I am just a commoner, but one thing I don't do is lie through my teeth. I hope you have a happy life,' and he turned and walked away.

'Dougie! Wait! Please let me try and explain!' but he was already gone, swallowed up in the Scotch mist which had crept up from the sea.

Ailsa collected Rosie and Bluebell and went to her room. She took a bottle of wine with her, showered and changed into her jammies, and phoned Connie. The first thing she wanted advice on was Max's comments.

'He's such an idiot. I can't believe he would just throw something so monumental into a conversation.'

'It might not be monumental – and from what you've said, I really think it sounds as if it was just talk at the time. Max would have been very young then, and stories like that grow arms and legs through the years.'

'I know, but it could be catastrophic. Anyway, I'm here to try and put problems out of my mind for a few days,' and she told Connie about Dougie.

'I was just feeling great about myself and starting to feel wanted again when his pal spilt the beans.'

'Well, you will play the Prince and the Pauper.' Connie knew her friend was upset but found the situation quite amusing. 'Try to think of the positives, you've had a few nights with a gorgeous guy fawning over you. Better than the starchy MacKenzie brothers or Stephen any day . . .'

'Yes, I know. I shouldn't have given him a false name, it turns out he hadn't heard of me anyway, so I could've just said my name was Ailsa.'

'Don't beat yourself up about it. It's not as if you slept with him. Even if you had, that still wouldn't be the end of the world. For God's sake, it's the twenty first century and you are a single gorgeously beautiful woman.'

'No, but that is what I think could have happened tonight.' Ailsa wiped back the tears. 'God, even the hotel owner, Bob, offered to babysit the dogs!'

'I think he was embarrassed that his friend knew who you were and told him, that's all that happened here. Just think positively, and be glad that he was there to make you feel good when you were feeling bad. Come on, Ailsa, it's no real biggie.'

Ailsa felt surprisingly good the next morning. Connie was a great friend to her, always the one to set out things clearly for her and the others when they refused to see the proverbial wood for the trees. She wished that things had happened differently between her and Dougie, but maybe it just wasn't meant to be. Life was just so complicated at home as it was. It was then that she realised as she had been thinking that this was the first time she had referred to Storm Winds as home. And home it was. Whatever happened in terms of her inheritance or who her real father turned out to be, between Sir Angus and the Colonel, she would fight to keep on the place she had grown to love over the past nine months. She would let no one take that away from her.

It was time to go home.

She packed up the car with her many purchases, the dogs on the passenger seat beside her, and was pulling out of the hotel car park when Dougie appeared at her door. She flicked the switch and opened the window.

'Sorry about last night . . .' He seemed embarrassed to admit it.

'Please don't be sorry, it's entirely my fault. I was selfish, I came here for a break, and wanted to be anonymous, and . . .'

'You don't need to explain, I realise what happened, and I didn't let you talk about it, so that's what I'm sorry about.'

'You know, I had a great time, and I'm glad I met you Dougie, you are a gem of a guy.' He leaned in her open window and gave her a kiss, then she pulled back with a smile and let in the clutch.

Storm Winds was silent in the dry autumn afternoon. The deep red and orange reflections of the early twilight seemed to make the house change colour in line with the landscape as Ailsa pulled up to the front door. The dogs ran through the house to the back to find either Jean or Miss Cochrane, and she noticed that there were voices coming from the blue sitting room. She walked in.

Hunter got up from the sofa with a glass of red wine in her hand, and the young man beside her rose too, with a bewildered and mortified look on his face. Joshua Bryant her estate worker also had a glass in his hand, but he looked less comfortable than Hunter.

'What is this?' Ailsa could think of nothing else to say to them as they stood silently watching her reaction.

'Darling Ailsa, you've come home,' Hunter said, in her most theatrical voice. 'We were just having a drink,' and she ceremoniously waved Ailsa to a chair, as if it were her own house. Ailsa stood where she was.

'I said, what's this? Why are you here Joshua?' For one horrendous moment she thought that something was going on between them. Hunter took a sip of wine, smiled and sat back down again.

'Ailsa, I was going to tell you this later on, when I had settled down here at Storm Winds, but now that you have forced my hand by talking quite ridiculously about me moving in to the Dower House, I felt I had to tell you . . .'

'Hunter, spit it out for God's sake, what are you trying to say?'

Hunter paused with effect before she sighed, as if this situation was all too much for her, then, in measured tones she said, 'Very well, I have no choice. I want to introduce you to Joshua.'

'I bloody know Joshua, I hired him.'

'Yes, darling, but I *sent* him. I sent him from Australia. Now, meet Joshua, my son, and your brother.'

Chapter Sixteen

Ailsa stood stock still in amazement at this latest revelation. 'What are you saying? I don't understand,' she said, finally.

Hunter gave that loud shrill laugh which had become her sarcastic trademark since coming back to Scotland. 'Sir Angus was Joshua's father too darling, what is so hard to understand?' Joshua shifted in his seat, looking anything but comfortable. In fact, he looked decidedly ill at ease. He took a gulp of his drink, as Ailsa sank into a chair in distress.

'I thought the Colonel said you were here on a work visa from New Zealand?' she questioned him, seeming to see him for the first time.

'Darling, that was the party line,' Hunter smiled, conspiratorially. 'I sent Josh here ahead of me. His name is not Bryant but Dillon. I kept my own name when I married Ricky Hammond in Australia, and of course Joshua was given that name too, as he wasn't Ricky's child but Sir Angus.'

'But none of this makes sense! You had just given me up for adoption! You left for Australia! How could you be pregnant again by my father?'

'Oh dear, darling. Of everything I expected, I did think you would be much smarter than this, you obviously don't take after your mother in that respect. I didn't leave for Australia straight away, I was here for a further two years! Ask anyone!'

'You conniving self-centred bitch!' Ailsa was almost foaming with anger. 'How dare you come here and stage this charade.'

'I dare, my dear Ailsa, because Joshua is the true Heir of Storm Winds, and I will help him to get back what is his.'

Ailsa reeled at this, as the whole sordid episode of Hunter's return became clear. She had heard that Sir Angus had died and had moved back with her son to claim his inheritance. Even if she was Sir Angus' real daughter and not the Colonel's, he, being male, would be in line for inheritance before Ailsa. She felt as if the walls were caving in on her, she felt dizzy with anger and shock, and she thought she would pass out. As she stood there, swaying, the door opened, and Miss Cochrane came in with fresh drinks on a tray for Hunter and Joshua, as had been ordered. She looked up in surprise when she saw Ailsa standing there and gave a little cry as she caught her swaying and moved forward to steady Ailsa and draw her down into a seat.

'I'm okay,' Ailsa took a sip of the wine which Miss Cochrane offered her. She looked at the woman who was sitting opposite her. Hunter wore a complacent look on her face.

'Get out. Both of you. Cocky, pack their bags and get Jim Hutton. I want them both out of my house today.' Miss Cochrane looked startled, but nonetheless nodded in assent.

'But Ailsa, darling . . .' Hunter patronisingly said, as if she were talking to a wayward child.

'Don't "darling" me, you selfish . . . don't ever lift my name in conversation again. I want you out, and I want you out today. Jim will take you to a B&B. If this stupid tale of yours has any ring of truth to it, then you will have to prove it. Joshua, you no longer work for me.'

'Work for you?' Again, that shrill sarcastic laugh. 'Joshua *owns* Storm Winds. It is his inheritance, and we will prove that he is the heir, not you.' At this last Miss Cochrane herself looked shocked into silence, then anger filled her soul and she spoke.

'Don't be ridiculous, this is Ailsa's house. It is her inheritance, not this stranger's.'

'Who do you think you are talking to?' Hunter flung round on the housekeeper.

'That's enough! I won't hear another word from you, Hunter. Cocky, please go and get Jim.'

'You can throw me out all you wish, darling, but I will be back very soon.' Hunter stood up and, blowing her a kiss, laughed, turned on her heel and left.

Jim Hutton escorted them out of the front door almost as if he was taking prisoners to jail, and shoved Joshua roughly into the back of the Jeep beside Hunter. He drove them to the hotel in Arnasaid, despite Hunter's protestations permeating the air throughout the few miles' journey, that she would not stay at a hotel, and that she had never been treated like this in her entire life. Jim put the volume of the radio up full bung to drown her out, and she eventually shut up and sat back in her seat. As they got out of the jeep, he unceremoniously threw their bags on the pavement in front of the hotel and drew away without a word.

The day passed in a daze after that for Ailsa. Miss Cochrane was really concerned about her. She watched the tears spill as Ailsa sat cowering over the fire in her library. She wouldn't talk about what had happened, refused to eat anything, and stared into space.

'That stupid, selfish woman!' Miss Cochrane swore under her breath, as she thought of all the things she would like to do to wipe the smile from Hunter's face.

Ailsa sat there for three days. Cocky stoked up the fire, brought her meals on trays and took them away again, untouched. She drank only water, she wanted her head to be clear to think things through. She showered on the second day, got into her casual jogging gear and sat back in the chair in the same position again, for another day of the same. In the evenings she wrapped herself in a blanket and sat there, sleeping fitfully until the dawn tapped on the library window with its breakfast of pale sunshine, rain or sleet, sometimes all three. The weather didn't help. It darkened the day, turning it into night. The storm winds came in from the North West, blasting the headland and bringing the first of the really wintry weather. Reports said that Glencoe was impassable for a day while they cleared the snow through the Great Glen, and the snow gates had been shut at Tyndrum. Deer crept down from the high forests, and the land was sodden with the onslaught of heavy rain and sleet.

The Cuillins were obscured for days by mist, which seemed to deaden out all sound, and the relentless surge of the seas broke with foaming anger onto the shores. The ferries to the islands were all cancelled, as the storms persisted.

Ailsa suddenly thought, after Miss Cochrane had given her an account of the weather which she thought would fall on deaf ears, that storm winds, the name of her beloved house, was a metaphor for her life since she had come here. The stormy turbulence of the relationships of the two families, the Hamilton-Dunbars and the MacKenzies had gone on for centuries, at daggers drawn in one shape or another, still prevalent in Ailsa's life today.

On the fourth day, Cocky took the proverbial bull by the horns and phoned Trannoch to speak to the Colonel. Nothing had been heard of Hunter and Joshua, and as far as Miss Cochrane was aware, they were still in the hotel in Arnasaid. She knew, as she had heard Ailsa and Hunter discussing it, that the fight and subsequent eviction of Hunter and Joshua was because Hunter, on behalf of Joshua, was trying to claim the inheritance of Storm Winds. Cocky knew Hunter of old. She knew that she was a cold, calculating woman who would stop at nothing to get what she wanted. Hunter had used that particular device in the past to get Sir Angus, and at the same time, the Colonel. She had confidently assumed that no one knew about her schemes, but, although the housekeeper's middle name was discretion, Cocky knew almost everything there was to know about her plotting and determination to get what she wanted.

Denbeath said that the Colonel was away for a week, visiting a cousin in France, and asked if there was anyone else who could help.

'Which of the sons are home?'

'Noel is out on the land, Malcolm is on a business trip to France, Thomas is in the estate office, and Max is in his study,' he answered promptly.

'Let me speak to Max.'

'Miss Cochrane?' The voice came on the line a few minutes later. 'What's up?'

'Mr MacKenzie, I am sorry to bother you . . .'

'Who's ill?' He was as abrupt as usual.

'Well, not exactly ill, but I don't know if you've heard . . .' Miss Cochrane was comfortably assured that the staff at Trannoch at least would have heard a version of what happened the other night. It was a tight-knit community in Arnasaid. The staff from the two estates fraternised with the people of the village, and word would surely have gone back that Hunter and Joshua were staying in the local hotel instead of at Storm Winds. Max MacKenzie, however, was not of that same social set which enjoyed a gossip. He purposefully detached himself from talk in the village, especially when it concerned his own family, otherwise he might hear a few things he had no wish to know.

'Heard what?'

'Well, there has been a disturbance here at Storm Winds. Mrs Hunter Dillon has now been asked to leave and is staying locally, we think at the hotel.'

'Good job.'

'But, Ailsa is worrying me.' Miss Cochrane drew in her breath, not sure how to continue. 'She had an . . . er . . . altercation with Mrs Dillon, and the estate worker Joshua, and she has taken it quite hard.'

'In what way, "hard"?'

'Well, I think they had a fight, and Hunter may have said things . . . about Ailsa's background. I wasn't there, but I know Hunter and what she can be like . . .'

'So, in what way has this "fight", or whatever it was, affected Ailsa?'

'Well, she has sat by the fire in the library for three days solid, not eating. She's sleeping there, and her mood just seems to be going rapidly downhill.'

'I'll be right over.'

'No, Max . . . I don't know if Ailsa . . . ' but Cocky realised the line had gone dead.

'More hassle!' she said aloud, and tutted in annoyance at her own inability to control the situation. Ten minutes later, Max MacKenzie drew up with a skid at the front door of Storm Winds. He strode down the hallway, meeting Miss Cochrane halfway, and, swinging his bag at his side, followed the housekeeper into the library.

Ailsa looked up from the fire, her face blotchy with crying, and red with sitting so close to the heat. Her blonde hair was in disarray around her face which was fraught with emotion, and her expression was none too friendly, as she saw Max grimly standing by her side.

'Well, you look a right mess,' was his friendly greeting.

'Max. What do you want?' she said, in a flat voice.

He said nothing but sat beside her on the other chair. He took her wrist and felt her pulse, which was slightly erratic. Her skin felt clammy, and her eyes were wide with emotion.

Ailsa pulled her hand away. 'What are you doing? Why are you here? I'm not ill, for God's sake!'

'What are you doing sitting here like this?' As usual, Max seemed to be devoid of anything remotely resembling a bedside manner.

'It's my house! I can sit here as long as I please!'

'You're wallowing.' He sat forward to face her, his elbows on his knees and his hands outstretched in a clasp.

'Don't be ridiculous. Of course, you have no idea what I have been through the last few days.'

'If you go on like this, you will make yourself ill.'

'Well, that's not your concern. I'm fine, I just need time to think, that's all.'

'Have you eaten?'

'I may have, but then again I may not have.' The glint was returning to her eyes.

'Ailsa, I could shake you!' He was not a patient man, and this interchange was not going his way.

'Oh, is that how you normally deal with your patients if they don't do exactly as you say, Doctor Doolittle?' When she saw his thunderous expression at this last, she had the grace to blush. He, however, chose not to reply to this remark.

'What I do know is that, whatever has happened, you are letting it take you over. If it involves Hunter, which I suspect it does, then she is winning as long as you stay here like this, in this inert position, basking in your own introspection.'

'Oh, spare me the psycho-babble, just do me a favour, and leave me alone. Anyway, it's not just to do with Hunter, it started the other night over at Trannoch, with you, if you care to remember.'

He looked at her for a long minute before he replied. 'Ailsa, I am sorry about that night. I really didn't mean to send you running down a rabbit hole on a wild goose chase.' She almost laughed out loud at this outrageous mixed metaphor. He continued, 'You know, there are people here who would like to help you, but you are just concentrating on your own anxiety and hurt rather than seeing that they may be hurt too.'

'Oh yeah? D'you mean like you? No chance. Just for your information, the only people I feel are really concerned for me are Cocky here, and Eileen.'

'That was whom I meant.' Ailsa thought he was implying that he himself didn't care, and for the first time in three days she began to stir.

'Well, I am doing just great on my own, so please go.' This time, her sarcasm bit through, and he got up with a sigh.

'Okay, have it your own way. I thought you had more in you than this, Ailsa. I am disappointed in you and how you are giving up.'

'Quite frankly, I don't give a rat's behind what you think of me.'

'Well, there you go. Miss Cochrane, it appears that your patient is too stubborn to listen to advice or take any help. Good luck!' he said breezily, and, without another word, he left.

Whatever Ailsa might believe, Max had affected a change in her. The fact that he thought she had 'more in her' and that he was 'disappointed in her' woke her up more than shouting or slanging each other could have done. It was his arrogance which had riled her. 'Who does he think he is, ordering me about like one of his ninny patients?' But, she had been really horrible to him, when he was only responding to Cocky's plea for help, and she felt bad about that. She went for a bath soon after he had gone, then took Rosie and Bluebell for a walk across the headland towards Arnasaid. She had on her warmest red coat, and halfway down the cliff path she stopped at the wooden fence, turned, and looked back at Storm Winds. 'I won't let you go!' She felt the tears streaming again, and she walked onwards towards Arnasaid.

The wind had picked up, driving away the rain clouds, and, although she had on her boots, the surface was slippery and wet on the path. She met no one. The wind tossed her blonde hair, which was getting really quite long now, and dispelled the bad feelings she had harboured over the last few days, making her feel more relaxed and energetic than she had done. She decided, as she reached the shores of the bay of Arnasaid, that she cared very much about things, her situation, whatever she chose to call it, and that she had got the energy to fight back.

Ailsa decided that she would concentrate on the children's Christmas Party and put the problems of inheritance on hold until she felt able to deal with it.

'I have the invitations ready to send out to all the usual societies,' Gennina said, a few days later, when they were both going through the preparations for the next big event at Storm Winds. 'There is the children's home in Dunlivietor, and all the local children from Arnasaid and Arnasaid Bheag. That usually makes up around seventy kids. Is that okay?'
'Of course, let's go for it,' Ailsa said. 'Do we have enough staff to help us with all the arrangements?'

'Yes, if we prepare everything, and get the usual caterers in, then we only need three staff on at the actual party. So, that will be Cocky, Eileen and Olivia, that pregnant Italian girl we have helping.'

Ailsa froze. 'Olivia is pregnant?' she said, incredulously.

'Yes, didn't you know? No one knows her history, and she won't talk to anyone about anything. Quite right too.' Gennina twirled her gum round her finger and popped it back in her mouth again.

Gennina eyed her employer curiously. 'Not that anyone knows. She hasn't been seen with a guy at all and does her work well, and thoroughly, if Cocky is to be quoted.'

'Does she have a boyfriend?' Ailsa asked innocently.

'No one knows,' Gennina said. 'You hired her, didn't you? I remember you said you felt sorry for her. Didn't you know she was pregnant then?'

'No, I didn't, but she may not even have known herself at that point.'

Gennina shrugged, then immediately went on to the next subject. 'The Colonel will be back on Saturday, and he has emailed an invitation to dinner at Trannoch.'

'Oh right,' Ailsa said, without relish. 'Another MacKenzie gathering. What could be nicer?'

'You know, you are really getting sarcastic in your old age, boss,' Gennina said, so sincerely that Ailsa laughed.

'Yep!'

Ailsa decided to tackle Olivia. The next day when she was writing in her library she heard the sounds of the hall being cleaned, the vacuum was heard only slightly due to the thickness of the old walls, and she peeped out to see Olivia.

'Can you come in for a minute, please?' Ailsa had waved above the noise, and Olivia, looking around her as if she was doing something wrong, could do nothing else but follow.

'Sit down, Olivia.' Ailsa hoped that the girl would feel the warmth in her voice.

'Are you happy here?' She could have kicked herself for such a lame opening, but with the girl opposite her looking like misery itself, she had plunged right in.

'I am fine.'

'Good. Erm . . . I see you have a condition, erm . . .' Lost for words, Ailsa pointedly looked at the girl's slightly swelling belly. She was very thin, so there was only a small bump. Ailsa had calculated the timings. She could not be much more than three months pregnant.

Olivia stared at her with a mixture of disdain and resignation.

'Yes, I carry a baby. A baby will be born out of rape, but I shall keep my baby, and nurture it, and love it just the same.'

'You are very brave, Olivia, and I intend to support you here. We will give you light work when you get too big, and I will pay you throughout your stay off work. You will of course keep your room here, for you and the baby.' Olivia looked at her, stony-faced, but a little of what Ailsa thought was gratitude also crept into her taught expression. 'I still think though, you should report this. It is not too late, and . . .'

'No!' she almost screamed back. 'I no go to Policeman!' She looked stricken again, and Ailsa was quick to try and calm her down.

'Okay, please don't get upset, it is what you want that is important.'

'He is too big a man,' Ailsa almost laughed at this comment, but Olivia had meant 'big' as in 'important'. Ailsa thought, that in her eyes, Stephen was a 'big' man. So he was. He was almost ingrained into the MacKenzie clan, he had worked there for years, and was like a fifth son to the Colonel. He joined them at dinner most nights, and on all their formal occasions he was always there.

'He said he would kill me, if I told anyone.' Olivia was now passionate in her exchange. 'He said he would kill me!'

Ailsa inwardly scoffed at this, putting it down to the usual drama of Italians, but tried to look serious as she replied, 'He won't come near you.'

'He is always with that family!' Olivia just voiced what Ailsa had been thinking. 'He was here at the Ball! I keep away from him, but every time I look, his eyes upon me.'

'Yes, I know, but in future when I have anything that would include him, here at Storm Winds, I will keep you away. You can have an extra night off.' Ailsa patted her hand kindly.

Ailsa's manner seemed to soften the hard lines of the Italian's brow, and tightness around her lips.

'Thank you, what you do for me.' With that, Olivia returned to her cleaning of the hall, and Ailsa gave a sigh and went back to her writing. 'The next thing I have to look forward to is dinner at Trannoch on Saturday!' Ailsa said to herself, then followed it with 'NOT!'

Chapter Seventeen

Hunter Dillon looked at herself in the mirror with a sigh of satisfaction. She was still a beautiful woman, and at fifty-seven years old could knock the socks off most women fifteen years her junior. Her navy skirt suit was beautifully cut, and her hair shone with the true natural lustre of an un-bleached blonde; hers was now mixed with grey, but the effect against her dark eyebrows and lashes was stunning. Her figure was full but not to the point of voluptuousness, her waist still narrow and her back straight. Her clothes looked as expensive as they had cost; Hunter still had money of her own, despite her late husband having gambled away most of their joint fortune.

Malcolm MacKenzie's export business was notoriously shady, and he had been investigated by the Internal Revenue in the previous year for tax avoidance, but Malcolm had a very good lawyer, the same firm that his father used, and had managed to squeeze through their clutches with only a very paltry fine. He had then decided to expand into property, which he had done so seamlessly, buying up individually top-range properties across Scotland, which had individually high-end price tags to go with them. When Hunter had contacted him a few days ago to meet and discuss some suitable properties, he not only saw a business opportunity but also a personal one, in the shape of the beautiful widow.

They met at the Cridland Hotel, which sat just off the main A830 road between Glenfinnan and Fort William. It was slightly too far out of the way to be used on a regular basis by most people they knew, although in the summer months, it was frequented by that set of people as it was a beautiful drive on a sunny day. The Thursday before the dinner party at Trannoch was not such a day. It was windy to the point of gale force, again the winds had been battering the coastline, and the sleet was adding to the snow of the week before making the road not an easy drive.

He had taken one of the Trannoch cars to the venue, whilst Hunter had ordered the one and only taxi in Arnasaid to make the trip. He wanted to avoid any speculation about their meeting, which may arise if any prying eyes had seen them getting into a car together; therefore, they chose to meet at the hotel. He had downed two whiskies by the time she arrived and was at a perfect vantage point to watch her elegant fluid movements as she walked across the floor towards where he was seated at the back of the dimly-lit lounge. She oozed sex appeal, and, when she sat, her long lithe legs crossed revealing a flash of toned thigh which set the blood racing around his veins.

'May I get you a drink, Hunter?' he asked, in what he hoped sounded like a calm and business-like tone.

'Of course!' Hunter smiled, showing a set of beautifully engineered and whitened teeth, and requested a glass of Prosecco. He called over the waiter, who was hovering nearby, and put in her order along with another whisky for himself. They stared momentarily at each other over the table before Malcolm pulled out a file which he sat between them, full of pictures of properties around the country, as was the proposed subject of their discussion.

'Now there is a lovely five-bedroom villa in the Inverness countryside, or I have a five story Edwardian town house in the centre of Aberdeen. Both of them are under £2m.'

Hunter fixed him with a look from her hypnotic dark eyes. 'I think these sound lovely little houses,' she said, with a smile, 'but I want to live around here.'

'Here?' Malcolm looked at her steadily. 'You mean around the Fort William area?'

'Not exactly. I mean, more specifically, the Arnasaid area.'

'Okay, but I think I will find it very difficult to find something of the same size and price as the ones I have mentioned, unless you go into Fort William, or some of the cities,' he said, taking a gulp of his whisky.

'Yes, I thought that, actually.' She lifted her glass to her mouth, and keeping his eyes in a locked stare, look a long sip. There was a suggestiveness in the stare that was not lost on Malcolm, and he felt his collar tighten and his forehead bead with sweat. 'You'll just have to show me what you've got . . .'

He had already booked a room. He was quite prepared to 'show her'.

Several hours later, Malcolm got his driver to drop Hunter off at the back entrance to the hotel in Arnasaid. With a discrete kiss, as an old friend might give, he let her go.

On Saturday evening Ailsa got ready for the dinner party at Trannoch with as much relish as she would make preparations for a funeral. She had dined there multiple times since she had arrived at Storm Winds, none of which were uneventful. She wore a red dress which sat just on her shoulders and had a deep V-necked back. It was plain but suited her perfectly. It was one of the dresses she had bought in Skye, when she had absconded, and it was simple and chic. Red was not normally her colour, but with her blonde hair and dark features she looked good in any colour.

She was desperately worried about seeing Malcolm again after the Ghillies' Ball. She knew he was making a play for her, and although she had been very attracted to him, at first, was now wholly put off by his philandering and salacious ways. Also, before he even tried to seduce *her*, there was Belinda. What a life she must have led being the spiritless and uncharismatic wife of someone so controlling. How Belinda had managed to survive being married to him for quite so long, was the question she kept asking herself.

She let herself in at the usual side door, after Jim Hutton had dropped her off. Again, Denbeath seemed to hear the grass growing and came into the hallway to meet her and take her coat. 'They are all assembled in the Great Room, Madam.'

He gave her coat to a passing maid, and she followed him meekly into the now familiar room where the clan MacKenzie and several guests were gathered. The booming voice of the Colonel greeted her with its usual gusto, and she was ushered over to a seat by the fire.

The dinner party had been extended to several local dignitaries, friends and acquaintances of the family. The room was much busier than usual, and drinks were being served by a bevy of footmen. The usual MacKenzie suspects were all gathered, the silent older brother Noel, of whom Ailsa knew so little, only nodded then went back to his conversation with a few other men. Malcolm was on the opposite sofa to the one on which the Colonel deposited her, and, as she tried to avert her eyes from his gaze, she was amazed to hear a pleasant, 'Good evening Ailsa, and how are you tonight?' There was something in his tone on which she could not put her finger, but she was pleased that, at least in front of others, he was prepared to behave himself.

She noticed Max turn from his place to look at her. He was having a conversation with Stephen Millburn and a couple whom Ailsa did not know but recognised their faces. She noticed that he still had on the splint, although it was a smaller version of the one he had been sporting the other day. Ailsa wondered momentarily if he had been in a fight, but as this was so far removed from what she thought Max the 'stuffed shirt' would do, she dismissed it from her mind.

Carys was looking amazing in a cobalt blue full-length dress, holding court with a large group of people, controlling the conversation as ever.

The couple sitting at the other end of Ailsa's sofa got up at this point, to greet other friends who had just arrived, leaving spare space at the side of her. Before she noticed the purposeful smile and realised what it meant, Malcolm had got up and moved across beside her. She felt her blood run cold.

'Ailsa, please don't worry, I am not about to repeat what happened at the Ghillies' Ball,' he said, with what he hoped was a charming smile.

'I'm not worried,' she lied. 'I am just amazed that you have the audacity to even speak to me after what happened.'

'I am genuinely sorry.' His attractive face was contorted with an expression of false contrition, and, although Ailsa was not fooled, she was pleased that he had at least attempted to put things right. 'I was drunk and had no right to try and kiss you like I did, . . .' He conveniently left out the fact that he had held her arms taught so that she could not move. It was much more than just a kiss. It didn't do much to dampen his spirits even now, as he continued, 'you are an extremely good looking woman Ailsa, practically irresistible, and . . .'

'Is he bothering you?'

Ailsa jumped, as the voice came from the other side of Malcolm, and she turned to see Max looming by her side.

Ailsa had no idea why she found herself jumping to Malcolm's defence, but she did. 'I am having a private conversation with your brother.'

'Yes, I can see that.' Max did not look at her directly but fastened his gaze with a frown at Malcolm. 'Just see you keep your hands to yourself, Malc.'

'Jealous?'

'I'll ignore that comment.'

'I am on my best behaviour, little brother' Malcolm grinned, as Max's face darkened.

'Just make sure you are.' He left Ailsa seething and Malcolm smiling from ear to ear.

'What did he mean?' But, before Malcolm could answer her, the call came from Denbeath that dinner was served, and they all ceremoniously walked the long corridor to the dining room. The table had been extended and easily seated the thirty or so guests and family members. The fire blazed in the grate, and the chandeliers flickered and sparkled light across the room. Ailsa was dismayed to find that she had been seated beside Max on one side. There was however a nicer older man on the other side of her who was part of the Round Table society she attended, so she knew him quite well. On Max's other side was the Colonel, who was heading up the table as usual, so at least she was only two away from a decent conversation.

'How are you feeling?' Max suddenly turned round, and faced her.

'Feeling? I'm fine!' She was momentarily non-plussed at the unexpected question. She had expected him to say something about the conversation with Malcolm, but he hadn't, and she was taken aback by this. She started buttering her bread. 'Why do you ask, are you looking to take my pulse?' She was gratified to see him smile rather than rise to her question. He stretched over the table to get the salt for his soup.

'Certainly not. Off duty.' His voice was a little gruff, but not as sardonic as it normally was.

'So, how did you bust your hand then?' It was said more nonchalantly than curiously.

He hesitated for too long before he said, 'Oh, it's nothing, I just punched Malcolm.'

The Colonel had finished a conversation with Stephen Millburn, opposite Max, just in time to hear this. 'You and Malcolm fighting?' he barked, in much too loud a voice for comfort. It seemed to Ailsa again as if the Colonel was unable to achieve the skill of talking quietly. Stephen heard and looked up with interest as the Colonel continued to plough right in there. 'Maxwell, you are the one of my four wayward sons whom I would expect to behave decently and not brawl with your brother. What did he do?'

'Now is not the time.'

'It's the time if I say it is!' The Colonel's face was going dangerously red.

'I don't want to discuss it, Father.' Max was beginning to look mutinous.

'Oh, really?' The Colonel's red face turned into a thunderous expression. 'Well, we'll see about that, Son. I'll speak to you both later.'

'Dad, we're not teenagers any longer,' Max said, half-laughing half-annoyed, but used enough to the Colonel not to let it bother him too much.

'Why did you fight with Malcolm?' Ailsa said, in a low urgent voice, when the Colonel and Stephen had turned away to have another discussion. Max looked at her long and hard. 'I think you know the answer to that question, Ailsa.'

'What? Why would I know . . .' Then her face suddenly cleared, and she swung round on him. 'The Ghillies' Ball at Storm Winds.' It was not a question, but nonetheless Max nodded in agreement.

'Shit,' she finished.

'Shit indeed.'

Ailsa was beginning to get angry again. Why had he done such a thing? It wasn't as if he had even come along in time to 'save' her. She had no idea if he saw anything or not, and she was upset and embarrassed by this disclosure. What business was it of his to interfere? She said as much to him in-between the plates of Balmoral chicken being laid on the table between them.

'Interfering?' He looked dumbfounded at the notion. 'I wasn't interfering with anything! However, had I come a little earlier than I did, and had I seen anything more than your stumbling away from my brother in obvious distress and him falling clutching his crotch, then I may have interfered further.' The sarcasm was evident in his voice.

'You are so full of yourself, it's sickening,' she said.

'Well, I can assure you, Lady Hamilton-Dunbar, that in future, I will leave well alone.' He began to eat, pointedly drawing a line under the conversation.

She had no idea why his conversation upset her so much. She hated his knack of seemingly putting her down in his confident way, calling her 'Lady Hamilton-Dunbar' in a way that seemed to make her feel foolish. She thought about that night, and the fact that events had overtaken her with the arrival of Hunter, so much, that she had put aside her encounter with Malcolm. She hadn't seen him after that. She had presumed he had just faded into the background. But now it seemed that Max had punched him, and it was this with which she struggled. He had apparently witnessed at least the end of the altercation, by his own description, and had mowed-in there to tackle his brother.

The other thing which annoyed her about all of this was that Stephen had been listening across the table to the conversation – he couldn't really avoid it, but she had hated to see the obvious amusement in his eyes as he listened to the exchange between Max and his father. 'I wish he would just piss off and leave us all to it!' she thought, as she caught his eye studiously taking it all in.

'May I escort you through, Ailsa,' the Colonel asked, as the dinner came to an end. Ailsa nodded thankfully, relieved at being out of the range of both Max and Stephen who had clouded the discussions over dinner with their own agendas. When the nod from one of the staff was given to the Colonel that everyone had finished, he stood, and the table rose as one in response. He walked round to Ailsa and offered his arm.

The Great Room was one of Ailsa's favourite rooms at Trannoch. It was a huge space and yet the decor made it seem cosy. The paintings were amazing, portraits of the MacKenzies since the seventeenth century, and landscapes of the beautiful surroundings and scenery of Arnasaid and the North West. Ailsa loved the dramatic colours and depictions of the mountains and sea which she had been so drawn to since coming to Scotland.

'Clementine painted that one,' the Colonel said, as Ailsa gasped aloud at the fact he was talking about his daughter-in-law. It seemed as if he tried to avoid discussing her. She stole herself before replying.

'She is very talented.'

'I agree, she is very talented. I so wish that things had worked out between them.' His voice sounded distant, almost as if he were talking to himself.

They sat near the fire, the flames dancing in the dimly-lit room, the shadows of guests walking the walls and ceiling in the casting light. A glass of brandy was put into her hand, and she started to relax. The Colonel began to talk.

'It was a great shock to me that Hunter came back. I loved her you know, Ailsa. I loved her with all my heart, and when she left for Australia she did so without a thought for me, after all, we had a good relationship, we loved, and I lost . . . that is the way of it.'

He looked so sad that Ailsa's heart went out to him.

'You must have felt bereft when you got the false information that she had died,' was all she was able to say to him.

He looked at her long and hard, as if trying to decide whether to answer that or not. At length he said, with a nonchalant shrug of his shoulders, 'Oh, I never believed that story, you know. I thought it was all too . . . convenient for her to die like that.'

'Convenient? That seems a strange word to describe faking your own death.'

'Well, Ailsa, the boys knew but were sworn to secrecy. As I said, I was heartbroken when she left, but I followed her. I carried on my affair with Hunter long after she had gone to Australia. I visited her twice a year and stayed over there for a few months at a time. She also came over here, no, not to Scotland,' he answered her questioning look, 'but to London. I have a flat there. The reason I say 'convenient' is that I was still seeing Hunter when she met her husband-to-be, but whilst Hunter, being the sort of person she is, saw this as an added excitement, I couldn't take it, and finished off our meetings. When I left for the last time she was not upset, but angry. The affair had lasted almost ten years, off and on, and a few months after I returned to Trannoch the letter came, via Sir Angus, to say that she was dead. I never believed it. I knew she was punishing me, and that there had been nothing between her and Sir Angus since you were born, Ailsa.'

She tried to take all of this in. She knew they had conducted an affair, albeit nothing like the one the Colonel had just described, but she also knew that she needed to understand the dates and timings. From what he had just said, it appeared that although both he and Sir Angus were having an affair with Hunter at the same time before she left for Australia, she was not convinced that he knew one way or another if he was her father or not.

'Colonel, I am sorry if this seems intrusive, but you and Sir Angus both seem to have had relations,' she spoke carefully, 'with Hunter, and I . . . I . . . that is, I . . .'

'I know what you are asking, Ailsa,' he smiled weakly, 'but I have to say that I have no idea if I am your real father or not. That is what you are asking me? Angus and I had no idea that the other was also 'seeing' Hunter at the time. The whole business is rather unsavoury.'

Ailsa looked at him in disbelief. 'Unsavoury' was one of the last words which she would have used to describe her situation, but the Colonel was of a different era and class, and this little 'problem' paled into insignificance to him in terms of his other considerations.

'I have something to tell you which I don't think you will be happy about,' he said, with a genuinely worried expression on his face. He signalled over a young man to give him another brandy, then he settled back in his chair. 'Malcolm has appealed to me to give Hunter a home here at Trannoch. I know you have asked her to leave Storm Winds and that she has stayed in the local hotel, but I feel I owe it to her to give her a place here. I hope you will understand, Ailsa, that I cannot just turn my back on her, and everything she has meant to me.' He seemed to sag in relief at owning up to what he had just said.

'Malcolm has asked you?' Ailsa was confused.

'Yes, he's not as bad as we would all make out, Ailsa,' the Colonel smiled.

Ailsa thought he was every bit as bad, and a bit more, but said nothing. She thought much more though. Malcolm? Why had he pleaded Hunter's case with the Colonel to let her stay at Trannoch? Was it merely because he thought she was a kindred spirit, and that they both were characters cast aside by their families? If what the Colonel had just said proved to be true, then Malcolm along with the other MacKenzie brothers had known, at the time, of the long affair between their father and Hunter. Was this the reason? An attempt by

Malcolm to get his father and Hunter back together again? She wanted Hunter as far away from the area as was possible, and now that Hunter was to stay at Trannoch, Ailsa knew that she would be part of her life in one way or another.

'Thank you for letting me know, but I have to tell you something you know already, that I am not happy about her being a part of my life. She is my mother, Colonel, and I realise this, although I will never recognise the fact. I think her return here is purely selfish, and the fact that she seems to have instructed her son Joshua to return too, which I am not sure is even palatable to him, makes me think her intentions are sinister to say the least. I also know that she is inextricably linked to both our families, but I will never, *never* let her get her hands on my estate.'

'Gosh, Ailsa, that is quite a speech. I don't blame you. Hunter is a law unto herself. She has dominated our lives for far too long, but, unfortunately, I am weak. I was her friend for so many years, and I cannot walk away from her now. Try to understand, Ailsa.' He did not plead but put it in such a way that she didn't really feel sorry for him as she knew his defences would never measure up to Hunter. That much was given.

Ailsa lay awake for much of the night. She heard every tick of her clock on the bedside table and opened the balcony doors and stood in the stormy air until her hair was soaked and her pyjamas made damp by the rain-soaked wind. Was her whole world to be upturned? She had begun to feel a part of this, to embrace the house, the people and most especially the landscape, was this to be taken away from her by the selfish actions of a beautiful widow who was also her mother? She slept deeply, when she finally did fall over, at around seven o'clock in the morning, and did not rouse until after eleven.

On waking, Ailsa called Connie and asked her advice.

'Well darling, DNA is one way of doing it, lots of people go down that route nowadays, and it's easy peasy. All you need is a hair sample and that's it.'

'But . . . but Sir Angus is dead and buried,' Ailsa stammered, desperately.

'I wasn't talking about your father, I meant the Colonel. Ask him to help you out, that you will pay for it etc., and, by a process of elimination, if he's not your Pop, then Sir Angus, dearly departed, is.'

Chapter Eighteen

The Colonel duly agreed to the plan, he felt he had nothing to lose, as he was certain he was not Ailsa's father, and Connie dealt with the rest. Hunter had apparently settled into Trannoch, and from the gossip which passed from the Trannoch staff back to Miss Cochrane and Eileen, she was causing all kinds of ructions; a fact which Cocky had not been short on prophesising, and then gloating that she was right in all her assertions.

The landscape was changing, winter was now well under way, and the rocky outcrops and steep cliffs overlooking the raging seas had become centre stage. Many of the trees had lost their greenery and the black tracery of the forests stood alongside the evergreen masses of firs, fighting for position on the bleak mountain slopes. The winds were freezing, and snow had now established itself for the winter in the ski centres of Glencoe and the magnificent Grampian range. Domineering Ben Nevis, the UK's highest mountain at over 4,000 feet, rose above it all, majestic and snow-capped, less than 20 miles from Arnasaid. The skies were fierce in their muddy blue and blackness, with hurtling clouds, full of rain, sleet and snow, crossing above like a marching army.

It was only a few weeks until Christmas, the days were short and the nights long, although the atmosphere was singing with the excitement of festive preparations. Lights were strung up around Arnasaid, a tree was strapped down with brace-like reinforcements on the grassy part near the car park; hardy lights and decorations clinging to the flailing branches in the slim hope that they would make it through to the New Year. Colourful posters, advertising everything from Christmas parties to concerts with mulled wine, adorned the wayside pulpit of

Arnasaid church, and the new hotel had sprung into action and filled its dimly-lit windows with decorations and fake spray-on snow. There had been an inflatable snowman standing guard on the decking at the front of the hotel for two days until Mr S decided to use his air pumped body to transport him across the sea to the Small Isles on a particularly stormy night, much to the astonishment of the passengers of a local fishing boat.

'The Colonel is not your father.' Connie had phoned Ailsa around a week after the test sample had been sent away. The results had been sent to Connie who had 'taken care' of the proceedings, and Ailsa had been strung up with nerves ever since, waiting on the results. 'Your Pop must, by a process of elimination, be sweet old Sir Angus, as you thought, honey. Apart from anything else, the Colonel absolutely is not your dad, and Sir Angus would have no reason to say you were his daughter and leave you half of Scotland if he thought you were not.' The line went quiet and Connie actually thought her friend had hung up. 'Darling, are you still there?'

'Yes, sorry.' The sobs were coming thick and fast down the line, and Connie started to feel alarmed.

'Ailsa, are you okay, sweetheart?'

'Yes. I'm okay. It's just, you know, the waiting and the fear that . . . that . . .'

'I know, darling. The fear that your inheritance would be taken away . . .'

'Not my *inheritance* Connie, my *home* and my *life*. It goes much deeper than money.'

There was silence on the other end, then a guarded voice from her friend. 'Yes, darling, look, I am sorry, I was thoughtless. I know how much Storm Winds means to you, and your new 'family' and friends. I shouldn't have opened my big mouth, but I am over the moon for you that everything is all right and your future is settled.'

'My future is far from settled with Hunter digging her claws into everything and demanding that Joshua is the one who should inherit Storm Winds. It's just all such a mess.'

'Well, maybe we should get him to do a DNA sample too! But wait a minute, didn't old Pop say that his inheritance goes down the female route? You're older than Joshua, so it really shouldn't make any difference, if he is your brother, he shouldn't have any claim on the estate.'

'When are you coming up again, Connie?'

'I'll definitely be up soon.'

The following Saturday was the Children's Party at Storm Winds. The tree had been chopped down from the slope behind the house and decorated with lots of hand-made decorations created especially by the children of Arnasaid Primary School, as suggested by the faithful Gennina. In fact, Gennina had done a brilliant job organising the party from beginning to end, and Ailsa was really proud of her. They had both gathered lots of winter foliage and decorated the mantelpiece in the ballroom. On Friday, they had spent the day covering the place until it looked really 'quaintly festive', to quote Gennina. The one concession to modern decoration-making was the simple silver chains and huge silver paper balls, which Ailsa had picked up on the internet. The balls hung from the ceiling and as they turned in the natural drafts, picked up sparkles of light like the disco balls of Ailsa's youth.

'Beautiful! Oh, Ailsa, I've never seen the place look so Christmassy! It's absolutely gorgeous!'

'I am rather pleased with the general effect,' Ailsa said, in a mock superior voice, and they both dissolved into laughter. As they hooted with mirth, they did not hear the knock on the door nor the footsteps across the parquet floor until the person stood in front of them.

'Excuse me, I didn't mean to interrupt,' Joshua said, running his fingers through his reddish-blonde hair. Ailsa turned her coldest look upon him. As far as she was concerned he was the enemy. Hunter's son, and her brother, if what the woman said was to be believed. As she looked at him, she caught his eyes, not on her, but on Gennina, who went bright red, and started to stammer at him. There was no mistaking the look which passed between them.

'Er . . . er, Joshua, was it me . . . er . . . did you want to speak to me . . . I wasn't . . .' It was going on quite long enough for it to become embarrassing, and Joshua intervened.

'No, Gennina.' His tone was warm, and too familiar for Ailsa's liking. 'Sorry, but its Ailsa I wanted to speak to, if that's okay.'

'Ailsa? You mean, Lady Ailsa!' Gennina looked shocked at the way the laissez-faire Australian spoke to her employer.

'Yeah, soz an all that! *Lady* Ailsa Hamilton-Dunbar! What a handle!' he said, with a wide grin.

'Gennina, do me a favour and ask Cocky for coffee in the library, will you please?' Ailsa said briskly, beginning to walk towards the door. 'Follow me, Joshua.' It was a command rather than a request, and Joshua did a funny little bow behind her back, as he winked at Gennina and followed Ailsa out.

'I don't know what you think you are doing here, I threw you and your mother out, and . . .'

'*Our* mother, you mean.'

'I will never, ever regard her as my mother, but that is none of your business. What do you want?'

'Aren't you going to pour the coffee?' he asked, nonchalantly.

'No. Coffee was a bad idea. I want you to say whatever it was you came here for and get out.' She got up and paced the floor for what seemed like ages, while he poured himself a coffee and stirred his cup calmly. This laid-back attitude only infuriated her further. 'What is it you came to say Joshua? Just spit it out and go.'

'OK.' He leaned forward again and took a biscuit off the plate. 'I'm going back to Australia. I can't be bothered with Mum's play acting and money grabbing any more than you can, dear sister.'

'Don't call me that! How do I know you are my brother? She tells us all whatever she wants to tell us. She's a conniving self-centred bully, and the only reason she is here is to try and get out of me whatever she can, no thought of reuniting the family, believe me.'

'I believe you, and I agree with you, Sis,' he said, annoyingly.

'I *said*, don't call me that. Until I have absolute proof that you are related to me, I don't want you to call me that. Do you understand?'

'Why, Lady Ailsa, don't get all flustered, I'll be out of your hair soon.'

'The sooner the better. Now if that's all you came here for . . .'

'Actually, no, it isn't.'

Ailsa gave a resigned sigh and flopped down onto her seat. 'Well? What else? Have you unearthed any other siblings since you came to Scotland who you want to try and make a claim on Storm Winds?' She was gratified to hear him burst into a hearty and quite natural laugh. He actually had a very charming laugh. No wonder Gennina seemed to have fallen for him. Maybe it was a very good idea that he had decided to go back across to the other side of the world, or her secretary would be in grave danger of splitting up her existing relationship for the dashing Joshua. But he had said there was something else, and Ailsa began to grow weary of this tête à tête.

For an answer, Joshua took a piece of paper out of his jeans pocket and handed it to Ailsa before he took another biscuit.

Curiously, Ailsa took the letter from him and sat on the window seat which overlooked Storm Winds' substantial parkland. She read the note through twice, then folded it up carefully, and looked across at her visitor, with only a slight tremor in her lip revealing any emotion.

'Well,' she said, flatly. She waved the letter in the air. 'So, this is a medical DNA result.'

'It is.'

'And, despite my hopes to the contrary, you are indeed my brother.'

'Yes, sorry about that.' He grinned again. 'But the news just gets better. I confronted Mum about this, and she absolutely went berserk.

'Why? I thought that was what she had said, and what she wanted?'

'Oh yeah! It is! But the other bit is that Sir Angus can't be my father.'

Ailsa looked at him long and hard. 'What? How?'

'There is another piece of paper,' he said. 'I've stolen it from Mum's secret box.' He touched the side of his nose conspiratorially. 'I didn't know she had a secret box until I went into her hotel room to look for her, when you arranged to have us dumped there, remember?' Ailsa looked sheepish. He stood up and stretched.

'What other piece of paper? What are you talking about?'

'A test which was done several years ago when Sir Angus was still alive, there's a date on it, she must have arranged it all. I've put it in a safety deposit box, so Mother darling can't get at it and destroy the evidence, but it is there if I need it. When I told her that, she was absolutely livid. Threw the box at the dressing table mirror and broke it, threatened me with all sorts if I didn't give it back to her,' he sighed and drew his fingers through his hair again, an obvious characteristic which apparently showed itself when he was agitated. 'I thought you had a right to know, especially since I am leaving to fly back home later today. I owe you that much for my part in the 'Hunter Dillon conspiracy'. It says that I am not the son of Sir Angus, but that my dear old dad happens to be Colonel MacKenzie. So, you see we are actually half-brother and sister.'

Ailsa looked at him a long time. His colouring, his height, his rugged good looks and yes, even his quirky way of pulling himself up to his full height were so like the Colonel; in some ways more so than the other sons. She suddenly and inexplicably felt drawn to him. In contrast to the way she had viewed him before, she felt all at once that he was an ally rather than an enemy, against Hunter rather than for her, and uninterested in inheriting anything, rather than the greed and downright avariciousness of their mother.

'Cheerio, Sis, it's been nice knowing you.' He made his way to the door.

'Wait, you are going back to Australia knowing all that?' Ailsa suddenly felt that she couldn't let him go, no matter how he had come into her life. He turned and looked at her. 'I only came here because Hunter said she needed me, but that was a pack of lies, obviously.' She could see the hurt in his eyes as he continued. 'My home is in Australia, not Scotland. Ricky left me the ranch, and although there is no money, I have been used to farming the land all my life, I don't need handouts from you or anybody else. Hunter knows who I am, and now you know who I am, and it is for the Colonel to find out, not for me to try and worm my way in there like my mother has done. I am going back to Australia.' He pulled the door open. 'Come and see me sometime, Sis,' and with a mock salute, he was gone.

Ailsa sat in her library for a long time. She thought about all the things which had happened since arrived at Storm Winds. How many lives had been altered since she came to stay here. She thought about Hunter, the Colonel, his sons and their respective families. She thought about Olivia, and Clem and Stephen Millburn. Olivia was pregnant, quite obviously with Stephen's child. How would her friend Clem feel when she found that little nugget of information out? Clem had been through so much, and Ailsa despised the thought that Stephen's child would be brought into the world at Storm Winds, but she could not turn Olivia away. She thought about Malcolm and poor Belinda, and quite suddenly about Belinda's daughter Melissa. The girl had confided in her to an extent, about her father, Malcolm, and she, Ailsa, had done nothing about it. But what could she do? All Melissa had said was that she had seen something, or to put it in Melissa's words, 'I saw him . . . I *saw* him.' Ailsa had surmised that it had been Malcolm she had been talking about, but with hindsight, could it have been someone else? But who? She had been talking about her mother at the time and almost accused her father of putting the pills into Belinda's hand and driving her to her death. No, it must have been Malcolm she was referring to, Ailsa decided. She had also said that David had seen it too but was too weak to do anything about it as he worshipped his father. 'Well, Gennina said that the children come home from school this weekend for the Christmas break, so I might see if I can talk to Melissa, at least to see how she is.'

She got up and looked around the library, gloomy in shadow and dark wood, with that essential musty smell which she had grown to know and love. She had long since discarded the painting of Hunter from its place on the wall, up to the attics where it belonged. She ran her fingers along the long table where she did her writing – that had been put on hold for weeks now, she just couldn't put her mind to it with everything going on – and along the bookcases filled with books of every genre, from every part of the world. They were relatively dust-free, kept that way by the scrupulous Miss Cochrane and her little brigade of merry maids. She came to her own personal favourite, a bookcase dedicated to children's books, hundreds of them, first editions mostly with beautiful dust wrappers which any collector would have given their eye teeth for. She would occasionally take one off the shelf and decant to her chair by the fire and read, transporting herself back to her own childhood. There was Enid Blyton, Elinor M Brent-Dyer, Arthur Ransome, Malcolm Saville, presumably all her father's old books as they were too modern for her grandfather. All the old classics: *Tom Brown's School Days, The Water Babies, Kidnapped, Treasure Island* . . . Ailsa stopped as a memory stirred. Treasure Island. Where had she heard that talked about relatively recently? Who would mention a book like that? Was it her friends, Connie or Jan, when they had exclaimed over the multitudes of old favourites as they examined her library? Miss Cochrane? No, why would she mention it . . . but . . . it was definitely in this room. Who? Why? As she strained to remember, the thread began to develop in her psyche. Sir Angus had mentioned it in this room. She had only had one conversation with him, and it had been in this room. Why had he mentioned that book? She thought for a minute, then decided it must have been part of the conversation about him loving Storm Winds, and in particular this library, which was his favourite room, and that he had hoped she, Ailsa, would grow to love it as much as he did.

She felt an excitement stirring within her as she thumbed her way along the brightly coloured dust jackets to settle on the book she had been thinking about. There it was.

She took it off the shelf and held it for a long moment before opening it. There was a letter inside the book boards, tucked under the front flap of the dust wrapper.

It was addressed: To my daughter, Lady Ailsa Hamilton-Dunbar.

When Miss Cochrane came in an hour later she found Ailsa sitting at the table clutching a folded paper and staring into space. The room had gone dark and was cold, as the fire had gone out. She set the teapot on the little table and made up the fire, then switched on the lamps and poured a cup of tea, which she took over to Ailsa. She noticed the book on the table, the tear stains and strained look upon Ailsa's face before she pulled out a chair and sat down beside the Lady of the house.

'So, you've found the letter?' Miss Cochrane asked, surprisingly.

Ailsa lifted her head slowly, the light coming back into her eyes. 'You *knew* about this?'

'Of course, I knew. I nursed him for years before his most recent illness took him from us. I knew his thoughts and his plans for the future.'

'So, why didn't you tell me? It would have saved a lot of heartache, not just for me but for Joshua and everyone else if you had just told me the truth from the start.'

'It was not my place or my truth, to tell. Sir Angus wanted you to find out for yourself, and you did. You got the DNA tests done, you found out Hunter, you found out Joshua, and, more importantly, you found out the Colonel.'

'Sorry, did you say, *more importantly*?'

'Yes, I did. Sir Angus hated the Colonel. They were adversaries in the old days, but they grew to hate each other. Your father hated the Colonel more than he had ever loved anyone, even Hunter. His hate destroyed him in the end. He knew Hunter was having an affair with both of them, but he could not let her go. She never loved him, it was the Colonel she wanted.'

'So why did she stick with my fa . . . Sir Angus? He was still married to Elizabeth Douglas, the Colonel was widowed by that time, why keep him on the sidelines, if that's what it was?'

'Storm Winds,' Miss Cochrane said, softly and simply. 'She wanted Storm Winds. Oh, she hated this part of the country, the weather, the traditions, yes, even the people, but she loved this house. She felt she belonged here, and . . . unfortunately your father felt that too.'

'And he was going to give it all to her,' Ailsa said, in a flat voice. 'Right up to the point before he was told she had died, he was going to leave Storm Winds to her, then the anger and the hurt seemed to hit him far more than it had done when she was 'alive'.'

'Yes.'

'I would never have tried to find him, I had been happy with my parents. They loved me, and I vowed I would never try to find my real birth parents. There was no need. I was happy as I was.'

'You sound as if you are trying to convince yourself of that, Ailsa.'

She looked angrily at the housekeeper. 'No! Don't try to say I wasn't happy, I was, I had everything I needed or wanted. I left everything I had built up and came up here to start a new life, but it wasn't easy.'

'Nothing worthwhile ever is,' Miss Cochrane said dryly.

Ailsa tried to get back to the subject, 'And then he got the letter to say she had died.'

'Yes.'

'But the letter did not come from Hunter's lawyer or anyone connected to her.'

'No.'

'It came from the Colonel.'

'Yes.'

'And Hunter knew nothing about it?'

'That we don't know. We do know that the Colonel and Hunter carried on their affair for years after she left for Australia. It was Sir Angus' belief that the Colonel wanted to cut the ties between Hunter and him, so they would be free to carry on their relationship in peace.'

'But, that seems ridiculous! Why bother? Why go to such lengths?'

'Because your father was waiting for her. He waited for her from the day she left to the day he got the letter saying that she had died. It hit him hard, Ailsa.'

'Then Hunter came back here about a year ago, it was not just recently, as she pretended. It was all a masquerade.'

'That's right. She came back here a year ago, desperate but not penniless. She had her own money, but she wanted more. Ricky Hammond had thrown her out and she had been staying with a friend for a few years before she decided to come back and hopefully get back into your father's good graces again. He almost died on the spot when she walked back into his life, but, unfortunately for her, he had begun to reconcile himself to the wasted life he had spent waiting, knowing what Hunter had done to him. She had cast him aside in favour of his greatest rival. She had been staying in London until she showed up back here, when she found out about you. No one but your father and I and Jim Hutton knew she had come back.'

'Oh my God, this is all such a mess,' Ailsa said, wearily. 'I can't believe he left me to find out everything myself rather than just getting his lawyers to tell me.'

'He wanted to test you, Ailsa. He wanted to find out if you were good enough.'

She looked at her housekeeper in amazement. 'My God, good enough? Good enough for what?'

Miss Cochrane took a deep breath and looked her in the eye before she answered. 'Good enough for Storm Winds.'

Chapter Nineteen

The wind from the sea wrapped her in its salty embrace, tore at her hair and billowed her clothes until she felt exhausted by it. The headland was ripped through by the treacherous sleet, sheeting its way into the land and covering all plants and grass with an icy film which was hardened almost immediately by the continuous sub-zero temperatures. The sea was dancing frothily in greyish-white frills which belied the magnificent heavy upsurging needed to produce such waves. The islands seemed to have shifted further away, out of reach of civilisation, behind a gauze-like veil which reached from land to skies. The sun was awake somewhere, hidden dimly in the elements.

'Ferocious weather, isn't it?' the postman shouted, above the wind. Ailsa had not even noticed that she had walked the entire headland and was now approaching Arnasaid.

She stopped and dumbly nodded. Bluebell and Rosie strained at their leads, they wanted to be on their way, it was too cold to sit, and even when walking they were close enough to the ground to feel the freezing air permeating upwards from the whiteness. She shivered and pulled her red coat tighter around her.

She wanted to visit Clem. Since that last day they had been together, and Ailsa had tried to discuss Stephen and her fears about him, she had felt guilty about not telling her friend exactly how she felt about him, and what he had done. It had been doubly difficult as she had had the distinct impression that Clem was trying to brush aside any attempts to talk about him. After the recent revelations about who her real parents were and the fact she had a brother, or rather, half-brother, as she now knew, she had thought long and hard about the situation with Stephen and Clem, and her own fears about what he might do to her based on what she knew about Olivia. It was the morning of the Christmas Party, the stage was all set back at Storm Winds, the tree and ballroom decorated, and the food prepared. There were buses arranged to bring the children to the party, but she still had hours before they were to arrive. With the heaviness of the revelations of the previous day pushing down on her shoulders, she was sluggish, had not slept much the night before and felt as if she was coming down with a dose of the flu or something. Her head and neck were sore, her joints aching, and her emotions in an absolute turmoil. In short, she did not feel well, and did not feel able to cope with the conversation she needed to have with her friend Clem. But, she was determined to have that conversation.

Looking to the side she saw someone coming towards her at a pace, they too struggling against the wind and holding a jacket hood tight against the gale. She moved to stand in the doorway of the Post Office to let the person past, but they were not looking at all and almost knocked her over before she managed to step aside.

'Oh my God! Watch where you are going!' she shrieked. Rosie and Bluebell went into a volley of barking at the same time as the person caught her, stood her back upright then pulled off their hood. Dougie was looking at her with a mixture of amazement and embarrassment.

'Ailsa! I am so sorry, I was battling against this bloody wind and didn't see you.'

'That much is apparent,' she said angrily. Her blonde hair was flying, her eyes flashing with annoyance and her face flushing with embarrassment as she took in the tall figure in front of her. Of the two, the windswept look definitely suited him more, and she was suddenly reminded that not only was her hair in a compete mess, as she had no hood, but that she had not a lick of make up on, and her eyes were baggy from the lack of sleep. Her head started to bang again just to make everything worse.

'I was on my way to do a practice with the band before this afternoon,' he said, as if this was an explanation or reason for him hurtling himself about the pavements of Arnasaid.

She was taken aback, as she had left most of the arrangements to Gennina, and it had never crossed her mind that it would be the same band playing as the one which had played at the Ghillies' Ball. Further from her mind was that Dougie would be part of the band, despite the fact she knew he had played there previously. With everything that had happened over the past few weeks it had completely escaped her mind, as Dougie himself had done.

'Ailsa, I'm really sorry, and it's . . . it's great to see you again. Look, I don't mean to barge in . . . too late!' he laughed at his own joke, then as he saw Ailsa's face was deadpan, he ventured to carry on, 'Sorry that wasn't even funny. I just wondered if you fancied catching up over a coffee? I mean, now that we are both here?'

'Thanks, Dougie, but no.' She was beginning to calm down and didn't want to sound ungrateful just because she felt bad and was embarrassed about her appearance. 'I'm on the way to see a friend, then I've got the party this afternoon, as you know, so, not really got a lot of time.'

'Of course.' He looked more resigned than disappointed. 'Another time maybe?' And before Ailsa could either confirm or deny the invitation, he had started to walk away.

Clem looked up as Ailsa came into the gallery. She looked neither happy nor annoyed at Ailsa's sudden appearance. 'Hi!' she said, in a flat voice, as she put a painting back against the wall. 'Well, what brings you out here today on such a day?'

'Are you busy?'

'As you can see I am presently bereft of shoppers.' Clem had a hint of sarcasm in her voice, 'So no, I am not particularly busy. What can I do for you Ailsa?'

Ailsa was not surprised at the change in her friend. She knew she had burned her bridges with Clem; although they had parted on friendly terms the last time, what Ailsa had suggested to her about Stephen had obviously eaten into her, a slow burn, so to speak, and she had been frosty with her ever since. What Ailsa wanted to say to her today wouldn't pacify her or help the situation, but what had to be said, had to be said, she could no longer keep it from Clem. She had to protect her even if they were no longer to be friends.

'I wanted to talk to you Clem.' Clem had her back to Ailsa at this point, but she could see her stiffen then slowly turn to face her.

'I see.' The voice was cold. 'I thought you had said everything you had to say the last time. Is this about Stephen again?'

'Clem, please don't think badly of me for wanting to protect you . . .'

'Protect me? What on earth are you on about, Ailsa? I don't need protecting, thanks very much. Stephen and I are trying to make this work and I don't know why you insist on trying to sabotage it with this idea of him giving that Italian girl a hard time. What's her name again? Olivia.'

Ailsa looked at her friend long and hard. 'I didn't mention Olivia the last time.'

'No, but Stephen eventually told me that the situation between the two of you came about because you accused him of something with Olivia. I think that is a ridiculous assumption and based solely on the fact that you let your jealousy overcome you when you saw him with her at the games. What is wrong with you Ailsa?'

'Look, I admit that I was a bit jealous when I saw him with Olivia at the games. You are right about that . . .'

'Great. At least you are being honest about it.'

'But it wasn't that . . . it was Olivia herself who said it.'

Clem looked at her in astonishment which quickly turned to anger. 'What? What did she actually say? Ailsa, I really am pissed off with you. You are supposed to be my friend and you come here with some bloody cock and bull story about the guy I am seeing, and don't think it has escaped anyone's notice that the Italian girl is pregnant. Are you going to say *that* was Stephen too?'

Ailsa took a deep breath but said nothing. Faced with this onslaught, she felt intimidated and began to question her own motives just as Clem was questioning them. Clem was a force to be reckoned with when she was in this kind of mood.

'Clem, it's not me saying it, I . . . I . . . am really sorry to be the one to tell you, but . . .'

'You *are* saying that. I can't bloody believe it!' She flung out her arms in a rage. 'Who do you think you are, Ailsa? You realise of course what you are saying? That Stephen had a one-night stand – or one day stand, or whatever the hell it was, and now the girl is pregnant? So, what exactly did this really reliable witness tell you? Eh? That she was somehow coerced into it by the unsavoury Stephen?' Clem was getting hysterical, and Ailsa was feeling quite scared at the reaction from the other woman. Was she right? Was Ailsa saying all of this through feelings of jealousy that the guy she had fancied, almost from the start, was now with one of her best friends? Or ex-best friend, as the case may be.

'Oh my God, you are saying that, aren't you?' Clem almost shrieked, as if the realisation just hit her all at once. Ailsa remained struck dumb, not trusting herself to speak. 'You are saying that, you think, or that stupid girl said, that Stephen somehow *forced* her into it? Did she say he raped her? Did she? Did she say that about Stephen?'

'Say what about me?' Neither of them had heard the gallery door as it opened to admit the person at the centre of the row. He stopped short when he saw Clem, tousled and fuming, the anger apparent, and Ailsa, with a stricken expression on her face. 'What's going on?'

Ailsa picked up her dogs from their place on the hearthrug and made to go.

'Oh, not going are you?' Clem's rage was still visible. 'I thought you would have been glad to tell Stephen to his face what you think of him. Don't you want to? That's strange, as I thought you would have revelled in your accusations, however sensational those accusations are.'

'I don't need to listen to this,' Ailsa said, with as much dignity as she could muster. 'I'm sorry, but I only did it with the best intentions. I had no idea of hurting anyone, least of all you, Clem.'

'Really? You surprise me! I think you planned this whole thing out! I think you . . .'

'Ok, Clem, give it a rest,' Stephen said seriously. 'What is it Ailsa?'

Ailsa stared at him for what seemed like an age but was only less than a minute. 'I tried to talk to Clem, but she refuses to listen. I only tried to be a friend, but it seems that, as usual, I have gone about it all wrong. I'm sorry Clem, I'll go and leave you in peace.' She left the gallery, tears streaming down her face.

The Christmas Party started at 2 p.m., and Ailsa didn't know how she would ever cope, after the fight with Clem, and she was beginning to feel all fluey again. Her temperature was hitting the roof, and she felt as if she had been battered and hung out to dry, and it was all she could do to get ready to welcome the children who looked forward to this party for weeks every year.

She had come home after the altercation with Clem, taken some flu capsules and a cup of tea before steeping herself in a long hot bath. As she soaked, she began thinking over what had happened that day. Why had she even bothered? It was obvious that Clem was going to stick up for Stephen, and although she thought she had been prepared for that, she had not been prepared for the venom which she had experienced during the exchange. Stephen had seemed surprised that she was there, although from what Clem said they had discussed Olivia since Ailsa's last visit. Had Olivia been exaggerating the attack? Ailsa thought this was possible, then firmly told herself it didn't matter what the extent of the attack was, whether he had been extra rough or extra cruel. If he either had sex with her against her will or had not stopped when she decided to say 'no', or whatever scenario there was, it was still rape. She had witnessed the girl, in the refuge of the bedroom at Trannoch, absolutely distraught and breaking her heart. She had not heard Ailsa come in the room, and there was no exaggeration there. It was absolutely real, she was sure of it. What had been fake had been Stephen's surprise that Ailsa was there, with Clem, accusing him again for a second time. She should really go to the police, although this was the last thing Olivia wanted, begging her not to, and it was Olivia's prerogative. There were other people to be considered though, Clem for one, despite what she might think of Ailsa at present.

Gennina had said that the MacKenzie children always came to the party, latterly to help, as they were mostly teenagers now. The oldest children attending were around twelve, in Primary Seven their last year of primary school. After the buses had emptied the children into the ballroom, the car pulled up the drive with the MacKenzies. Melissa came in holding little Aria's hand, Ryan, Aria's brother walking truculently into what he considered to be a 'lassies' party', to quote him. David, Malcolm's son, was a responsible prefect at his school, and proceeded to take charge of some of the hordes of children in the hall. Melody, the only grown up one of the MacKenzie children, took a glass of wine from the adult's drink's table, and perched on a small table at the side to view the proceedings. Ailsa moved over and sat beside her.

'Melody, it's good to see you here,' Ailsa said warmly.

'What do you want me to do?' she asked, flicking a tendril of her beautiful auburn hair from her face. Her emerald eyes pierced Ailsa's as she spoke, and Ailsa suddenly realised, with shock, that Clem could have spoken to her daughter about earlier. She felt very vulnerable and exposed, like a one-woman band with a mission, and perhaps it was made worse since she felt unwell. Ailsa had never had that mother-daughter grown up relationship with her adoptive mother, who had died before the two really got a chance to become close as adults, so it hadn't dawned on Ailsa that Clem may have taken Melody into her confidence, until now.

Luckily Gennina came over at this point, armed with the running order of the party on a clip board, and spirited Melody away.

The band were excellent. Ailsa tried not to catch Dougie's eye, but did find that every time she involuntarily looked up, his eyes were upon her.

The party went like clockwork. There was Scottish country dancing, which had been taught to the children for the last six weeks during their gym sessions, so that they could participate with all the right steps.

The dining room had been set up with long trestle tables where they all sat and gorged on the usual party goodies, which gladdened the hearts of the children, before they were ushered back through to the ballroom where the lights had been dimmed and the only light came from the twinkling of the Christmas tree. The children were very excited when they saw the darkened room and there were whispers of, 'Santa's coming! Its Santa,' and Ailsa sat at the side to watch the fun.

'You need to come up to the tree, Ailsa,' Gennina said briskly. 'This is the bit where Santa comes in and you help with giving out the presents. Is that okay?' she asked, doubtfully as she looked at Ailsa's white face and weary expression.

'Yes, of course,' was all she said, and Ailsa made her way up to the tree.

The band played 'Jingle Bells' and the children all sang and clapped, then the door opened, and Santa came in carrying a sack. The expressions on the faces of the younger children were a sight to behold, and Ailsa felt herself buoyed with the festive atmosphere.

'Ailsa, this is Santa,' Gennina said, with a giggle.

'Santa' took her hand and gave a mock bow. He stood up straight and Ailsa looked into his eyes. It was Stephen Millburn.

When the children had all dispatched to their buses, the remaining people were joined by the rest of the MacKenzie clan for some refreshments; Gennina had explained that this was the usual custom after the Christmas Party. Ailsa had arranged for a buffet afternoon tea, and as they milled about, she picked out Melissa MacKenzie, sitting in a window seat, apart from the rest, with a small plate of crisps and a sandwich. Ailsa nodded towards the window seat.

'May I?'

'Why, what do you want?' Melissa looked at her sullenly. 'If you have come to discuss what I think you have, then I'm not interested.'

'It was good to have you helping this afternoon.'

'I didn't do much.' Again, that petulant expression which reminded Ailsa of Malcolm, her father.

'But what you did do was appreciated. This is my first time doing the Children's Party and I had no idea what to expect.' Her head had started to spin again, and her throat felt like cut glass. She was beginning to burn up too. Her face was flushed with the fever which was beginning to take a grip of her.

'You may as well just say what you are going to say.' Melissa had that canny knack of being blunt without sounding rude. 'It's something about what I said at the funeral.'

'Yes,' Ailsa felt that she owed the girl honesty above all else. 'Yes,' Ailsa coughed a chesty cough. 'I think we should talk about what you said. You said something like *I saw him*, which I am not sure about and need to be clear about who you meant. You also said that your brother David had seen him too, but that he wouldn't admit it. What did you mean by that, Melissa?'

Melissa was very quiet as she took all this in, but she looked at Ailsa and suddenly said, 'Are you okay, Ailsa? You don't look well. Are you ill or something?'

'More wine, Ma'am?' Olivia had been walking about with a tray, filling people's glasses. After she topped up Ailsa's, she made her way over to a little clutch of people consisting of the Colonel, Stephen Millburn and a few others. Ailsa watched her go. Olivia smiled up at the Colonel as she emptied some red wine into his glass, and then, turning to Stephen, smiled up at him too. They exchanged what looked like a few pleasantries and she topped up his glass with a beaming smile. Then she moved away to another group. Ailsa was astonished. How could she react that way to the man who had in her own words, 'molested' her?

Suddenly, she felt quite faint. She thought she was going to be sick as scenes from the past months flooded her mind and coldly touched her soul. She stood up, swayed, and, for the first time in her life, fainted. Ailsa had no idea of the sensation she had caused until she was back to normal. When she had stood up from the window seat and subsequently fell at Melissa's feet, the party had come to a standstill. Of the adults who remained, several then rushed to her aid, doing all the usual first aid things while Max was sought for his help. The room was cleared, and only a few stayed, whilst Jim Hutton, the ever-faithful, was dispatched to Trannoch to fetch Max's bag. Ailsa was carried up to her own bedroom, still delirious and semi-conscious.

The result of Max's diagnosis was that she was suffering from flu, not 'pretend flu' as he lost no time in letting the little audience know that this common misconception was his personal frustration with his patient base. They mistook a head cold and ordinary feverishness for flu, but Ailsa's happened to be real slam dunk flu. He gave her an injection, and a prescription and a packet of strong painkillers to Miss Cochrane, who was clucking about the room like a mother hen. Gennina had found Ailsa's pyjamas, and the rest of the little group dispersed when she began to get Ailsa ready for bed.

'She is going to be really ill for the next two days, feverish, and probably delirious, as she is now,' Max explained patiently to the housekeeper. 'I will call in every day, but meanwhile, give her the antibiotics and painkillers, and help her to drink plenty. Do you want me to arrange for a private nurse for her?'

'Certainly not!' Miss Cochrane looked positively aghast at the mere idea. Gennina can leave her estate duties for the next few days and help me here.' At which Gennina looked askance, she was no nurse, but did not dare to contradict Miss Cochrane, who was very determined.

'Okay, well, you will probably need to change the bed linen each day, maybe during the night, as she will sweat profusely as she is beginning to do now, and we can't have her lying on a wet bed. The injection I have given her will start off her medication, but she needs to be sponged regularly to keep her fever down. The strong paracetamol will help very shortly with this too.' He took out the thermometer and tutted at the apparently very high reading. He packed up and left shortly after, leaving Miss Cochrane and Gennina looking at their employer with mixed reservations, but not speaking a word of their worries.

'I'll get the room next to mine made up for you, if you like?' Miss Cochrane spoke hopefully that the younger woman would consent to stay in at Storm Winds and help with the patient.

'Okay, just let me phone for some clothes and stuff.'

It was the next evening before Ailsa was fully wakened and semi-coherent. Max had been in to see her in the morning, and, although she was awake, she was 'spaced-out' to quote Gennina, and knew nothing much of what passed that day. By the third day she was sitting up in bed, reading for a short time, although she still slept most of the day. Max faithfully attended her, much to her displeasure, when she was well enough to notice.

'Now, just you listen here,' Miss Cochrane said, on the fourth day, when Ailsa was well enough to sit by her fire in her bedroom, and had even found the energy to moan about the fact that Max MacKenzie was there each morning, despite the fact that she had taken the trouble to enlist with a doctor in Fort William, as she did not want to be a patient of his. 'Maxwell MacKenzie was here on the spot when you fainted and has looked after you since last Saturday, when you couldn't even lift your head.'

'As have you, Miss Cochrane.' The voice came from the door as the doctor appeared in time to hear these words.

'Thank you, Doctor,' Miss Cochrane said humbly, and left the room with a tray in her hand.

'Cocky is exhausted,' he said shortly.

'I know she is,' Ailsa said, with a stubborn set to her jaw. 'I'm sorry, but I just can't help that I was unconscious and couldn't make any decisions.' For the first time since she became ill, Ailsa felt tearful.

'You should give her some time off. I have a retired nurse who works occasionally for the practice who could help you out for a few days.' He spoke gruffly, and, it had to be owned, with a certain amount of patronising authority in his voice which maddened Ailsa.

'I don't think she would be happy to take some time off,' Ailsa said sulkily.

'Is that for you to decide, or are you going to actually ask her?'

'Of course, I'll ask her! You can send that woman of yours over, although God knows I don't need anyone else interfering,' she said, pointedly looking at him, 'And, I'll give both Cocky and Gennina the rest of the week off. Will that satisfy you?'

'You know, you really have a terrible attitude on you.' Max shoved the thermometer unceremoniously in her mouth. 'Now just try and shut up for a moment, hot tempers make the mercury rise.'

Ailsa looked at him with steely dark eyes, though she did keep her mouth shut until he pulled the thermometer away. 'Are you always this nice and homely with your patients? I wonder you actually have any at all.'

'And I wonder you have any staff the way you treat them. Look Ailsa, I am actually worried about Miss Cochrane, she looks done-in, and she may well have caught influenza from you, you know.'

'Yes, of course I had thought of that,' she snapped 'although I wasn't exactly in the position to decide who would look after me over the last few days.'

'No, I realise that. I'll send Nurse Stewart over today, and I'll go and see Miss Cochrane now.' Before Ailsa could answer, he had shut his bag with a snap and left the room with her seething in his wake.

Miss Stewart arrived later that day and reported to Ailsa that both Miss Cochrane and Gennina were down with the flu and in bed. 'I'm afraid I will be looking after them, as a priority, as you seem to be on the mend.' Her tones were more strident than Miss Cochrane's had been in the early days, and Ailsa could just imagine her terrorising the wards of the Glasgow Royal Infirmary in days gone by.

'The patients would be terrified to be sick at all!' she mused, more to herself than anything, but Miss Stewart's sharp hearing picked up some of it and frowned.

'Well, you're lucky to have that fine doctor looking after you all. I've known Maxwell since he was a wee boy, and he is a better man than I have ever known.'

'Really? You do surprise me!' and to herself she said, untruthfully, 'And I bet you have known plenty.'

Chapter Twenty

Both Miss Cochrane and Gennina were down with the flu bug, Gennina still at Storm Winds, in the bedroom next to Miss Cochrane's apartment, and the doctor came in to see them every day. On the following Thursday, a full five days after she became ill, Ailsa was still shaky and unfit for anything but sitting up for an hour, then bed for the rest of the day. Miss Stewart looked after all three of them, her bark was worse than her bite, although she was a fearsome creature in her own right and stuck rigidly to the nursing rules she had learned over forty years ago.

The Trannoch household was wakening up on the Friday after the Christmas Party, and the family gathered at the breakfast table. With the children home from school it was a much bigger crowd than normal, and dishes clinked, piles of food were spooned onto plates, toast crunched and newspapers rustled as they all consumed their breakfasts.

Denbeath arrived with the mail on a silver tray, such was the tradition still upheld at Trannoch, and proceeded to dish out the letters.

'Daddy, Mhairi has asked if I can go to her house for a sleepover on Saturday, can I go?' Max's daughter spread her toast liberally with marmalade as she spoke, then licked her fingers one by one.

'You mean, may I, not can I,' Max said, with a smile.

'What's the diff'rence?'

'I know what the difference is cos I'm much older than you,' her brother Ryan piped up. 'Can I means am I able to, and may I means am I allowed.' He puffed up with importance at this explanation which had been drilled into him by his Housemaster at school.

'You're only twelve, that's only two years older than me, anyhow!' Aria snapped back, ignoring the explanation completely.

'You can't be expected to know everything, Aria,' David laughed at his little cousin. 'You're only in junior school, but you're top in most of your class subjects, anyway,' the school prefect spoke kindly, wise in his years.

Aria ignored this, 'Daddy, everybody has wee blue envelopes the same,' she said, pointing to the letters at each of the places. 'I've not got one, neither's any of us 'cept the grown-ups, they all have.'

'Don't they teach you to speak decent English at all at that school?' Malcolm said, from behind his paper. 'Ten grand a term for each of them and you can't even string a proper sentence together.'

Max threw down his napkin in a rage at this. 'Yes, well you include your own offspring in that, and it's my twenty grand a term which sends Aria and Ryan. Aria is only ten for God's sake, stop picking on her.'

'Only stating a fact, little brother.'

'Right you two, stop it right now.' It was the Colonel, of course, booming across the table as if he was behind a megaphone. 'I'm sick of all this bickering at my table.'

'Aria, of course you may go, pet.' Max began to open his own letters.

'An invitation!' Carys said, with an upturn of her nose as she opened her blue envelope. 'Oh, it's from *Lady Hamilton-Dunbar* she continued, with a sniff of derision. 'When did she start signing her full title?'

'Good morning, everyone!' Hunter swept into the room at this point, taking centre stage as usual. 'No kippers this morning?' She filled her plate from the dishes on the sideboard and sat down beside Malcolm. Max looked at her and shook his head, but said nothing.

'It's for tonight!' Carys continued. 'That's a bit short notice! Does she think we are all just sitting around waiting for her to summon us?'

'You will go, unless you have a prior engagement,' the Colonel said, with decision, and Carys did not flinch one iota at this, but sneered and began to eat her poached egg daintily.

'We don't have any other engagement, Father,' Thomas rushed to say, and Carys looked at him in anger. Secretly she wouldn't miss it for the world, any chance for a catty word here and there was good in her book.

Hunter had begun her breakfast when she realised that she didn't have one of the blue envelopes. 'I see my daughter has forgotten to include me!' She threw back her head with a snide laugh.

'You can be my plus one,' the Colonel said, beaming across the table at her, and oblivious to Malcolm's raised eyebrows and sulky expression.

'Oh, can I?' she gushed. 'Terrific! What a splendid idea!'

'Daddy, doesn't she mean 'may I'?' Aria asked her father seriously, and he exploded in laughter. He then read his own invitation.

'What is Ailsa doing inviting us all round when she is still recovering from 'flu?' he spat out to no one in particular.

'Maybe she wants us to cheer her up, darling, after her illness.' Hunter stabbed a piece of bacon and waved it in the air as she spoke. 'Maybe she wants to show off her little figure. She must have lost a pile of weight since she became ill. She takes after me, of course, in her slight figure. She must look positively scrawny now.'

'She does no such thing, and cheer her up, indeed. She should be taking it easy and not throwing dinner parties, she's still got a day's worth of antibiotics to take.'

Hunter ignored Max. 'It says an evening buffet, not a dinner party. How very modern,' she quipped, as she read over Malcolm's invite.

'Well, I will have something to say to her when I see her anyway,' Max said, getting up from the table.

Ailsa was in her library that evening, when Miss Stewart arrived, the nurse's expression quietly seething, and a black scowl adorning her lined face.

'A car has just drawn up, Lady Ailsa, and people have arrived,' she said, her voice tight.

'Oh? People?' Ailsa glanced down at her jogging trousers and hoodie.

'Yes, Jim has met them and shown them into the front sitting room. They are dressed, evening wear, I mean, and one of them showed Jim this.' She handed Ailsa an invitation.

Ailsa read it quickly with rising alarm. 'Where did this come from? I didn't write these, or print them as it seems to be – where did they get them? Who has arrived, Miss Stewart?'

'All of the MacKenzie family adults.'

'*What?* Where the hell did these come from? Who wrote them? Is Jean still here?'

'I believe so, Ma'am, and I have taken the liberty of asking Jim to talk to Cook about the buffet on the invites, but she will be none too pleased.'

'She'll be absolutely bloody furious!' Ailsa sprang to her feet. 'Miss Stewart, can you and Jim manage to serve drinks and nibbles, while I run-up and dress? I can't believe this has happened! Who the hell . . .?'

'I think you had better just do as you say, Ma'am.' Miss Stewart's face spoke loudly of her feelings that this was over and above the call of duty.

Ailsa turned back when she got to the door. 'Is Max there too?'

'Yes, the doctor is here, and he lost no time in informing me that I should not have let you do this tonight, but I was as much in the dark as you are and had no answer to give him.'

'Shit,' Ailsa retaliated, and walked out of the door and up the stairs as quickly as her weak legs would carry her.

'My sentiments entirely,' Miss Stewart said to herself, as she turned on her heel and prepared to cater to the guests.

'Ailsa!' The Colonel sprang to his feet ten minutes later, as a thinner, listless Ailsa joined them in her front sitting room. Music had been put on in the background, and some small tables had been set with crisps and hastily prepared canapés, whilst Jim Hutton served drinks. Miss Stewart had met her in the hall and informed her that Olivia had volunteered to help and had been commandeered into action. She was helping Jean in the kitchen, so there would be a buffet of sorts but not for an hour or so yet.

'Good evening, everyone.' Ailsa said weakly and took a glass of red wine from Jim. 'Thank you for coming. Please help yourselves to nibbles as the buffet won't be ready for an hour yet, I do hope that suits you all?' It was said with a polished confident voice, so different to the Ailsa who had arrived at Storm Winds almost a year ago. Everyone started to relax and talk amiably.

She sat next to the Colonel, as usual, trying to ignore Hunter who appeared in the corner of her eye, talking to Malcolm. Max, on the couch opposite, frowned deeply at his patient, and when the Colonel stood up to fetch another drink, he leaned forward, his voice wringing with consternation.

'What are you thinking of, entertaining so soon after you have been ill?'

'Actually, I wasn't thinking at all about entertaining,' she said, looking straight at him, almost willing him to carry on with this questioning.

'What's that supposed to mean? Do you think we just all came here uninvited?'

'Not at all, in fact, I know you were all invited as Miss Stewart let me see one of the invitations, but I didn't write or send them. She came into the library where I was sitting *resting,*' she emphasised the word, 'and told me you had all arrived. It's not that I didn't want you all to come over, I always enjoy a bit of MacKenzie company, it's just that I didn't invite you, and I have no idea who did, or why.'

Max studied her face as if looking for any trace that she might be having him on.

'So, you don't believe me?' She suddenly flared as she took in his look. 'You know, you can be a right pain in the butt at times, Max.'

'Oh, really?' He was starting to get angry too. 'Well, the only reason I came over tonight was to tell you what I thought about you, for not following my instructions.'

'Well, I am so sorry if I have not been able to do what I was told, and instead chose to burst your bubble with the truth.'

'I was concerned for you, you've had a really bad bout of flu and . . .'

'Oh, shut up about the God damned 'flu. I am sick of hearing about the stupid 'flu, and to be perfectly honest, I am glad, *glad* that everyone has come over tonight, because I am sick and tired of being told what to do by a jumped-up doctor who thinks he is the big 'I am'.'

Max looked at her in disgust, at this tirade, then amusement, and he finally burst out laughing. 'Well, you certainly told me, Lady Ailsa,' he said, and got up to go and talk to Stephen Millburn and Thomas who were at the other side of the room. When the flush had gone from her cheeks, she looked up and caught Hunter's eyes on her, looking at her daughter with a knowing expression. Ailsa quickly looked away.

Jean Morton, Cook at Storm Winds, did the party proud with a magnificent buffet, which she and Olivia then laid on the table in the dining room for people to fill their plates and sit around in groups at the tables placed for their convenience. It wasn't a huge group, so, while unexpected, it was manageable from Jean's perspective. A raging fire burned brightly in the grate, and the still open curtains revealed that it was snowing heavily outside. Ailsa noticed that Clem was not present as Stephen's partner, and wondered if she had received an invitation and decided not to come, or if the mysterious letter writer had somehow left her out. Hunter kept out of Ailsa's way, although she did try and catch her glance now and again with a pathetic, but what she considered to be an endearing smile, and which Ailsa studiously ignored. Ailsa asked Jim Hutton to join them for the meal, but he staunchly refused saying he 'knew his place' in such a serious voice that Ailsa didn't press him. Besides, as he pointed out, the party needed a server of drinks, especially Malcolm who was knocking them back like there was no tomorrow.

Ailsa was people watching. It was only the MacKenzies, granted, but they were a really fascinating bunch. For all their talents, they were dysfunctional as a family, and it was interesting to watch the way they interacted with each other. Hunter was like a sleek beautiful predator, with Malcolm at her heels, and the Colonel apparently unaware of the developing relationship between his son and his ex-lover. Ailsa had guessed at it, as she had witnessed many meaningful glances between the two recently. Thomas, sweet and endearing, was totally unable to be anything other than a lap dog to Carys, a cold and calculating woman, second only to Hunter. Carys seemed to be completely devoid of feeling for anyone but herself. Stephen Millburn, the unofficial adopted son of the MacKenzies was harder to read. Ailsa still felt such mixed emotions for this man. Firstly, she had fallen for his rugged good looks and charm, but latterly thought him to be a philandering, cold man, who, when he didn't get what he wanted, moved quickly on to the next best thing. She had basically gone to hell and back mentally, over Stephen, but still did not know what he was capable of in terms of the molestation accusation by Olivia. Malcolm was a salacious, insecure man, the most handsome of the MacKenzies, but also the most self-centred and selfish man she had ever met. He was the most spoilt of the MacKenzie brood, and poor Belinda's death hung heavy on Ailsa's mind, as she was convinced that it was partly the outcome of her marriage with Malcolm. Max, she could not work out. Everyone seemed to admire him but her. What was it about him that drove her to the deepest dislike she had for any of them, in him? His attitude towards her was one thing, but he was patronising and controlling, and, if she was honest with herself, she would own that it was his apparent lack of respect towards her, whilst all around her fell at her knees, figuratively speaking, which really galled her.

She could not see this, as yet, though. In her own mind she was very proud of the title bestowed on her by Sir Angus, and, although she did not wish people to use it as an everyday nome de plume, she wanted others to be as respectful of the family history as she herself had grown to be. Although people teased her about her title, Max seemed to somehow not even acknowledge it unless he was patronising her and this was something which confused and exasperated her in equal measure. She could not work him out.

Then there was Noel. She could not remember having a single conversation with the man who was Clem's ex-husband. As the oldest, he seemed to take the heavy weight of responsibility on his shoulders, but he blended calmly into the background. Noel was not witty and sarcastic like Max, or sensitive like Thomas or sexy like Malcolm. In fact, he was, on the surface, a very ordinary guy who did not put himself forward in social situations. Noel was a dark horse.

They moved back through to the sitting room, where a fire was blazing, and a collection of bottles of various spirits and wines had been put on a sideboard to save Jim Hutton playing footman for much longer. Miss Stewart had departed from the social gathering, to see to her patients for the last time in the evening, and had then retired, exhausted, to bed.

There was a baby grand piano in the corner on which Ailsa had been taking lessons, but she was not nearly accomplished enough to perform yet. Carys obliged her, with a supercilious air, by playing beautifully for half an hour. Malcolm also, surprisingly, played a few modern musical hits, his chubby fingers gliding surprisingly lightly across the keyboard. By this time, as most people in the room were more than merry, they joined in with a sing-song. Ailsa, though she possessed a nice soprano voice, sat quietly in the corner sipping her second glass of red wine. She had determined not to get too tipsy and listened with quiet enjoyment to the music.

The Colonel, who had a rich baritone voice, sang 'Oh Holy Night', and Stephen Millburn, with a tenor any choir would be proud to call its own, sang several songs from 'Les Misérables', including 'Bring him home,' Ailsa's favourite. Thomas then took to the ivories, and, after several tunes, Malcolm was called for again to sing, but he was not in the room. Ailsa, being the most sober of the lot, noticed that Hunter too, was missing. So, she was right, there was something going on with them both. They slipped back in, half an hour later, and five minutes apart, with Ailsa not being the only one to notice that they looked slightly flushed and dishevelled.

'May I sit with my insubordinate patient?' Ailsa looked up and saw Max hovering above her, a drink in his hand, pointing to the place next to her on the sofa and close by the fire. His face had an almost imperceptible glaze of comfortable placidness, brought on by the alcohol he had drank, and an unusual look for him.

'If you're going to lecture me again, please don't bother.'

He sat down anyway. 'How much have you had?'

'Not as much as you, apparently, and none of your business,' she said sweetly, 'and actually, now you mention it, I have just finished this glass, so I am going to fill it up.'

'I'll get it for you.' Max almost snatched her glass and went over to the table to replenish it.

'Wow, alcohol suits you, you should do it more often,' she said sarcastically, as he sat back down beside her.

'Ailsa, I'm sorry, I'm really not that good at new friendships, and I feel I have not really been very nice to you.'

She stopped in her tracks, almost chocking on her wine, as she searched his face for any sign of sarcasm but found only sincerity which rocked her backwards in amazement.

'So, I'm a 'new friendship' am I? Well whatever I thought you would say . . . '

'No, I don't imagine you would think I would have said something like that, but hey, I am having a good evening, and I wanted to set the record straight.'

'Did you just say, "*but hey*"?'

'I might have done.'

'Don't ever say that again.'

'Okay,' He actually grinned at her.

'Well, I suppose I haven't really held out the hand of friendship to you, either,' she said this, realising with surprise, that this was really how she felt.

'Fancy starting over again?' He moved slightly closer to her in a clumsy, boyish way.

'Okay, why not?'

The door opened on the rise of voices as they sung a well-known Christmas song together, and Ailsa was the first to notice the solitary figure in the light of the doorway.

'Next year all your troubles will be miles away . . .'

'Oh my God, what the hell . . .'

'So, have yourself . . . a . . .'

It was a few moments before the room at large noticed the figure, and people exclaimed as they began to compute what was happening.

The music stopped, everyone stopped. The atmosphere crackled with fear and shocked anticipation.

Olivia stood with both arms outstretched, holding a gun, a revolver, pointed and swaying as her eyes roved the room, apparently seeking someone.

'Olivia, what the hell are you doing?' Ailsa sprang to her feet, but Max's strong grip pulled her back down and slightly behind him, out of the way.

'What do you think you are doing?' someone shouted.

'Who is she? What are you playing at?'

'What the hell . . .?'

'Put that thing down and be sensible!' The exclamations came thick and fast.

'I have something to say.' Her Italian accent was deep, her voice tremulous, and the gun swung about erratically.

'Who are you, what are you doing here?' Hunter tried to take command of the situation but was silenced by the Colonel.

'I have something to say, sit down, all of you. I no be interrupted,' she said, again, and like one body, they all sat down. 'You think I just small Italian nobody, you are wrong. You wronged me you people, for this you . . . you must pay.' The gun was shaking now with the obvious emotion of the girl, and the tension in the room was electric and palpable. 'I bring you all here tonight, I, Olivia. No her.' And she pointed the gun at Ailsa, amidst the gasps of the room. 'I bring you here as I tell you what you all done to me.'

'She's absolutely mad! Can't someone stop her?' Stephen began to rise in his seat, but as he did so, a bullet ricocheted by his side, sending a fresh shock wave through the room. Ailsa gasped, and Max put his hand behind him, found hers and gripped it hard.

Malcolm, Noel and Stephen, who were sitting in a little group, looked fearfully at each other, and Noel sprang to his feet. 'Look, whatever you think we may have done, this is no way to address the situation . . .' Another bullet rang out to the left of Noel, and the group cowered in submission.

'I say you listen, and you *will* listen!' Olivia screamed out, and the room silenced again. 'As you see, as you all know, I with child.' Her quaint Italian translation was lost on them as they stared, transfixed, into her eyes. 'I not conceive naturally, I was molested.' The silence morphed into shock. 'I was molested, I cast aside, but I am here to claim the father. That is what I come to do!'

Noel again stood up, but this time he was incensed with anger. 'You stupid bitch!' He shouted. 'You stupid, stupid . . .' again a bullet fired, and this time Noel screamed in agony and dropped to the floor. They swarmed in towards him, heedless of the fact that Olivia still had the gun, and, as Ailsa looked towards the door, she was gone.

Max was first to his brother's aid, tying a tourniquet to stop the bleeding whilst shouting instructions to get ice and a blanket. There was no further thought of the Italian girl. Ailsa, left behind in the crowd, almost in a daze, floundered towards the front door, which was lying open, the swirling blizzard of snow flying into the hall.

Miss Cochrane, with a huge shawl wrapped around her, and curlers in her hair which would have been funny at any other time, rushed unsteadily up to Ailsa. 'What was that? Ailsa, did I hear a gun shot?'

Ailsa, still in shock and dazed by the episode, turned to her and slowly nodded, then walked into the icy wind and swirling snow.

'Ailsa! Oh, my dear God, come back! Where are you going?' the ill Miss Cochrane shouted, in vain, as the solitary figure vanished into the blackened night.

Chapter Twenty-One

She didn't get far, as Malcolm caught up with her, holding a coat sent by Miss Cochrane.

'Get inside, Ailsa. You are ill. I'll go after that stupid girl, now go, and no arguing!' He tried to look concerned, through the haze of alcohol, but his expression was dark and almost threatening. Ailsa, drenched in snow, suddenly came to her senses and turned to go back to the house. After she took a few steps, she looked back again and saw Malcolm running towards the headland as if wild horses were after him. Suddenly something snapped in her brain and she heard the *kerchink* of ideas which had been milling around in her mind but going nowhere.

Malcolm.

– I saw him, I *saw* him! –

'Oh my God!'

Ailsa started to run in the direction Malcolm had just taken, her legs slipping underneath her from the heavy fallen snow and weakness in her limbs, pulling the coat around her to try and take away some of the iciness of the wind which battered her, and the snow which danced dizzyingly in front of her against a blackened sky.

Malcolm

She stopped at one point and looked back towards the house and saw a line of uneven dancing beams coming from a group bearing torches, which only hastened her flight, as help was on the way. Malcolm had gone along the left-hand side cliff path, in the opposite direction from Arnasaid, and one which Ailsa seldom took. This was because it was this path she had gone with Bluebell and Rosie just before she had fallen over the side, and she had no wish to repeat this episode. She could see Malcolm, still in the distance, slipping and sliding in the heavy snow, getting precariously near to the edge in his pursuit of Olivia. She stumbled along, her head pounding with the thoughts she could not escape, that Malcolm was the one who had taken advantage of Olivia, not Stephen Millburn at all. The reasons all falling into place. That night when she had come across Olivia, the girl had not said who her attacker was, it was Ailsa who had put two and two together to make many more than four, after she had seen the two of them at the Highland Games. It was why Olivia, earlier on in the evening, had smiled up at Stephen as if she knew and liked him, not hated him for what he was supposed to have done, and when she had shot Noel earlier, who was sitting beside both Stephen and Malcolm, she had presumed the girl had tried to hit Stephen, but the bullet had been for Malcolm, and Olivia had missed. The other thing which was beginning to click with Ailsa was Belinda, whose own daughter Melissa had practically accused her father of driving Belinda to her to her death. 'I saw him . . . *I saw him,*' was what Melissa had said, and her brother David had seen the same as she had, which was presumably Malcolm attacking his own wife, but they had done nothing about it. Poor Belinda. Poor, poor Melissa and David. What must they have gone through when Belinda died? The guilt must have been tremendous.

Malcolm had even tried to attack her, at the Ghillies' Ball, and, if the circumstances had allowed, she might have been raped by him that night too. She stopped for breath, her lungs felt as if they were about to collapse, her legs were just about giving way beneath her, and her head was swimming with pain and misery.

Malcolm

Then there was Max. It had been Max who had come to fight off his brother. To save her, as he had saved her more than once. She had mistaken his concern for her as patronising control and dislike, and Ailsa's eyes spilled over with tears as she thought about the way she had treated him. She had been horrible to Max. She had misjudged him, she had misjudged Stephen and she had misjudged Malcolm, although his crimes had been staring her in the face all this time.

Malcolm

As she stopped there, now sobbing with deep emotion and fear, she saw Malcolm standing, a few feet away from the edge of the cliff, Olivia teetering on the brink. His back was to Ailsa, his arms flailing in the air as he shouted at the Italian, who she could just see behind the shape of him. They were beginning to struggle; it looked like Malcolm had a stranglehold on the girl, his hands on her.

He was trying to wring her neck.

'No!! No!!' Was all that Ailsa could shout, the sound deadening against the wall of snowstorm between them. She scrambled forward – the path was beginning to get rocky here, and with the snow rapidly turning to ice she could hardly stand.

The sound reached him, and he momentarily let go, and swung round to face her. She was about fifty yards from them by this time.

'Ailsa, get back to the house!' he screamed manically.

'No!' she said again. 'Leave her alone, Malcolm!'

'Ailsa, go away!' he screeched again. 'You idiot! You have no idea! Get away from us, or I'll do the same thing to you, I promise you!' As his eyes were on Ailsa, the silent figure slipped to the left and drew both hands up in front of her, the gun poised.

'No!' It seemed Ailsa was incapable of saying anything else, but as she lunged forward, her hands flying to her mouth in shock, the shot rang out through the snowy air, and Malcolm, who had taken a few steps in Ailsa's direction suddenly froze in his tracks, his face seared with pain as he staggered back round towards Olivia, swayed a little, tripped, careered forward and disappeared over the edge of the cliff.

Olivia fell to her knees in the snow, her face running with tears and the gun lying by her side. Ailsa ran over to her and put her arms around her, both bodies wracked with sobs. The dancing lights seemed to quicken, then neared the two, kneeling together in the snow. For Ailsa, time seemed to halt. She felt as though she were underwater. Loud voices floated around her, arms gripped her gently and pulled her up, blankets wrapped her, brandy forced its way into her mouth and she remembered nothing of being half-carried, half-led, back to the house. All she could remember was looking up and seeing the black universe spilling out the snow, which darted at her from all directions, finding her face and numbing the pain away.

It was Hogmanay, and Ailsa was standing on the headland. The day was wintery sharp with frost, the landed snow glittering like millions of stars in the weak afternoon sunshine. She had left the dogs at home and was making the pilgrimage back to the place where Olivia had shot Malcolm. It had been a calm, clear day although the wind was now quickening slightly. The Small Isles sparkled in the winter water, the blues and greens glorious against the jagged coastline. The picture was angled slightly differently at this part of the headland, but beautiful all the same. The Cullin ridge on Skye, icy white and darting upwards; the onset of sunset the backdrop.

She had spent a very quiet Christmas, no visitors from London, and only Miss Cochrane there with her on Christmas Day. This had been her choice. Jean Morton had prepared a simple Christmas dinner for them, and, at Ailsa's insistence, joined them to eat. Her friends had asked her to come south to join in their festivities, but she didn't have the energy to do so. Gennina brought her boyfriend for Christmas drinks later, which again, was a quiet affair, and they only stayed for an hour. Miss Stewart had gone back to her home in Arnasaid. The Colonel had visited her early on Boxing Day. He had invited her over for Boxing Day lunch, but Ailsa was still very much unnerved by the happenings and could think of nothing worse than spending the day with the MacKenzies. She was inclined to be jittery and tearful.

Malcolm was *not dead*.

This was something Ailsa struggled with but tried to accept. What helped her bear it was the thought that it would have been heartbreaking for David and Melissa to lose both parents in the one year. He had been airlifted by the helicopter ambulance whose crew had spent over two hours in atrocious conditions trying to free him from the outcrop of bushes on the cliff side into which he had fallen. The bullet had hit him in the chest, puncturing a lung and only just missing his heart. He had lost a lot of blood. The police had been called, of course, and had started an investigation, but no charges were brought. Noel's bullet wound had been, in the main, superficial. The main protagonists had been primed by the Colonel to say it had been an accident. The MacKenzie clan had wielded their own special weaponry of power, and the case was subsequently thrown out.

The most astonishing part of all of this was that Olivia was moving into Trannoch to raise her baby as a MacKenzie, and, when he was well, Malcolm was to come back to Trannoch, but to live separately to Olivia. She had been in hospital for two nights' rest after the incident, then she had stayed with a student friend in Fort William. After the initial shock had worn off, Olivia had agreed to come and live at Trannoch; the Colonel had been very persuasive. He wanted his grandchild to be brought up there, and this situation suited both Olivia and Malcolm. Olivia, as her baby would be brought up in one of the wealthiest families in Scotland, and she herself would want for nothing; and Malcolm, thanks to the Colonel, would stay out of prison. In addition to this, the Colonel had visited Malcolm only once in hospital alone and had a long talk with his son. He informed him what the family arrangements would be and warned him that if he ever touched Olivia again he would sling him out on his ear, completely disinherit him, and instruct the police to re-open the case, with the family as witnesses.

Following the Colonel's visit, Ailsa had gone to see Clem. Thankfully, Stephen just happened to be there too, and she had made her peace with them. They were so understanding of the mistake she had made, and so forgiving, that Ailsa had felt quite overcome. Any feelings or emotions for Stephen she had felt in the early days had now vanished. She was happy that he and Clem were now firmly together.

Ailsa had never been to her villa in Italy, and, on impulse, decided to book a last-minute flight. As the plane touched down she felt a certain trepidation – was she running away? Yes, she probably was, but she needed to get her thoughts in order and come to terms with what had happened. Being on her own in Italy might not help her to work everything out, but at least she would be away from everyone who reminded her of the terrible events of that evening.

She filled the days walking, thinking and scribbling notes for her writing which she hoped she would be able to resume very soon. The villa was a moderately sized one, with three bedrooms, and an outside pool, with a view of the ocean. She just needed to be alone. She ate in a tiny restaurant, around the corner, and discovered they made the best pizza she had ever eaten. She had even managed to read a book she had been meaning to read for some time but never got round to. She found it hard to focus, such were the tumultuous thoughts coursing through her brain, but she tried to soak herself up in the gentle post-Christmas atmosphere, and come to terms with what had happened.

A small terrace led out from the main sitting room and overlooked the garden and the sea beyond, where she thought she would like to spend most of her time in the summer. There was lots of work to do to the place, mainly decoration, and she had determined that when she arrived back home she would make enquiries with the cleaning and caretaker agency, who managed the place, to find a decorator.

She had her laptop with her but used it only for the internet and keeping up with events as they progressed in her absence. The little holiday did more to heal her wounds than anything else would have done, and she enjoyed the experience, despite everything. Orbatello, in south west Tuscany, has the hills and forests behind it, and the ocean in front, and is one of the places Italian people go to holiday. Right now, she felt happy just being away and becoming accustomed to a different place. There weren't a lot of English-speaking people there, not like the main Italian resorts, but this made Ailsa like it even more, and think that when things got back to some sort of normality, she would do as she had always promised herself she would do, and learn Italian.

It felt good to touch down at Glasgow Airport, and find her car and Jim Hutton waiting for her. He threw her small case into the boot and she snuggled down in the back for the long drive up to Arnasaid, which was roughly twice as long as the flight to Italy.

She had missed the dogs so much, and the rapturous welcome they gave her gladdened her heart. Miss Cochrane met her at the front door; so very different a meeting from that first one where she had been received with the icy politeness which had made her feel small and unwanted. This time the housekeeper hugged her and drew her into the warmth of the house. She sat at the kitchen table, Jean cooking a simple lunch of soup and sandwiches, and Miss Cochrane fussing around her, making her tea and asking about Italy. They talked about Orbatello, but not about what had happened before Christmas. Miss Cochrane skirted around the edges, saying 'that Italian girl' had moved in to Trannoch now, and that the MacKenzies were not having their usual Hogmanay Party this year, but that she had been invited over for a midnight toast and some steak pie, as was the custom. Ailsa shook her head in resolute determination. She would perhaps stay up for the bells but would be in her own house, in her own sitting room, with her dogs, and the fire blazing, and most definitely not at Trannoch. Miss Cochrane nodded as if she had expected this.

After having something to eat, she donned her red coat and stepped out into the cold late afternoon. There was something she had to do. She had been thinking about this when she was in Italy. She felt compelled to return to the scene of the crime on the headland with the hope of obscuring it from her memory. She crunched across the garden grass, through the short forest path and onto the headland, where the day opened up its wonders, and the clear skies and sea gave her a slight lurch in her stomach. When she caught sight of this view, she felt she was truly home. She walked further towards the cliff edge, then veered off to the left. After around ten minutes' walk, she stood there looking at the space where Malcolm and Olivia had been, just over a week ago, and could almost hear the screams and shouts. She heard the sea thundering in the background, just as it had done that night, and 'heard' the shot ring out, then 'saw' Malcolm stagger and fall over the side and Olivia drop to her knees. After that it was a blur, and her mind had gone as cold as the snow that night. Just recalling the scene set her mind and heart racing.

She felt a range of emotions move up her body into her head, inescapable tears coursed a pathway down her wind-blown cheeks.

She jumped as she heard a scraping of feet on the stones behind her, and turning, saw the serious and concerned face of Max looking down on her.

Max

She didn't know how she felt at that moment, she was so raw, so tired, so scared of herself and her own emotions. She looked up at him, his hair blowing softly in the sea breeze, his face, his eyes and his stern brow, and another tear escaped the corner of her eye, tracing delicately down her cheek.

'Hi! You're back!' he said, studying her as if he thought she would collapse at any moment. 'Are you okay?'

'Mmmm, fine thanks.' She felt new and old emotions overwhelm her and couldn't trust to either sort them out, or to say anything else.

'How was Italy?' he managed, conversationally.

'Good.' She pulled herself together. 'Can't wait to go back in the warmer weather.'

'Italy was always a favourite place for me. Florence is my favourite city, although I know most people prefer Rome.'

As he talked, he came nearer until they were almost touching. The sky fell, the mountains moved in to surround them, and the smell of land and sea came together.

Without a word, he picked up her face in his hands as he bent forward and kissed her tenderly on the lips. He then folded his arms around her. He enveloped her. His warmth kissed her cheeks, her eyes, her hair, as he held her. She imagined that if he took his arms away she would fall. She looked across to Skye and felt they were floating out to sea. The ground was no longer there.

The sunset was gorgeous. Pinks turning to deep reds, flowing gently over the mountain peaks, the snow glowing warmly. The clouds were gathering over Storm Winds, and the wind was beginning to rise. There would be more snow.

'Nice sunset,' he said.
'Nice sunset,' she agreed.
'Come on, let me take you home.'

He had known his feelings for Ailsa for a long time, but couldn't reach her. After the incident, right here on this very spot, he knew without doubt how he felt for her, but she had refused to face what she had only just begun to believe.

She turned and looked straight into his eyes.

Max

It had always been Max.

Acknowledgements

I would like to thank my family. My daughter Emma, my Mum and my big brother Ian, all of whom had unending faith in me, and made me believe I could 'do it.' They have kept me going, doing what I love, writing; not pushing me to get a 'proper job.' My two other siblings Lorna and Colin, and my friends for their support.

I would also like to say a huge thank you to Margaret and Dan Miller, my brother-in-law's parents, who introduced me to the Mallaig/Arisaig (Arnasaid in the book) area through their very generous giving of their lovely holiday home. We have all spent so many wonderful holidays there, and have grown to love the surroundings and scenery which inspired me to write in the first place.

Chris Bryson of Spotlight editorial, for her love of language, her 'book-shepherding,' her faith in my storytelling and her encouragement and heart-felt advice. She has been my rock through this process.

Michelle Fairbanks of 'Fresh design,' my wonderful cover designer, who showed endless patience when I wanted her to design the cover I could 'see.' And she did. I would also like to thank Shutterstock for the images.

Leila Dewji of I_AM self publishing, for her expertise, advice, help and professionalism throughout the printing process.

Storm Winds is the name of a small boat I saw many years ago. If memory serves me it was bobbing in Arisaig harbour. This of course, was the name I chose for my estate house.

The house *Storm Winds*, in the cover design is Arisaig House near Arisaig. Thank you, your house is the one of my dreams.

If you have enjoyed this book, please leave a review on Amazon. The author would love to hear what you thought of her work.

Coming Soon

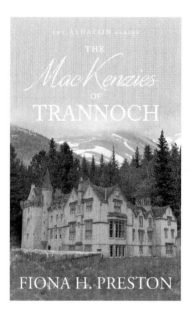

The MacKenzies' shadows from the past, walk the walls of *Trannoch*...

Great rivalry continues between the two magnificent estate houses in the North West of Scotland, as bitter in-fighting among the MacKenzies threatens to destroy everything Ailsa has built at *Storm Winds*.

Ailsa and Max are working hard to reconcile their differences in upbringing, and aspirations for the future, but can their diverse lives ever come together? Meanwhile, the dangerous and conniving Hunter proves she will stop at nothing to get what she wants.

Trannoch takes centre stage as a terrible incident touches not only the two estates and their households, but also the people of Arnasaid. As the awful events unfold, both money and titles become useless against the forces of evil darkening their lives...

About the Author

Fiona H. Preston was born and brought up in South Lanarkshire in Scotland, and still lives there now. Having worked for most of her life in a large corporate organisation, she decided to leave that world and concentrate on her writing. She has a BA Hons in Humanities. Her interests are many and varied, including music, amateur dramatics and collecting childrens' books and she has travelled extensively in the UK and Europe. Her favourite place is the North West of Scotland where this story is set. She shares her life with her close family and friends and her two Yorkie dogs.

Printed in Great Britain
by Amazon